Gerc

DARWIN'S BETRAYAL

The Story of a Voyage and a Theory

Translated from Spanish by
Juan Carlos Cattaneo and Lely Bartolomé

Bartolomé, Gerardo Miguel
Darwin´s Betrayal: a voyage to the mystery of mysteries / Gerardo Miguel Bartolomé. - 1ª ed. - Ciudad Autónoma de Buenos Aires: Gerardo Miguel Bartolomé, 2020.
256 p. ; 22 x 15 cm.

Traducción de: Juan Carlos Cattaneo.
ISBN 978-987-86-5350-1

1. Narrativa Argentina. 2. Biología. 3. Evolucionismo. I. Cattaneo, Juan Carlos, trad. II. Título.
CDD A863

ISBN 978-987-86-5350-1

Published as a paper book for the first time in December 2005 in Spanish with name *La traición de Darwin* by Editorial Zagier & Urruty Publications.

Cover by Ricardo A. Dorr and Gerardo Bartolomé.
Book layout: Ricardo A. Dorr.

Index

To my wife Paula,
who tenderly supported me from the beginning
and helped me with her clear intelligence.

To my son Francisco,
whose creative enthusiasm is always a source of inspiration.

To my parents Lely & Felipe,
my sister Alejandra
and my brother Jimmy
who always believe in me and my work.

Chapter 1

Secret Instructions

Late 1875. It was one of those rare days in December in which a soft breeze allowed one to dress elegantly without suffering the heat. A young man, barely 23 years old, waited impatiently to be received by one of Argentina's most important men, Dr. Rufino de Elizalde, the Argentine Government's Minister of Foreign Affairs. He wasn't sure why he was there. His uncle, who was a friend of Dr. Elizalde, had told him of the Minister's wish to have a meeting with him, but had not wanted to let him know the purpose of the meeting. He just told him to put on his best clothes and muster patience, since the Minister had an extremely tight schedule which usually meant that his visitors suffered long waits.

The young man had seen a waiter in his finest livery go by with a tray loaded with beverages and sundry morsels, so he believed the wait would be even longer than expected. When the door to the Minister's office opened to let the waiter in he overheard the voices of several people. A grandfather clock against the wall across the room from him struck 4 o'clock. His appointment had been for 3:00 pm. He was not used to being idle, and having to wait hours on end put him in a bad mood; however, he had been warned that this would happen. When the waiter came out he stopped by him and said:

"Dr. Elizalde says he is sorry to have to make you wait, but for reasons of State the meeting has extended beyond the scheduled time. He asked me to offer you any food or drink you may desire since he will be delayed for a further half hour."

The young man just asked for a glass of cool water, while he grumbled impatiently, unaware that the interview with Dr. Elizalde would change his life.

While he waited he tried to remember what his uncle had told him about the minister. He had already been the Minister of Foreign Affairs during Mitre's presidency, and would have been the next president if it hadn't been for the "crazy Sanjuanino", as they called Sarmiento, who snatched it from him. The president who succeeded Sarmiento, Nicolás Avellaneda, needed Mitre´s support, so many of the latter's followers had been given important positions in the Government. The presence of Rufino de Elizalde on Avellaneda's cabinet was an unmistakable sign of Bartolomé Mitre's (the most powerful politician in Buenos Aires) backing. The young man was not interested in politics and his uncle's account baffled him. All he knew was that he was about to meet one of the most powerful men in the country.

He suddenly realised that time had gone by inadvertently and he had not drunk the water the waiter had left. When he reached out for the glass he was startled by the sound of the door opening. He expected to see the people that had been in the previous meeting file out, but all he saw in the doorway was a slim man, around fifty years of age, with thick sideburns, who smiled and addressed him in a pleasant though somewhat mocking tone:

"Francisco Pascasio Moreno, naturalist and explorer of remote and hidden lakes, come in, your Country needs you!"

Young Moreno opened his eyes wide and got up. He found the greeting rather amusing and it changed his mood. He gave the Minister a firm handshake and walked into the office expecting to find the people that had been there before him, but the room was empty.

"Surprised?" asked Elizalde.

"I thought that you were in a meeting with several people, and as I did not see them leave ..."

"Aha! You are quite perceptive. You know, this office has a little secret which is very useful to politicians. It has two doors, each one with its own waiting room, so that visitors will not know who was there before them ..."

"Or to allow you to leave without being seen by whoever is waiting for you."

"Very good Francisco! That too. I will not deny having used that stratagem myself, ha, ha! Very well, let us go and sit in the armchairs; we will be more comfortable there."

Moreno turned and looked around the room. It was large and rather crammed with furniture and ornaments. The walls were covered with magnificent wood panelling where pictures of personalities and battles hung. One in particular caught his eye.

"That's the Battle of Caseros. I was there," said the Minister, "when we defeated the Tyrant[1]."

"Of course, February 3rd, 1852, almost 4 months before I was born."

They both sat on the soft armchairs. Elizalde spread a map of the continent on the low table. Large portions of the map were marked with the words Terra Incognita, unexplored territory.

"Your uncle told me of your expedition in search of the Limay river headwaters. I understand that the lake that feeds it stretches into the Andes."

"That is correct. The Indians call it Nahuel Huapi which in Mapuche language means 'big lake'. One of its branches reaches as far as a pass they use to cross over into Chile."

"Your uncle also told me you are a great naturalist, interested in geology and anthropology."

"I see my uncle told you a lot about me. It is true; I am interested in science in general. I find anthropology to be one of its most fascinating fields. In this last expedition I found a cave that had been occupied by ancient Indians. There were paintings on the walls of the cave, and we found bones and arrowheads, probably from before the discovery of America. I also have a collection of skulls and Indian weapons from previous trips. The truth is I could talk for hours about exploring unknown territory, but I believe you didn't summon me here to talk about this."

"That is right, Francisco, you don't mind my using your first name, do you? Actually I asked you to come to offer you the possibility of organizing an expedition that will be of great importance for our country's future. What do you know about the Santa Cruz River?"

"Not much. Last year I sailed there with Carlos Berg, the naturalist, but we were only able to see the mouth of the river. The rest of my knowledge is from having read about the expedition led by FitzRoy and Darwin. I also know that Piedrabuena sent a group of adventurers who were the first to reach the lake which is the river's headwater and that recently an expedition organized by the Navy managed to carry a boat up to the same lake."

"Right, and a few days later a Chilean expedition reached the same place. If we don't react soon, Chile will keep most of Patagonia, maybe even all of it. Look here, Francisco, Sarmiento's government lost precious

1. Name by which the "Unitarios" (political faction favoured by the citizens of Buenos Aires) referred to Juan Manuel de Rosas.

time. He did not know how to consolidate Argentine sovereignty over Patagonia and the Chileans took advantage of our lack of action. Our president, Dr. Avellaneda, has decided that the territorial expansion of Argentina is his most important State policy. While Alsina has been assigned the task of dealing with the Indian malón[2], I was entrusted with asserting our rights over Patagonia."

"But doctor, I don't understand where I come in."

"Let me give you some historical background so you can better understand the situation. The countries in South America were born from the remains of the Spanish Empire as continuators of its administrative jurisdictions. It is what is called the principle of *Uti possidetis juris*. Thus Argentina derives from the Virreinato del Río de la Plata (with the exception of Uruguay, Paraguay and Bolivia who did not join the May Revolution in which your famous ancestor Mariano Moreno participated) and Chile received what used to be the Capitanía General de Chile. It all would have been very simple, but, there always is a but, the good Spaniards never got down to delimiting the territories they had not explored and that were dominated by the Indians. Have a look at this map."

They both bent over the copy of an ancient Spanish map.

"Look at these territories that were declared unknown: the Puna, Chaco and Patagonia. As there were no borders defined by the Spaniards, there were serious border disputes in these three territories. In Chaco we had a very serious dispute with Paraguay which was finally decided by a bloody war which was finally won by our then president, Mr. Bartolomé Mitre. In the Puna there is a potentially explosive situation involving us, Bolivia, Perú and Chile. And in Patagonia the dispute is with Chile. Our position is that the Andes should be the natural border between our countries, but Chile does not agree and they would like keep it all. If we don't react, they will. So far they have been bolder than us. They founded Fort Bulnes and Punta Arenas while Argentina 'slept', which established a strong Chilean presence in the area, and most European powers will consider that they have better grounds for their claim."

Moreno stared at the map with disbelief written all over his face. He could not believe that all this Terra incognita that he always considered Argentine territory could be lost. He noticed, however, that the tone and

2. Indian raiding party, usually quite aggressive, where white men were killed and the women taken prisoner.

attitude of Elizalde was not that of one defeated. He was sure he had not been summoned to be told that it had all been lost.

"I imagine, Mr. Minister, that you have a plan and that, I cannot imagine how, I am part of it, right?"

"Right. There is a plan. There is a strategy that must be carried out exactly as planned for us to have a chance of retaining Patagonia. What I am about to disclose is strictly confidential. Together with President Avellaneda and Mitre we designed a plan to take advantage of a situation which is unique. It is our last chance and we must not squander it. There is a very tense situation between Chile on one side and Perú and Bolivia on the other over the Puna. We believe that in a relatively short time, two or three years, perhaps, there will be war over this territory. If Argentina were to join the war, Chile would surely be defeated. Chile cannot fight on two fronts, Patagonia and the Puna. Our plan is to escalate tension with Chile in the same measure as the tension with Perú and Bolivia does, thereby keeping the threat of a conflict on two fronts for Chile latent. What we want to achieve is to force Chile to try to resolve a possible conflict with Argentina before taking on Bolivia and Perú."

"Then why is an expedition necessary if the plan is for Chile to relinquish its claim on Patagonia to avoid a conflict with Argentina?"

"One moment, not so fast."

Elizalde got up and walked over to a cabinet from where he fetched a more modern map of southern Patagonia.

"I did not say that Chile would simply relinquish its claim. The plan is to get Chile to accept an international arbitration, which it does not want at this point because they know that as things stand now they can keep it all. In an arbitration one must prove and support one's position. We must generate 'sovereign actions' that will allow us to uphold our claims that Argentina owns the region. That is why we must explore, name places, discover things, know and inhabit the territory. We must take advantage of the little time we have to generate all the 'sovereign acts' we can before the arbitration."

"I get it ... but doctor, why explore the Santa Cruz River, and not other parts of Patagonia that are easier to reach?"

"Take a good look at this map. Chile, by founding the town of Punta Arenas, has managed to control the Strait of Magellan. It is lost for us, there is no way we can recover it. What we can do is limit the Chilean presence by territorial pressure. That is, surround Punta Arenas with undisputedly Argentine territory. Our plan is to 'Argentinize' this land

The young Francisco Moreno.

like pincers, advance quickly from the south and from the north. In the south we will create a settlement on the island of Tierra del Fuego, here," he pointed at the south of the island, "is the *Beagle* Channel. Chile might control the passage between the Atlantic and Pacific through the Strait of Magellan, but we will control the Channel FitzRoy discovered. North of the Strait of Magellan, on the continent we already have a settlement on Pavón Island, but we must extend our presence to the foot of the Andes. If we manage to do this we will be in a very good position for the arbitration and thus limit Chilean presence on this side of the Andes to just Punta Arenas and the Strait of Magellan. Look here," he said, tracing his finger over the area with a smile on his lips, "the whole of Patagonia east of the Andes and the whole, or most, of Tierra del Fuego will remain Argentine."

Moreno was fascinated by the idea that such a daring plan existed to snatch most of this unexplored land from Chile practically at the last moment. He loved the idea of being a part of this plan but still couldn't see how, or what, his contribution could be.

"Francisco, our offer is that you lead an expedition up the Santa Cruz River and reach the Andes."

"But Dr. Elizalde, that was already achieved by Second Lieutenant Feilberg's expedition. What can I contribute that has not been done already?"

Elizalde leaned back in his armchair. He then he sipped some water from the glass on the table next to it, taking his time to answer.

"My dear Moreno, you ask some incisive questions which oblige me to dwell on subjects I did not want to go into, but I can see that a person as intelligent as yourself needs, and deserves, to know all the details."

He stood up, strolled over to the window and gazing into space, continued.

"As part of this strategy, in 1873 the Ministry of War assigned the Navy the task of organizing an expedition up the Santa Cruz River. This was entrusted to young Feilberg, who managed to reach the headwaters but he did not perform any sovereign act; nothing to prove he had actually been there. They did not draw any maps, did not discover anything new, it is as if they were never there at all. It is not that I don't believe they were there, but during an arbitration hearing Chile could easily doubt the existence of the expedition and we would have nothing, absolutely nothing, to prove it really happened."

Elizalde turned to look at Moreno and walked back to the armchair as he continued.

"Naturally, it was not Feilberg's fault, it was the person who gave him his orders who was at fault ... The military are as bad exploring as they are playing music, ha, ha! That was why President Avellaneda put the responsibility of this matter in the Ministry of Foreign Affairs. We decided to change the style of the expedition completely. We need a naturalist who will discover places, bring home strange bones and rocks, that will describe the surroundings, draw maps and diagrams, in short, someone who can prove beyond any doubt that he was the first one to explore these places, and that our country knows and controls the land. When your uncle told me of your trip to the Limay headwaters I realized that you had exactly the profile we need."

Moreno was afraid Elizalde would notice the rush of pride that came over him. To conceal it he gulped down some water and nearly choked.

He tried to say something intelligent, but all he could manage was "And when do you think this expedition would take place?"

"The first thing we must consider is that it would have to be in summer since it is very cold down there, so I would believe it would be around November or December '76."

"I could do it as early as March or April." When he finished saying it he felt like a presumptuous fool.

"I am sure you could, my good friend, but first we must do our homework, and regarding this, I have not told you everything yet."

Moreno stared at him and thought "what else must I know?"

"We must keep in mind that all this will be sent to an arbitral commission which will be formed by European powers. Tell me Francisco, which power do you think will be leading this commission?"

"Before you talked about 'homework' and now you are examining me. I feel I'm back at school," he joked. "I would say the leading power will be England."

"Very good! That is why we must prepare to convince England. What usually happens during an arbitration is that the litigating parties will fabricate evidence about their rights and sovereignty, so the commission will mistrust every piece of evidence that is put before them. You must be aware that the British are particularly suspicious. So, Francisco, who would the British trust when analysing each country's presentation?"

Moreno thought a while, he had no answer. "I suppose they might trust us more than the Chileans," he ventured.

"Wrong, my friend. The British only trust the British. So to strengthen our position we must include someone British in our plan.

"I guess you have already thought of something," said Moreno.

"We have. Concerning the southern branch of our pincers, we are negotiating with a small Anglican mission to have them acknowledge Argentine sovereign rights in Tierra del Fuego."

"Thomas Bridges' mission? The priest from Malvinas[3]?"

"The same," answered Elizalde, "I see you know about them."

"I've heard of him. There have been previous attempts by Anglicans to set up missions in the area but they all ended in disaster. The first one by FitzRoy and a second one led by a clergyman named Gardiner who died tragically. Bridges has, in some way, continued their work, but I would never have expected him to cooperate with Argentina."

3. Falkland Islands. Argentina claims the Islands.

"The thing is, Francisco, that we are trying to seize the opportunities that come our way. Bridges has clashed with the Chileans several times, so he might think we are not as bad as they are. Furthermore, he has quarrelled with the people in the Malvinas so he is on his own. He is a very special sort of person, difficult to deal with but he is in need of a protective umbrella and he can sense that we can provide it. His priority is to protect the Indians and we are offering guarantees in that area ... But that is the plan for the southern part of our pincers. The plan to involve someone British in the northern branch is a bit more complicated." He gave Moreno a defiant look, "any ideas?"

Moreno could see that Elizalde was rather proud of having a well-thought-out plan, so he didn't bother guessing.

"I don't know why, but I get the impression that you already have some ideas."

"Naturally," said Elizalde, "but I'm going to give you a few clues so you can venture an answer." He looked Moreno in the eye, "We want to involve an Englishman who has already been there and happens to be a world-renowned naturalist."

"Darwin?!" Moreno exclaimed.

"Exactly. What can be better to support our position than having it endorsed by a scientist of such prestige who, also, already knows the area?"

"And why would Darwin want to get involved in this quarrel?"

"It is not as complicated as it appears to be. John Coghlan, the Irishman (at the club, I once called him English, by mistake, and he nearly threw his lit cigar in my face), is an engineer and he frequently contracts for the government. As his work often involves excavating, he has found several skeletons of long extinct animals. He has an arrangement with Darwin by which he sends him whatever he finds so that he may examine, catalogue and use them for his theories."

"You may not know him," he went on, "but John is quite a character. He got his engineering degree in France, and worked all over Europe before coming to Argentina, with a recommendation from none other than Baring Brothers. He built the warehouses at Catalinas[4], laid down the tracks for several railway lines, built bridges, and sewer systems all over the Province of Buenos Aires. He is tireless and also loves exploring. He actually made quite an interesting trip up the Salado river. He has mellowed a bit since his wife died, however, but he still corresponds with

4. The Buenos Aires port area.

Darwin, who even sent him a portrait with a personal dedication, which he had framed and hung in his library and proudly shows it to anyone who visits him."

"I have seen Coghlan a couple of times but we haven't been introduced. I did not know he corresponded with Darwin," said Moreno with interest.

"But that is not all. Following my instructions John wrote to Darwin about this expedition we are planning to the place where he was forty years ago. Naturally he did not mention who would be leading it because at the time we had not decided that. In his letter he asked Darwin, based on his experience during the expedition with FitzRoy, if he could indicate where fossils could be found and offered to send him anything found during this trip."

Robert FitzRoy wearing his Vice-Admiral uniform, by Francis Lane.

"And what did he answer?" asked Moreno anxiously.

"There has not been an answer yet, I expect it should arrive any time now." Elizalde looked at his watch and jumped. "How time flies! Francisco, I thought that the best thing is for you to go directly to Coghlan's house that is close by, at 25 de Mayo 135.

Moreno looked at him mockingly, "I still have not accepted."

"You are right," answered Elizalde, "but before you answer me, I want you to know that our plan includes the publishing of a book on the expedition with details of discoveries, places, and al related data. The book will be printed at the Government Print Shop and distributed all over the country and overseas too. Naturally, to conceal the plan behind it, it should concentrate on scientific data... Very well, Francisco, do you accept?"

"Of course I do!" answered Moreno, "I never dreamed I could have the fortune of being offered a job I want so badly to do."

"Good. Now, before you leave, let's go over it: you must organize an expedition which will go up the Santa Cruz River and not only find the headwater, but also explore all the area adjacent to the Andes. You must name mountains, rivers, lakes and anything you find. We need descriptions and diagrams. You must also look for, find and bring back fossils and samples of animals, plants, the weirder the better, find Indian paintings and also contact the local Indians. Finally you must involve Darwin in the results of the expedition."

Elizalde looked at his watch again, drank a bit of water, and suddenly exclaimed, "I almost forgot! You must also find the marker Feilberg says he left at the river's headwaters. It will help us 'certify' that Feilberg was there and thus prove we have been exploring the zone for several years."

"What was the marker like?" asked Moreno.

"An overturned boat, an oar stuck in the ground with an Argentine flag."

"Not a very good marker for that area. I don't believe it survived the winds."

"Probably not. The first storm must have blown the whole lot halfway across the steppe," and added in a whisper, "if they ever were there in the first place."

Elizalde got up, indicating that the meeting was over. Moreno fetched his hat. At the door he turned and said, "Doctor, what if I don't find Feilberg's marker?"

Elizalde looked at him in surprise, "Easy, if you don't find it ... you find it anyway."

Seeing Moreno's bewildered expression, he added, "I have a box where I keep a wind-torn flag which may be useful. Good afternoon, my friend."

They shook hands and he closed the door.

Moreno was in a pensive mood as he walked towards John Coghlan's house. He had just been offered to go on a trip that might change his life. Nearly fifty years earlier, something similar had happened to Charles Darwin. He had devoured several of the British naturalist's works. He had read Darwin's account of his voyage on the *Beagle*, with FitzRoy as Captain, thoroughly. In this book he had read the chapters related to the two years he spent on Argentine soil with special interest, and had gone over the report on the three-week expedition up the Santa Cruz River, which never reached the headwaters, several times. That story was what drove him, even as a teenager, to want to explore Argentine territory and to collect and classify fossils and animals. He liked to refer to himself as a 'naturalist' because he had learned the word and the meaning behind it through Charles Darwin's work.

He had also read the book with which Charles Darwin had created quite a commotion, On the Origin of Species. Over twenty years after his trip around the world on the *Beagle*, the British scientist used the evidence he had collected during this trip to contend, almost prove, that animals had not been created as they now exist, but had evolved, modifying according to the changing conditions on Earth, over thousands, maybe millions, of years. His theory rocked the world, dividing society into those who adhered to the biblical theory of creation, or 'creationists' and those who defended Darwin's theory, known as 'evolutionists' or 'Darwinians'. How many lifetime friends had fallen apart after arguing bitterly over these beliefs in well to do clubs, not only in London, but in all the great cities in the world, including Buenos Aires!

Darwin was not daunted by the effect his theory had on British society, and he went on to give the Bible another blow. He wrote a book in which he now claimed that not only animals, but Man himself had evolved from a lower form, such as monkeys. There was no room for Adam and Eve in Darwin´s world.

Apart from his theories on animal evolution, Darwin, as a geologist, explained that Earth's topography is not static, but has been perpetually changing over millennia and is still changing. The manner in which an

Charles Darwin in his old age

area changed was of great importance for a geologist, like Moreno, to understand the forces and the direction of these changes.

Moreno could not help noting certain similarities between himself and Darwin. "He was almost my age when he received the offer to participate in the most fantastic voyage he could imagine." Suddenly the angry shout of a cab driver who had to make his horse swerve to avoid running over him startled Moreno and made him realize that he was very near John Coghlan's house. The house was not pretentious, but you could see that Coghlan was far from destitute. He knocked at the door. A maid opened the door and escorted him to a dimly lit room. She whispered something that Moreno didn't catch but he assumed she meant for him to wait there until his host came.

While he waited, he examined some of the many fossils and bones that were on display. As he approached the wall to look at one close up he noticed Darwin's portrait, the one Elizalde had told him about. It had a handwritten inscription: "To my dear friend John Coghlan, whose valuable effort supporting my work deserves more than just this remembrance. Charles Darwin."

A hoarse voice behind him said, in Spanish, "To my dear friend ..."

Moreno interrupted him, "whose valuable effort supporting my work deserves more than just this remembrance. I Speak and read English, Mr..."

"Coghlan, John Coghlan. Please take a seat." They shook hands and sat down. "How did you learn English? It is not that common in these lands," he spoke with a heavy British accent.

"My mother taught me, she is from Irish stock. Thwaite is the name. Her father was a soldier in the British Army who came with the expeditionary forces that attempted to take Buenos Aires in 1806, and decided to stay here."

"I've heard of many cases similar to your grandfather's. The Irish soldiers found the place attractive, not only because the local society girls flirted with them, but also, being Catholics, they felt they could escape Anglican pressure and be able to practice their religion in freedom. Many chose to escape from the English as soon as they had a chance. I guess you know the type of relationship there is between the Irish and the English, my friend Moreno," Francisco's expression showed that he didn't. "Ok, the English are like an elder brother who ill-treats us. At home we are constantly quarrelling, but when we are far from home we find we have a lot in common; I, for one, have countless English friends. However we Irish believe we are old enough to have our own home; that is, separated from the British Empire, but our big brother refuses to let us go."

Coghlan was a large man who appeared to be a little over fifty years old. His thinning hair was going grey, but seemed to have been red once. He had a ruddy complexion with little veins criss-crossing under his skin, something found often in the British.

"Well, Moreno, you don't look Irish but from what I heard of your travels, the Celtic blood is still alive in you since you have proven to be quite obstinate when it comes to achieving your objectives, are you not?"

The young man smiled, understanding it was a compliment.

"I take it that if you are here it is because you have had your meeting with Dr. Elizalde and accepted his offer, right?"

"Correct. I must add that not only am I flattered by the opportunity I am given to serve my country doing something that fascinates me, but also pleasantly surprised by the existence of such a detailed plan to protect our Patagonia. Dr. Elizalde told me of your relationship with Darwin and that you even wrote him to see if he would be interested in this expedition. Was there any response?"

"Unfortunately there was, and it was not good. Yesterday morning the British ship Arrow arrived in Buenos Aires and that same afternoon the mail it carried was distributed. In his letter Darwin says that as it is over forty years since he made that trip up the Santa Cruz River, there is little he can remember of it. He also says that he went through the notes he took at the time and considers there is not much useful information in them. In short, he does not seem to be very interested in this expedition." Suddenly Moreno felt that the whole plan was falling apart. The idea of involving a prominent Englishman in the plan was crumbling right at the start.

"How strange, I understood you had offered to send him any fossils we could find," said Moreno, unable to hide his disappointment.

"I did, but in his answer he says that both the river bottom and the cliff walls were basaltic or of alluvial origin, and that this sort of rock does not contain fossils. He also mentions that at the current stage of his work he is interested in complete skeletons and not bits and pieces, and he does not believe your expedition could haul that amount of material."

"So, is that it? The plan to involve an Englishman is lost?"

"Well, not quite," said Coghlan, "in his letter he says that what would be of great help to the Argentine expedition is the geographic and geodesic data compiled by the *Beagle*. He says that that information was in FitzRoy's possession, and since he had died, he would help us get in touch with FitzRoy's cartographic assistant, John Lort Stokes."

"A third-rate contact is not what we need, Mr. Coghlan," said Moreno visibly crest-fallen.

Coghlan stood up and walked over to the library. He searched for a few minutes and finally picked a book from one of the shelves, returned and handed it to Moreno. He took it listlessly and read the title.

Discoveries in Australia; with an Account of the Coasts and Rivers Explored and Surveyed During the Voyage of the *H.M.S. Beagle*, in the Years 1837-38-39-40-41-42-43. By Command of the Lords Commissioners of the Admiralty.

John Lort Stokes when promoted to Admiral, by Stephen Pearce

Moreno looked at Coghlan inquisitively. "Take a look at the author," said Coghlan. Moreno turned back to the book.

Author: John Lort Stokes.

"Stokes," said Coghlan, "Vice-Admiral John Lort Stokes happens to be one of the most prominent members of the Admiralty. He is considered to be the most experienced British explorer alive. He was Captain of the *Beagle* on its third voyage where they explored the coasts of Australia and New Zealand. He is something of a living legend. He is our man. It is he we must write to and get him interested in our trip."

He looked at Moreno whose face showed he did not have a clue of how to do that.

Coghlan added with pride, "Fortunately my friend Darwin has already done part of the work for us. He sent me a copy of the letter he sent to Stokes, in which he explains the scientific and exploratory nature of this expedition and asks him to assist us in any way he can. We could not hope for a better introduction! What we must do now is to write to Stokes right away. Let us get down to it right now, so we can take advantage of the fact that the Arrow is still moored, and will be returning directly to England. One of my staff will wait for us to finish writing the letter and will take it straight to the ship."

Coghlan led Moreno to his desk, then fetched paper, pen and ink. Moreno sat down to write, but his mind was blank. He did not know what to say or how to begin. "What do I write?" he asked.

"Tell him of your journey up the Limay river, your adventures with the Indians, your discoveries. Stokes is an adventurer himself so he will be delighted to read your first hand experiences. He will see you as an explorer in his own image. Then describe the expedition you are planning up the Santa Cruz River, which is no less than to continue the one he made with FitzRoy and Darwin forty years ago. Have you read the chronicles they wrote on that trip?"

"Only Darwin's."

"Perfect. Remind me to give you FitzRoy's. They are more detailed than Darwin's but also more tedious." Then he added, "finally you should request his assistance. Ask him for all possible data he may have: maps, drawings, illustrations, coordinates, camping sites, etc."

Moreno looked doubtful, "And do you believe he will give us any of this? Why would he do that?"

"He will do it if your letter tickles his fancy. If he sees in you the young Stokes, and senses that if you get as far as the Andes it will be as if he were there with you. Make him feel that your expedition is the continuation of the one he formed part of forty years ago. It all depends on your writing skills, my dear Moreno ... excite him ... I'll help you with the English spelling, that is a little tricky."

They worked for hours, night crept in and they continued writing in the gloom, choosing every word carefully. Finally, in the wee hours of the morning, still not altogether satisfied with the final result, they finished it and it was sent directly to the Arrow that would take it to London where it would be delivered by hand at the Admiralty to one of the living legends of the Royal Navy, the greatest explorer of Australia and New Zealand, Tierra del Fuego, the Galapagos Islands and other faraway places around the World and, above all, friend and assistant of Robert FitzRoy and Charles Darwin: Vice-Admiral John Lort Stokes.

Chapter 2

A Gentlemen's Agreement

Sitting at his desk planning the expedition he hoped to start by the end of 1876, Moreno was interrupted by Pedro, his manservant.

"Mr Moreno! Several parcels have arrived with mail from England."

Moreno turned and saw Pedro holding an envelope, two boxes and a cylinder which, he suspected, contained maps.

"Leave it all on the table and hurry over to tell Mr. Coghlan. Quick!!"

As Pedro left, Moreno opened the cylinder. Inside he found three sheets larger than his desk.

The first one was a detailed map of the mouth of the Santa Cruz River. It showed the estuary and surrounding hills, with depth indicators marking several points in it. This information would be very useful to the Captain of a large ship! Mount Entrance and Shingle Point were the names given to the headlands that delimited the entrance to the estuary. From a point inside the estuary, marked on the map as Weddell Bluff, 300 feet high, two vectors were drawn resembling the ones that indicated the visible angle of a lighthouse. The angle projected out to sea with an aperture of no more than 10 degrees. "The *Beagle*'s crew must have built a stone landmark at this point which can probably be seen when you are within these vectors," thought Moreno.

Lighthouses and stone landmarks are built in places where there are hidden dangers... In this case, the map showed that the estuary concealed a deadly trap for those who were unaware of it ... right in front of the entrance to the estuary there was a rocky underwater reef running parallel to the coast and exactly where the logical course a ship unaware of the danger would be. "Of course," thought Moreno, "the true entry channel is further south. If a ship attempts to sail in this course, it would hit the reef and sink. The landmark is there to warn them: don't come in this way". The map also had thick arrows drawn to indicate the direction of tides and their speed in knots (as much as 6 knots![1]), further down a legend warned: Tides of up to 33 feet. "So these dotted lines show the coastline at low tide." Moreno said to himself, "Weddell Bluff must only be seen from inside the estuary when you go past Keel Point."

Still fascinated by the first sheet, Moreno looked at the second one. This one showed three views of the mouth of the estuary as seen from the sea. They showed the coastline as it was seen from the ship's bridge. The top view was from the North East. The angle of this view was indicated above (250 degrees). The headlands were visible, but a legend below warned Entrance not possible from the North. The second view was from a 300-degree angle, almost directly east. A legend at the bottom of the diagram warned that sunken rocks did not allow access. The drawing showed the headlands and between them a cliff was visible inside the estuary, and on the highest point of this cliff there was a stone landmark. An arrow and a legend explained Weddell Bluff visible from here. Finally, the third view showed the only course possible to access the estuary, the southern one, although a legend warned Entrance only possible at high tide. Not only were the rocks and the shallowness a menace for the ship seeking the shelter of the estuary, the speed of the tides were an added problem for a vessel that relied on wind to advance. A Captain would have to be patient and wait until the tide coincided with winds from the right quadrant. "It obviously is not a suitable port for a Ship in distress". However, as a reward, Santa Cruz Port offered refuge for the ship and crew, which, Moreno knew, was what the *Beagle* had searched for in 1834.

Finally, the third sheet showed the whole course of the Santa Cruz River from the estuary all the way to the Andes, although these were in the hazy area of Terra Incognita. Several mountains on the range were named (one was Mount Stokes!), the expedition must have seen them in the distance but were never near them.

Moreno opened one of the boxes. In it there were a great deal of neatly folded sketches. The title on the first one was Views from Observation Points on Keel Point and Weddell Bluff. It showed a simple view of the horizon from Keel Point and from Weddell Bluff; Shingle Point, Mount Entrance, Sea Lion Island, *Beagle* Bluff and several other significant points were drawn as seen from Keel Point and Weddell Bluff, and above each the degrees which represented the angle of the view to the magnetic

1. Knot is a measure of nautical speed. One knot is one nautical mile per hour.

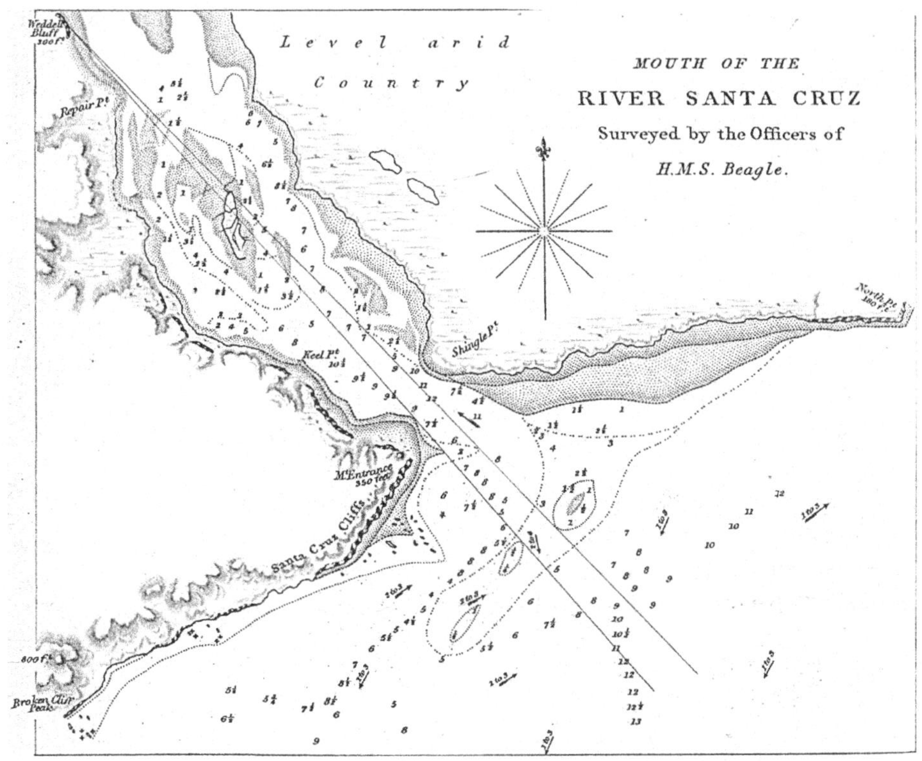

Map of the estuary of the Santa Cruz River,
surveyed by the officers of *HMS Beagle*

North. Below were the instructions on how to calculate the coordinates for each one, that is, how to calculate the coordinates for each point starting from the coordinates of Keel Point and Weddell Bluff plus the angle to the magnetic North. Moreno knew quite a bit of geodesics and understood how you can calculate the coordinates of faraway places that are visible, even though they are out of reach, and so be able to place them on a map. His delight at having all this data available made him smile. "These sketches will allow us to identify these mountains by their silhouette," he thought.

His curiosity made him continue looking through the contents of the box. A at the bottom of it caught his eye. The title of this sketch was View from No-God Point. "View from No-God Point?" thought Moreno, "what a strange name for a view point. Why would they have chosen such a name?" The last sketch was made from a place called Western Station. On the map of the Santa Cruz River each one of these viewpoints was marked and Western Station was as far west as FitzRoy and Darwin's expedition had reached. On the map he noticed a plain named Mystery Plain. The reason for this name was that the British expedition never found out what hidden wonders were beyond it.

The sound of a door opening and approaching footsteps brought him back to the real world.

"Moreno! Moreno! What was in the mail?"

By the heavy British accent he recognized John Coghlan. Coghlan opened the door to Moreno's study and, seeing the boxes and maps on the table he shouted in triumph, "He accepted our request!!"

"I suppose he did. All I did so far was to look at these maps," said Moreno.

"Don't be uncivilized, man! When you receive a parcel, the first thing you do is read the letter that comes with it. Open it now!" he ordered.

Moreno had not paid much attention to the envelope. The handwriting was rounded and clear and written on heavy white Admiralty paper. He carefully opened one end of the envelope and took out a three-page letter.

To: Francisco P. Moreno

From: Vice-Admiral John Lort Stokes

Dear Mr. Moreno,

Thank you very much for your kind letter. I am very pleased to know you are projecting an exploration trip along the River Santa Cruz, where over forty years ago our exploring party, led by the late Vice-Admiral Robert FitzRoy, advanced up to a place not far from the impressive Andes. I cannot but wish you and your group every success.

Your accounts of your trip to the headwater of the Limay River and your adventures with the aborigines made me fondly remember those distant days when I, being young and daring as you are, engaged in similar explorations. On one occasion, when we were attacked by Australian aborigines, I suffered a severe shoulder wound from a lance that very nearly cost me my life. Although I can now talk about this episode as an exciting anecdote, at the time, since I was in charge of the expedition, the lack of precise information on the lay of the land and possible dangers not only put my own life at risk, but also that of those who were in my command. That is why I find it very wise of you to seek all possible documentation and data on the region you are going to explore, and I understand that your request is part of this planning.

However, the maps, memoirs and sketches you request are not only hard to come by (it has been many years since our voyage) but they also require authorizations which are not easy to get. Obviously, by the time you receive this letter you will be aware that a great deal of this data is accompanying it, so it will be clear I have taken the trouble of securing them.

Given the fact that Robert FitzRoy is deceased, the only way to have access to his files was to contact his widow who has been, since his death, a lady-in-waiting of the Royal Family at the Royal Palace in Hampton Court. My own files are at my family estate in faraway Wales. Finally, the most important part of the data I have sent you, and the data I could send you shortly, belongs to the Admiralty and requires a well-founded request to secure the relevant permissions to make copies of them. These are some of the reasons why I took almost two months to answer you.

You will surely ask yourself why I took the trouble in the first place. You have certainly, through your spontaneous and sincere style, captured my fancy; but this is not the main reason why I have decided to back your expedition. My help, however, will be given on the condition that, in exchange, you accept to fulfil a request I will detail later.

We could say that I offer you a gentleman's agreement, to give you the data you need if, and only if, you agree to honour my request which, I assure you, you are perfectly capable of fulfilling.

If you do not agree, then you must, as a true gentleman, return all the parcels unopened.

I shall let you know what my request is later, but I will say that it has to do with the recognition that FitzRoy, unjustly, has never received.

So, my dear Mr. Moreno, if you accept the commitment, you must answer this letter stating your acceptance and you may then proceed to open the boxes that accompany this envelope. On the other hand, if you decide not to accept it, then you must return them unopened.

Expecting your answer, I remain,

Truly Yours,

Vice-Admiral John Lort Stokes

Moreno and Coghlan looked at each other.

"What will you do?" asked Coghlan, "will you accept his offer?"

"What choice do I have? The Argentine strategy for Patagonia needs this data and the involvement of some high ranking officer in the Admiralty, like Stokes. But Coghlan, you know the British better than I do, what could his request be?"

"To be honest, I'm as baffled as you are. It might be a monument with a bust of FitzRoy, or a square or a book in his honour ... But that doesn't matter much now. What we must do is answer his letter at once and take it directly to the ship that is still at its mooring, so your answer can get to England sooner."

They both cleared the desk and after choosing paper and pen to match the occasion, they got down to writing the letter, as they had done several months before. This time they were more relaxed, however. They wrote a short note and soon Pedro was on his way to the port to deliver it so it could continue its way to Europe.

They now faced the exiting task of going through the contents of the parcels and cataloguing the data. Coghlan ordered mate[2]. As a true Criollo[3] Irishman, he had adopted the local custom of drinking mate and indulged in it whenever he could, specially while reading a good book, or a friend's letter or writing his diary, so how could he not indulge in it while examining the chronicles, maps and sketches of the voyage that had such an impact on recent history?

Moreno, who had already seen part of the contents of the parcels, showed Coghlan the maps and sketches. The Irishman, being an engineer, had a perfect understanding of the method for calculating coordinates, and also made Moreno note a series of details he had overlooked. The name "No God Point" with which an observation point was marked also baffled him, and he could not imagine what had prompted it.

A box still remained unopened. Once opened, they found more maps, coordinate calculation rationale and sketches in it. But there was one other item that caught their eye. It was a thick folder that held a manuscript in the clear round writing of Vice-Admiral Stokes. The first page seemed to be a letter addressed to Moreno:

Dear Mr. Moreno,

If you are reading these lines it means that you have accepted the gentleman's agreement I offered.

What I shall be narrating in the following pages is a story only three

2. Indigenous tea that is brewed in a gourd and sipped through a metal straw called bombilla. Consumed mainly in Argentina, Uruguay, Paraguay and southern Brazil.

3. Creole. In this case, an Irishman turned local.

persons know of. The purpose of doing this is so you understand the reason for the request I shall be making at the end.

I joined the Royal Navy many years ago. I was not seduced, as most young men were, by the glory and victories during the Napoleonic Wars, but enthralled by the fantastic adventures of Captain James Cook's exploratory voyages. My dream, during my youth, was to be in command of a ship exploring unknown lands. I sailed on three exploratory voyages in the brig HMS Beagle. *On the third one I eventually was appointed Captain and spent six years exploring Australia's shores; my dream had come true.*

I must confess, however, that the burden of being responsible for the well-being of over eighty people in dangerous country is overwhelming. Cook himself was killed by aborigines on his last trip, which goes to show that safety must be foremost in the leader's priorities, even above the exploratory objectives of an expedition.

Every time the ship and crew were in a difficult situation and I, the Captain, was expected to make an effective decision, I experienced the extreme loneliness of command and the burden of responsibility, and with it the fear of failure, through which I could bring harm to those whose safety I had been entrusted with. On those occasions I resorted to a little trick by which I felt there was someone I could turn to for advice. I made believe Robert FitzRoy was sitting next to me and would tell me what he would do in that situation.

FitzRoy was, in my view, the model of the Captain who is truly prepared to face adversity, his crew had a blind faith in him and his leadership was undisputed. From him I learned everything I would later need to comply with the demanding survey tasks assigned to me by the Admiralty.

FitzRoy was a man called upon to do great things, which no doubt he did. But destiny would have him take on the role of guardian, for which he was condemned by society, in particular by the scientific world, and was thus denied the recognition he deserved.

This role of guardian has to do with his attitude towards the scientific discoveries which were the result of the famous second voyage of the Beagle. Curiously, he contributed, through his intelligence and scientific mind, to piece together the theory he later endeavoured to ridicule and would eventually lead to his tragic end. He took on this role, however, and stuck to it even though he was aware that his reputation would be shattered and with it any goal he might have planned for his life.

On the other hand, Charles Darwin was, and is, another great personality that I was fortunate to know and admire, although we have not seen

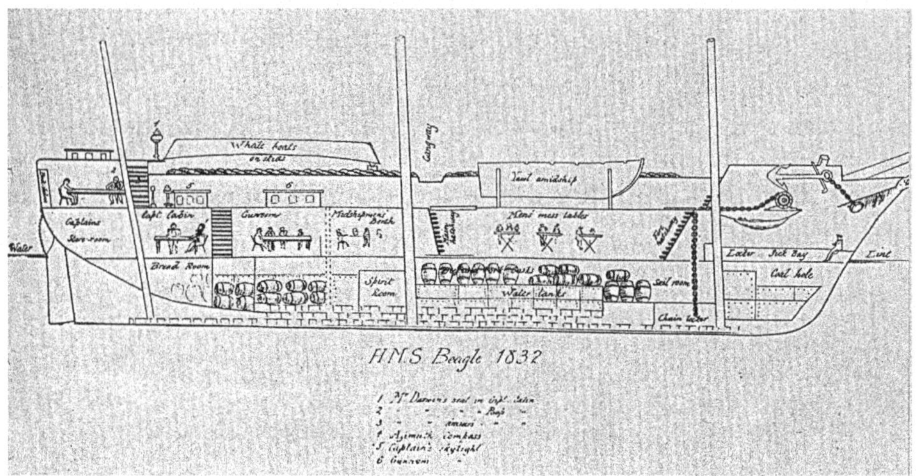

Section plan of *H.M.S. Beagle*

much of each other lately, mainly due to the depression he fell into after our Captain's death.

I endeavoured to honour both FitzRoy and Darwin by naming and important river and a bay, respectively, after them during my survey and discovery voyage to Australia.

When did this story commence? It is hard to say. I met FitzRoy when he took command of the HMS *Beagle, at the age of 23, as a result of the death of its Captain, Pringle Stokes (who, in spite of having the same surname, was no relation of mine), who committed suicide. Pringle Stokes could not cope with the responsibility I have mentioned before and shot himself when he realized that, due to errors he had incurred in during the survey, the Beagle and its crew would have to endure a further year in the distressing channels of Tierra del Fuego.*

FitzRoy took command firmly and carried out the task he had been assigned: to finish the survey and complete the Beagle's first voyage. On his return to England, he immediately got down to planning the second voyage, of which Darwin would be part of.

Perhaps that is why I am inclined to think that it all started in Plymouth, where we were outfitting the HMS *Beagle for its second voyage, which would take it around the world.*

It was a horrid autumn afternoon, when English weather is at its worst: mist, cold, wind and a persistent drizzle. Captain FitzRoy came aboard in the company of a rather shy young man with light brown hair ...

"Stokes!" bellowed the Captain, "Stokes, come over, I want you to meet someone."

Young John Stokes approached, eyeing the Captain's companion with distaste. Years at sea had made him feel uncomfortable, even suspicious, around 'landlubbers' as they were referred to on board. This young man appeared to be two or three years older than himself. He was 19 years old at the time.

"This is Charles Darwin, who will be the Naturalist on board during our trip. Mr. Darwin will be sharing the map room with you. While you draw maps Mr. Darwin will desiccate animals or use his microscope, or make great discoveries," this last comment in an almost humorous tone.

Stokes shook Darwin's hand in a not too friendly manner, so the Captain, who knew his men well, added:

"Mr. Darwin comes from Shropshire County, very close to your native Wales, Mr. Stokes. He has recently made a geological trip to the Welsh mountains, so I am sure you will have plenty to talk about."

"Of course we do!" Stokes' expression had changed and he pumped Darwin's hand vigorously, "only on our trip we will miss the Welsh mountains, since at sea there are no mountains to climb."

"Behind each port there will be mountains we can climb," said Darwin on impulse, "Even here, in Plymouth, we can climb mount Edgecombe, if you are so inclined."

"Count me in!" said Stokes. That instant was the start of the friendship between Darwin and Stokes that would last over fifty years.

"Mr. Stokes, while I supervise the loading, please show Mr. Darwin around the ship and where his quarters are," and then to Darwin, "I will see you this evening for dinner on shore. I shall take you to a place where they cook the best lamb you can eat. See you, gentlemen..." and he strolled away towards the bridge.

Stokes took Darwin on a 'guided' tour of the *Beagle*. He showed him the map room, where not only would they share their working hours, but was also their cabin, in which they would sleep in hammocks that hung from the ceiling. Darwin was appalled at the cramped quarters, but he was assured that with time he would get used to it.

While they went over every nook and cranny, Stokes gave Darwin an account of the ship's history. The *Beagle* was the 41st vessel of the Cherokee class, of which over a hundred had been built. The ships of this class were often called 'coffin brigs' because twenty-six of them had sunk in high seas. The *Beagle*, however, had been modified in several ways which had improved its handling, making it faster and safer than the rest, as had been proven during the very successful voyage to Tierra del Fuego, surveying the channels around the Strait of Magellan. Stokes had been on that voyage and FitzRoy had been Captain for the last stretch of it.

Stokes practically recited the ship's data: launched in June 1818, 242 tonnes displacement and 90 feet long. The crew would be augmented by several supernumeraries that included Darwin, three Fuegian Indians and the Anglican preacher who was going to attempt to establish a mission in southern Tierra del Fuego.

"Mr. Stokes, could you tell me how these aborigines came to England and what is planned for their future?"

"I do not know what is planned for them; I suggest you ask the Captain about that. I can tell you how they got here, however. When we were in Tierra del Fuego a party from the *Beagle* landed on one of the islands to do some surveying and take readings to calculate coordinates. While they were on the island and distracted, a group of Fuegians stole the whaleboat. The Captain pursued them and we managed to capture a small group that had the oars. The Captain decided to release the older ones so hoping they would return the boat while we retained the children as 'collateral'. The Fuegians never returned. We continued searching for the whaleboat and captured one older Fuegian whom we named York Minster. We finally never recovered the boat, but found we had four new passengers who seemed to be quite content to be on board with us. The Captain decided to take them back to England to be educated and on the next trip return them so they could take education and civilization back to their people. That is, the plan would be for them to establish a small colony with a clergyman. The Fuegians will be arriving in a few days and then you will have the chance to meet them. Originally there were four of them, but one died. The younger ones are around twelve years old, the boy we called Jemmy Button and the girl Fuegia Basket. They are tremendously pleasant and very intelligent. The elder one, York Minster, is sullener and we believe he is around twenty-eight.

During this tour, Stokes kept introducing people to Darwin, who could retain neither names nor faces, no matter how hard he tried. He was only able to remember Wickham, who was second in command, and young King who would be sharing the map room with him and Stokes, and who was the son of well-known Captain King, FitzRoy's superior during his first trip on the *Beagle* and who now commanded the *H.M.S. Adventure*, a much larger ship than the *Beagle*.

"Where do we eat?" asked Darwin.

"There is a main galley for the crew and a smaller one for the officers. That is where I take my meals, but you will have the privilege of dining with the Captain in his quarters. It is a rare privilege that is not often granted, Mr. Darwin."

In the end, darkness and the persistent rain brought the tour to an end, and they agreed on meeting the next day to start stowing Darwin's belongings on board. Darwin was afraid he would not be able to load all the items he had planned to.

The outfitting and loading took a few more weeks. Whenever he had a free moment, FitzRoy would take Darwin to visit the city, which had a rich seafaring history. Amongst other things, it was from where the British fleet, under Francis Drake, had set sail to confront, and defeat, the formidable Spanish Armada at Calais, France, in 1588.

"The legend has it that before leaving to battle, Drake played cards in the taverns near the port, as if to let everyone know that the Spaniards did not worry him, but that is not so." FitzRoy was well versed in military history and enjoyed showing off his knowledge, "The truth is that to leave Plymouth Port the wind must blow from a specific quadrant and this must coincide with receding high tide. This combination happens, on average, only once every four days. So in fact Drake stayed on playing cards while he waited for the conditions to be favourable. We must do the same in early December when we are ready to leave.

They continued walking along the wharfs. The port was protected by a powerful citadel. Its cannon controlled the access to the port, but it had also played an important part in land battles.

"A castle in the city was built by Henry VIII. However, during the Civil War the city sided the Parlamentarians and was besieged for almost four years. Although there was a Parlamentarian victory Charles II was restored and he built here the citadel that we now see."

FitzRoy continued his account, "there," he said pointing at a long pier that jutted out to sea and disappeared into the mist, "is the pier from which the famous Mayflower left, taking the first British colonists to North America, the 'pilgrims'. They surely had good memories of Plymouth since that is the name they gave to their first colony." FitzRoy continued his account, "there," he said pointing at a long pier that jutted out to sea and disappeared into the mist, "is the pier from which the famous Mayflower left, taking the first British colonists to North America, the 'pilgrims'. They surely had good memories of Plymouth since that is the name they gave their first colony."

"As you can see, Mr. Darwin, this port has been a witness to great historic events. One day someone will note that you and I set out from here to circumnavigate the world," this said on a humorous note.

On the ship activity was hectic. Every nook and cranny was used to stow provisions and equipment, since they would not return to England for at least four years. One of the technological novelties that the *Beagle* harboured were installed in the map room: twenty-two portable chronometers that were the most accurate time pieces in Great Britain. Stokes was very excited about this equipment and he explained to Darwin what they were used for.

"To draw maps, or to determine where one is, we use coordinates. Latitude indicates the position relative to the equator, while longitude indicates the angle relative to the Greenwich meridian (Greenwich is near London). To measure latitude a sextant is used, I must confess I have not seen one as accurate as the Captain's. The sextant measures the angle of the sun or a star at its highest point (if it is the sun, this occurs at midday) relative to the horizon. As a ship is constantly moving it is not possible to get a good reading on board, so we usually must land in the morning and wait until midday to take a reading. To measure longitude, we must record the exact time at which the sun reaches its peak. The chronometers are set to Greenwich Time and keep it with great accuracy. As we know the Greenwich Time at the moment the sun reaches its peak we can establish the distance we are from the meridian. The more accurate the chronometer, the smaller the error. We carry twenty-two because in this way we can average the reading and thus increase accuracy. Our estimate is that the error will be less than 20 seconds of a degree, which means that on any point on earth the error will be less than two thousand feet. Never before have there been such accurate measuring and I will be in charge of making them." Stokes face glowed with pride in a way Darwin had seldom seen.

Almost two months went by before the ship was finally ready to set sail. As from that moment the crew was required to stay aboard so they could be mustered as soon as the weather and tide conditions were right. Days went by one after the other. December advanced but Nature seemed not to want to give them permission to leave. Darwin was convinced that they would never leave. When Christmas finally came, the Captain gave the crew permission to go to church for the Christmas Service. After the service many crew members went to bid farewell to the taverns and several got back to the ship stone drunk. On the morning of the 26th the weather conditions were perfect to set sail, but the crew's condition was not. FitzRoy was forced to postpone the start of the voyage for another day. Fortunately on the 27th the weather conditions remained favourable and they were able to sail.

FitzRoy would not let the indiscipline go unpunished. He prepared the commencing speech he would give the crew that afternoon at sea, but he also prepared the punishment for those seamen whose drunkenness had been notorious. Darwin would soon discover a new facet of the Captain's personality, a personality he would never quite grasp and that would eventually lead to tragedy.

Chapter 3

The Seed of an Idea in the Middle of the Ocean

What I remember most of those first days on board was Darwin's seasickness. The start of the trip was not promising, even though the Captain gave a memorable commencing speech from the bridge, which we would remember for years to come.

Once the *Beagle* had sailed past the outer breakwater and sailing was steady, FitzRoy ordered the crew to assemble on deck facing the bridge. From there, shouting over the sound of sea and wind, the Captain rendered a speech intended to boost morale and create what he called the espirit de corps (team spirit). This was common practice in the Royal Navy. He commenced by reading a legend that was written on a wooden plank on the bridge: "England expects every man to do his duty."

He continued, "These were the famous words spoken by Admiral Nelson before the Battle of Trafalgar, in which he defeated the enemy, but lost his life. Nelson did his duty, and that is exactly what we will do, our duty. We shall be away from our country and families for over four years, but we shall return proud of having completed the mission we have been assigned. We shall survey and map the southern part of the American Continent so our ships can traverse safely from one ocean to the other. We will find and mark dangerous rocks, treacherous currents and hidden hazards, but we shall also find the shortest routes and the safest harbours where vessels in distress can ride out storms or wait for help to arrive. To dominate the passage between the oceans is paramount for Britain to rule the seas.

But unlike previous expeditions, our voyage has an added task which is new to the Royal Navy. Apart from the geographic survey we will also make a scientific survey of the whole region. Thus we will search for, classify and take samples of insects, animals, plants and even fungi and also make geological observations. That is why we have Mr. Charles Darwin aboard as a supernumerary, that is, he is not a member of the crew, but shall be treated as an officer. Mr. Darwin has my full support and confidence in achieving our goal. So, gentlemen, to Glory we steer!"

At that very instant two volleys from the ship's cannon marked a perfect closing to the speech. The crew, ecstatic, gave three cheers. FitzRoy had them eating out of his hand. He knew exactly how to handle them. He was their leader and they worshipped him.

When they were all about to return to their duties, the Captain ordered them to stay. What followed was not so nice. Three midshipmen escorted the three seamen charged with drunken behaviour on Christmas Day, who were duly flogged in accordance with the Navy's regulations. In this way FitzRoy also proved he could also be ruthless. Each man must now decide whether he would be among those who 'steered to Glory′ or those that would be whipped.

The men attended the sad ceremony in silence and they all understood that not only did England expect them to do their duty, the Captain did too.

During the first few days the *Beagle* made quick progress. The wind was stiff and the seas were rough, so the ship heaved a lot. Darwin lay in his hammock in the map room feeling miserable, trying to overcome his seasickness. Stokes explained that 'landlubbers' always were seasick at first, but after a few weeks most of them got over it. Darwin feared he was not a member of the majority and wondered, terrified, if he would be able to endure a four year trip in these conditions.

Stokes continued saying that in heavy storms even the most experienced seamen got seasick. "I would say that the only ones who I never saw seasick even in the worst conditions are the Fuegians. When we brought them to England, in our previous voyage, we went through some really fierce storms and they never appeared to be bothered at all."

As days went by and the *Beagle* moved south, the climate turned progressively more benign – they came from a very crude British winter – and the sea was also more serene. Darwin was able to venture on deck and enjoy the good weather. He put together a sort of a funnel made of fishing net and wire that, left to trail in the water for a couple of hours, allowed him to collect marine species. In this way he started his work as the *Beagle*'s Naturalist, while he waited for the first stop at Santa Cruz de Tenerife, Canary Islands.

Early on the 6th January, Stokes shook Darwin awake. "It is almost dawn, we have arrived! Hurry on deck."

Darwin dressed quickly and hurried out. There was hectic activity on deck in spite of it being so early. Many men had got up before their shift to gaze at the magnificent Teide.

The sun had just cleared the misty horizon and could be seen large and orange. With the sun behind him, Charles could see before him an island with a small village made up mainly of white houses, above these a mist obscured the view, but above the mist loomed an imposing mountain that appeared to be of volcanic origin. The top half of its perfect cone was covered in snow, in spite of the fact that they were practically on the latitude of the Tropic of Cancer. The early morning sun gave the snow a yellow-orange tinge that stood out against the dark sky behind it.

This mountain had been sacred for the now extinct natives of these islands, the Guanches. The Spaniards had kept the name the aborigines had given it: El Teide.

"It is much higher than I had imagined," said Darwin.

"It is about twelve thousand feet high, higher than any mountain in England or Wales and probably higher than the Alps."

"It is the most spectacular mountain I have seen. I guess it is because I have never seen one so high, but also because I have always seen mountains as part of a chain while this one is alone and isolated, rising from the sea, which makes it stand out."

"Not so alone or isolated," said Stokes pointing in the direction of the ship's bow, "look over there, on the horizon," another island could be seen, dominated by another mountain, in this case with no snow on its peak, "that island is the Grand Canary. I measured the mountain with my instruments, though I would need to measure it form solid ground to get a really exact reading, and it appears to be close to six thousand feet high, which, for such a small island, is really large."

"What are the rest of the islands of the archipelago like?"

"They are all very rugged, though none with mountains as high as these. Why do you ask?"

"Because I believe that both mountains are volcanoes, probably still active. These Islands are no less than mountains that rise from the bottom of the sea. Constant eruptions have pushed them above sea level. I would think that the whole archipelago has the same origin. When we land I shall verify if the rocks are the result of lava."

"We shall have to wait a couple of hours for that. We cannot land until the port authorities allow us to, and their offices have not opened yet."

Both young men remained silent, their elbows on the handrail, admiring the view the morning offered them. After a few seconds Stokes spoke.

"Tell me Mr. Darwin, I suppose that four months ago you had no idea that you would be invited to be the naturalist on an expedition that would take you around the world. So, how would your life have continued if you hadn't received FitzRoy's invitation?"

"My father, who is a country doctor, wanted me to be one too. But when I started medical school I found that blood and human suffering had a disturbing effect on me. I believe I would never have got used to it, as I think I will never get over seasickness. He was not pleased when I told him I would not be a doctor. I thought that being a minister[1] would be similar. He always used to say that there was not much he could do against sickness and that his main task was to comfort and uphold his patients so they could heal or come to terms with their disease. So I told him that a minister´s job was not too different from a country doctor's only he treated the illness of the soul instead of the illness of the body."

"But to be a minister one must have very strong beliefs. From what you say you don't seem to have received the 'divine call'."

"True, I suppose I hoped to receive the divine call, as you put it, later on. But to be honest, I chose that profession to please my father."

"You seem to have great respect for your father."

"Of course I do, but it was not that I wanted to please him out of respect, but because my father is a very wise man and he clearly knows what is best for me."

"I see... then I guess that now that you will be away from your father for so long you will miss his guidance?"

"I thought I would, but I must have matured, however, since I feel I am doing the right thing regardless of his not being here to give me his approval."

"What did he think of the trip?"

"At first he thought it was a trick of mine to avoid being a doctor or a minister or anything. But then he found out about FitzRoy and spoke to my uncle, another wise man, and he was persuaded that it was a unique

1. Protestant Ministers, as opposed to Catholic priests, may marry and have children, and their social standing was not very different from a doctor's.

opportunity. He imagined that on my return, as a naturalist, I could become a professor at Cambridge and that perhaps that was my true calling. In short he believes I did not get the 'divine call' but I did get 'the call of nature'."

"Ha,ha! In Wales the 'call of nature' is something quite different!"

"I can just imagine!" said Darwin trying to stop laughing, "in Shropshire we call it that when one has to hurry to the bathroom!"

The boys laughed for a while and then fell silent again. After a few minutes Darwin asked:

"And you, Mr. Stokes, how did you get here?"

"I joined the Royal Navy when I was fourteen. At an early age I had read the chronicles of Cook's voyages in the faraway Pacific. I wept when I read the part where he was killed by the aborigines in Hawaii. It was not easy, but I finally convinced my mother to allow me to go to the Naval Academy. I was soon sailing all over the world. It was, and is, my life's dream. My greatest ambition is to be in command of a ship on an exploratory expedition to Australia. I do not believe I will have a chance."

"Why not? You are acquiring experience, and the Captain seems to have great faith in you. You will climb one step at a time; you are on the right track."

Suddenly they noticed that the rest of the crew was tense. "The Captain is coming," they were told, and sure enough, FitzRoy appeared, wearing his best uniform.

"Why is everyone standing around doing nothing? Are you a group of lazy ruffians on holidays?" he evidently was not in a good mood, "Wickham!"

The lieutenant materialized.

"Aye, sir!"

"Hoist the greeting banners so they can be seen from the port. Sullivan! Prepare one of the boats immediately; we shall go to port to arrange our landing authorization."

Jemmy, One of the Fuegians, was close by and said:

"Japtain, no need. Already Spaniards put boat in water."

Jemmy was the smartest of the Fuegians. He had learned to speak English reasonably well, but with a heavy accent. What seemed strange was that he appeared to have forgotten his native language. He communicated with the other Fuegians, York and Fuegia, in English.

"Jemmy, I cannot see anyone coming."

Darwin in 1840, watercolour by George Richmond

FitzRoy used a fatherly tone when addressing Jemmy. It was clear he was his favourite and felt proud of him.

"Jemmy be right. Japtain believe Jemmy. Jemmy see. Use metal eye to see reason."

"Sometimes, Jemmy, I forget you see so much better than we do. You are probably right. Stokes, lend me your telescope, please."

He looked through the telescope and smiled.

"Sullivan! Cancel the boat. They are coming to us."

He gave Jemmy a pat on the back and went towards the bow, his humour had changed. Jemmy smiled and looked around. When he met Darwin's eyes he said "Japtain good man."

What was not good was what the Spaniards told the Captain. They had received news that there was an outbreak of cholera in England. As

Young Robert FitzRoy, by Philip Gidley King

a precaution, to avoid an epidemic in the island, they would have to wait twelve days before disembarking.

The Captain called a meeting in the map room with Wickham, Sullivan, Stokes and Darwin.

"Gentlemen, we have two possibilities. We either wait here for twelve days or we continue to the Cape de Verd islands. We must consider the possibility of being quarantined there too, although I do not think it probable. My first reaction is to continue to Cape Verd, but I need to have the pros and cons clearly set out from every possible point of view. Let us start with you, Mr. Sullivan, do we have enough food and water to allow us to sail to Cape Verd and stand a quarantine of … say, twenty days?"

"Aye, sir. We have enough provisions for three times that, not counting the rain water we may collect".

"Perfect. Mr. Stokes, we must take readings and calculate coordinates as often as possible at different latitudes and longitudes so as to be able, at the end of the voyage, to detect inconsistencies and correct them by distributing them. How would the lack of Tenerife's coordinates affect this plan?"

"Hardly any effect, Captain. The Cape Verd islands' longitude is similar to the Canary Islands, and with the stop we have planned at Fernando de Noronha island we have the Atlantic crossing covered."

"I would like to offset the loss of precision this will cause, though." Looking at the map he pointed at a place in the middle of the ocean. "We will add a stop here, at St. Paul's Rocks, to take readings."

"Excuse me, Captain," Interrupted Darwin, "why can't you take readings of Tenerife from aboard?"

"The ship's movement would not allow Mr. Stokes to take a reading of the sun's peak with the precision that is required. You explain it to him, Mr. Stokes."

"Aye, Captain. We have defined three orders of precision to measure coordinates. The ones of the first order have a precision of less than twenty seconds of an angle. The ship's movement, even in calm weather, generates angles of up to five degrees, which is a thousand times greater than the precision required. The readings taken at sea when there is no land near are used to navigate, to know where you are, but cannot be used to draw maps."

"Well put, Mr. Stokes. Mr. Wickham, what would the delay be in the sailing plan if we stop at St. Paul's Rocks?"

"I would have to re-plot and calculate, but I don't think it would be more than a couple of days."

"Perfect, if we add an extra day to take the readings, it would add three days to our schedule, much less than the twelve days we would spend here. Finally, Mr. Darwin, how do you think missing Tenerife would affect your work?"

Darwin was taken by surprise. He never thought the Captain valued his work and his opinion and was rather pleased to be put on the same footing as the officers.

"It is hard to say, Captain. It will be pity not to be able to study the nature of these rocks from a geologic point of view. These islands, as others in the Atlantic Ocean, seem to have been formed by volcanic activity. But what I can't examine here I will be able to at the Cape Verd islands, which I understand have a similar appearance, and I am very interested in examining some rocks lost in the middle of the ocean, like St. Paul's Rocks."

FitzRoy thought for a moment and then said:

"Very well, gentlemen, we shall skip the Canary Islands and continue directly to the Cape Verd Islands, where I hope we will not be stopped for some ridiculous quarantine, and include a stop at St. Paul's Rocks in our route. Gentlemen, let us sail. Mr. Wickham, weigh anchor immediately!!"

The first time I heard from Darwin a disturbing comment regarding the direction his observations were leading him to, occurred when we were on the boat returning to the *Beagle* from taking readings, measurements and observations at St. Paul's Rocks.

The *Beagle* was waiting about two miles from the little island lost in the middle of the Atlantic Ocean. They had not been able to anchor on account of the great depth, so the Captain decided that the ship should wait relatively far from the islands to avoid the possibility of it being accidentally thrown on the rocks. A party that would make observations left the *Beagle* in two boats. This party included Wickham, Stokes, Darwin and several seamen.

The island's size was just about one square mile and not more than forty feet above sea level at its highest point. The waves pounded the rocks fiercely. Inland the island was practically covered with birds, their nests and offspring. The birds were not used to seeing humans and therefore were quite tame, so they were able to catch many specimens and collect a large amount of fresh eggs.

While Stokes waited for midday to arrive for his readings, Darwin wandered over the island with his geologists hammer, collecting rock samples, birds, insects and several types of crustaceans. A few minutes after midday Stokes declared his task finished and the party returned to the boats. Launching the boats and boarding them safely turned out to be extremely complicated, since the sea was rough and there was no beach where they could slide them gradually into the water. When they finally managed to get them afloat and manned, the seamen started to row, but the headwind would hinder their advance and make their return slower.

Darwin sat next to Stokes and asked him how his readings and calculations had been.

"Fine. The latitude is 55 minutes north of the equator, so tomorrow, when we cross it, you will go through the line crossing ceremony, as all those who cross the equator for the first time must. And your observations? Did you discover anything interesting?"

"From a geologic point of view, the island is definitively volcanic. It is probably the top of a volcano that must be several thousand feet high and rests on the ocean floor. In this it is similar to the Cape Verd Islands, only this one emerged at a later date. Not very different from what we saw of the Canary Islands or what I have read of other islands in the Atlantic, such as Ascension and St. Helena. All this data leads me to believe that the ocean floor is full of volcanoes, but only a few have reached the surface. Maybe there is whole mountain range down there."

Darwin gazed at the horizon his mind was wandering elsewhere.

"But what is stranger and even disturbing, Mr. Stokes, is not geological; it is the flora and fauna."

"But what can be so disturbing about the fauna? I only saw two types of birds. "

"Exactly, only two types, a type of gannet (booby) and a tern (noddy). I couldn't find any insects, except some tics that surely live in the birds' plumage. Why do you think that when God created the world and filled it with animals and plants he only put these two types of birds on this island?"

"I have no idea."

"Well, I believe that when God created the world this island wasn't even here. It emerged later and that is why there were no animals on it. These two types of birds are roving species, they arrived later and found a favourable environment where they could live and reproduce."

"It sounds dead logical and interesting, Mr. Darwin, but I find nothing disturbing about that."

"The thing is that I believe that the same happened in Cape Verd and Tenerife, only long before. The Canary Islands and the Cape Verd Islands emerged from the bottom of the sea without flora or fauna and were populated as the volcanic activity kept pushing them up. Cape Verd has higher mountains, more plants and animals because they emerged earlier and more time has passed. Cape Verd, the Canaries and St. Paul's Rocks are different stages of the same phenomenon. But, and this is the disturbing part, It doesn't seem possible that the six thousand years the Bible says that separate us from creation is enough time for these momentous changes to happen."

Stokes followed Darwin's reasoning with a mixture of admiration and concern. "What makes you so sure that six thousand years is not enough time for these things to happen?"

"You see, Rome was founded about seven hundred years before Christ, which makes it close to two thousand five hundred years ago. The Italy and Europe they describe is not different from what it is today. The Vesuvius and the Etna, just to mention two well-known active volcanoes, are

Young John Lort Stokes, by Lely Bartolomé

not significantly higher than they were then. Furthermore, from what I have heard and read, the area around Naples has received around fifty feet of volcanic ash since the Vesuvius buried Pompeii. Fifty feet in two thousand five hundred years, at that rate, how long would it take to create a mountain the size of the Teide?"

"Let me see, twelve thousand feet at fifty feet every two thousand years ..." Stokes made some quick calculations in his head, and exclaimed, "four hundred and eighty thousand years!"

"Exactly, and that not counting that the height should be calculated from the bottom of the sea, in which case it would be closer to a million years from creation. If we apply the same reasoning to the Pico de Coroa at Cape Verd, it will also give a figure that is at loggerheads with the Bible."

Both young men fell quiet while the boat rocked on the waves and the seamen, oblivious to their conversation, toiled at their oars, eager to reach the *Beagle* soon.

Darwin continued:

"Shortly before leaving England, Professor Henslow, my tutor at Cambridge, presented me with Lyell's book 'Principles of Geology'. What he suggests in his book is that the world is ever changing and that the periods of time in which these changes occur are much longer than what the Bible declares."

"Have you discovered all this in one morning on a solitary island in the middle of the ocean when the trip has hardly started? It's amazing! You are a genius! What else will you discover in the next four years of our journey?"

"No, you must not think that. I haven't discovered anything yet; I have simply put forward a hypothesis that must be backed by solid arguments to become a theory. I will now dedicate the next four years to find and compile the necessary evidence that will allow me to present this theory to the Royal Society[2]."

The boat was now close to the *Beagle* and they could already see members of the crew moving over to starboard to see and help them up.

"I must confess, Mr. Stokes, that I was getting restless because I was not sure what my function was as the expedition's naturalist. I could see the Captain had great expectations about the discoveries I could make, and the bigger his hopes the worse was my fear of letting him down. But ..." Darwin turned and gave St. Paul's Rocks a last glance, "... these rocks lost in the middle of nowhere have changed everything. Now I have a mission to carry out on this voyage."

"How happy the Captain will be! A scientific breakthrough will put his expedition on a higher footing than any other."

"I agree, Mr. Stokes, he will be thrilled, I can hardly wait to tell him."

2. Royal Society of London for the Improvement of Natural Knowledge.

Chapter 4

The Real FitzRoy

We finally arrived in South America. Fernando de Noronha, Bahia de Todos los Santos, Abrolhos and Rio de Janeiro were places we surveyed. My friend Darwin discovered the tropical jungle, and its exuberance, both in animal and plant life. Nowhere else, during our trip, was he able to collect such a variety of specimens. However, I can positively declare that what most shocked young Charles about the Brazilian Empire was seeing slavery up close and what affected him most was to discover a different feature of Captain FitzRoy's personality.

The *Beagle* had arrived at the first area they had to survey. The port of Bahía and its access were not accurately portrayed on any map. The Captain surveyed and recorded most of the area, but decided to interrupt the survey and sail to Rio de Janeiro to report to the Admiralty Headquarters in charge of Royal Navy ships in South America. In Rio they found several Royal Navy ships at anchor. After the normal formalities, FitzRoy was instructed to finish the survey of Bahia, and to then proceed to the River Plate. Darwin and Augustus Earle, the expedition's artist, would stay in Rio de Janeiro until the *Beagle*'s return. Charles used this time to explore the surrounding jungle. From his dwelling in Botafogo he could see the mountain that dominated the area, the Corcovado. It was two thousand feet high and one of its sides was a sheer vertical wall almost a thousand feet long. At its foot there was a dense jungle and a salt water lagoon.

Darwin and Earle befriended an Irish tradesman, Patrick Lennon, who showed them not only places of interest, but also the inner secrets, not always pleasant, of an imperial society whose economy was heavily dependent on slavery. The experience reinforced Darwin's views on the inhumanity of slavery, so widespread in that country, where it would continue to exist for a further fifty years.

The *Beagle* returned almost two months later, with the sad news of the death of three crew-members, brave Morgan and two boys, almost children, Boy James and Musters. They caught a fever during an expedition up the Macacu river from which they would never recover. They died on their way back to Bahía. These deaths deeply affected the crew's morale.

The death of poor little Musters was such a heavy blow to me that many years later, during our next voyage aboard the *Beagle* under the command of Mr. Wickham, we stopped at Bahía to visit young Musters' tomb.

For a Captain the death of a crewmember is a heavier blow than for the rest of the men, since he feels that these deaths were caused by his decisions. These events had a deep effect on FitzRoy's spirits, and surely had a lot to do with the terrible mood he was in for the next few days. Those who did not know him were to discover a new side to FitzRoy's character. It almost ended Darwin's trip.

On 5th January the *Beagle* left Rio de Janeiro and set sail for Montevideo. Normal routine slowly returned. After several months, Darwin resumed his meals with the Captain, in his quarters. Lunch on 6th July was one Darwin would never forget.

It all started during a conversation, which started as so many others before. FitzRoy summarized what he had seen during his second visit to Bahía and Abrolhos. The Captain told Darwin that he had found out the origin of the name Abrolhos; Portuguese sailors knew of the existence of dangerous coral reefs in the area, so they would give those who were going to that area the advice to 'keep your eyes open when going there', which in Portuguese is 'Abra os olhos quando passe pela regiao'. The name derives from the contraction of the first three words. "And that is exactly what one must do when one sails in that area," said FitzRoy, "keep your eyes open."

He then told Darwin about the mangrove at the mouth of the Macacu river where the tragic events that led to the death of the three seamen had started. After this Darwin started to tell FitzRoy of his observations in and around Rio de Janeiro while the *Beagle* was many miles north.

"One thing that shocked me, Captain, was the sight of three heavily armed, very fierce looking men we ran into on our way up the Corcovado. Mr. Patrick Lennon, who accompanied us and was our guide, told us that they were slave hunters. These men are paid per captured slave, dead or

San Salvador de Bahia, Brazil, by Augustus Earle

alive. Turning in a pair of ears is enough to be paid their fee. They were in that spot because many slaves who escape from plantations around Rio de Janeiro choose the jungle around the Corcovado to hide in."

Lennon had told Darwin that not long before one of his own slaves, who had escaped, returned, terrified, because he was being hunted by a group of these men, and he knew that if he was caught, they would kill him.

On the same trek Lennon had shown Darwin and Earle a rock that jutted out over a precipice three hundred feet high. Sometime before a group of escaped slaves had settled down in the vicinity. Eventually they were discovered and surrounded by a group of slave hunters. After some deliberation they gave themselves up, except for one woman who ran to that rock and jumped off, plunging to her death. She chose death to slavery.

"There are distressing stories," said FitzRoy, "I recall one that Captain Paget, from the HMS Samarang, told us. On a plantation he asked one of the slaves what he would want most in the world, and he answered that he would want to see his children again, because they had been sold to another plantation. Slavery requires very conscious and responsible owners for the system to work in a humanitarian way."

"Not even with conscious and responsible owners, Captain!" said Darwin, "I would say that Patrick Lennon is one of the most affable owners with his slaves, however the fact that they have absolute power over these people's lives makes them lose perspective of the meaning of 'conscious and responsible'. One afternoon Earle and I were at his plantation and we witnessed something shocking. Lennon had an argument with his foreman over something of no consequence, but the argument escalated until they were shouting at each other. The Lennon told his foreman that he would sell his daughters, both slaves on his plantation, so he would never see them again. With Earle we managed to cool things down, but the next morning Lennon insisted that he would sell the girls to teach his foreman a lesson. We talked him out of it, I think, but I suspect that as soon as we left he sold them."

"My dear Darwin, I am definitely not in favour of slavery, but we must bear in mind that it has been around for thousands of years. It is mentioned in the Bible, it existed in ancient Rome and in England Serfdom, during the Middle Ages, was a form of slavery. Although I am proud that there is no slavery in the United Kingdom, you cannot deny that it works adequately in the United States of America and in the Brazilian Empire, as we have recently seen. They are both fair societies with a thriving economy."

"How can you say that, Captain?! You can't call a society fair while there are people who can be killed, sold, raped or have their children taken away from them!"

At this point Darwin's tone was impassioned, while FitzRoy's was cold, he evidently was trying to check his temper.

"Mr. Darwin, while you were in Rio, I had the opportunity of visiting a plantation in Bahia that had slaves. I saw where they lived and slept and I can assure you that their dwellings are superior to the ones of most farm hands in England. At my request, the owner assembled a group and asked them if they would rather be free and their answer was NO."

Darwin lost his composure altogether, and, almost shouting, asked the Captain if he honestly thought the slaves would say anything different considering they could be beaten or even killed a few hours later. The Captain rose and stared at Darwin with fury in his eyes.

"This is too much, Mr. Darwin. Do you think I cannot tell whether a person is sincere or not? But if you believe I am either a fool or stupid, then there is no room for both of us in this cabin, nay, maybe even on this ship!"

FitzRoy was beside himself. He threw open the cabin door and shouted, "Wickham!! Come and escort Mr. Darwin out of my cabin!" Darwin did not wait for Wickham to arrive.

"I do not need anybody to show me out of your cabin, Captain," he said defiantly and stomped out. As soon as he was out, FitzRoy slammed the door, which was a message in itself.

Wickham took Darwin to the officer's mess, where they were finishing lunch. The Naturalist trembled with fury at the prospect of being left out of the voyage. He was sure FitzRoy would drop him at the next port and send him back to England. The rest of the officers did not share his fears. They knew their Captain well, in good and bad moods, and they knew how things would turn out.

Sullivan brought Darwin some food and Wickham sat across the table to tell him what FitzRoy was really like.

"Very well, Mr. Darwin, you know what the name FitzRoy means, don't you?"

"Yes, it is from the old Norman-French fils du roy, son of the king."

Slavery scenes, by F. Denis and C. Famin

Rio de Janeiro with the Corcovado in the background, by Augustus Earle

"Exactly. He descends directly from the illegitimate son Charles II had with Barbara Villiers. But you see, two persons live within the Captain, whom he himself calls Fitz, the son and Roy the king. Fitz, the son, is the loyal friend, educated, trustworthy, understanding of human nature and responsible leader. But there is also Roy, the arrogant king, who has a bad temper, does not allow dissent, he humiliates and is partial to drastic measures. Today you met Roy."

"Well, Mr. Wickham, it will be Roy who shall throw me off the *Beagle* and stop me from doing my work. It doesn't change the outcome."

"Don't be so sure. The other feature of his personality is that Fitz is the one usually in charge of his person and he keeps Roy under control, as a prisoner. Only sometimes Roy escapes and takes control, which is what you have just experienced. The good thing, however, is that Roy does not manage to stay in control for very long. After a while Fitz will take over again and things go back to normal. That is exactly what will happen in about an hour or two, you'll see."

"But then, Wickham, The Captain is totally unpredictable."

"Not really. Actually he is quite predictable. Only you must make sure, before making a request or propose something, if it is Fitz or Roy you are speaking to. If it is Fitz, then there is no problem, the Captain will be absolutely rational. If it is Roy, however, it is best to avoid him and wait till Fitz returns.

"And how do you know whether it is Fitz or Roy?"

The officers laughed. Darwin was asking about one of their best guarded secrets. Sullivan said, "we send Wickham to the lion's den to see in what mood he is in." They all laughed again.

"It is true in a way," said Wickham, "I am the first one to see and speak to the Captain every morning, so I will make a comment or ask a question Roy would react to. For example if I told him the main deck is still dirty, Fitz would say: 'when you change the watch, make sure that the outgoing crew clean it before retiring.' Instead, Roy would roar, 'find the culprit and put him in irons till dusk!'"

"When Wickham leaves the Captain's cabin," said Sullivan, "he will say 'the tea was spilt' if it is Roy, or 'the tea has not been spilt,' if it is Fitz, and so we all know how to handle ourselves around him."

"So now, my friend, you are one of us. You must keep our little secret," said Stokes.

Darwin was still worried, "what should I do now, Mr. Wickham?"

"Continue with your usual activities. I suggest you collect marine animals with your net. Give me time. I will go and see the Captain later with the pretext of going over the sailing plan, and I will see what I can do for you."

Two hours later, while Darwin was intent on collecting a series of small marine animals that live on the surface, Wickham appeared on deck.

"Mr. Darwin, the Captain requests your presence in his cabin, I must add that he has not spilt his tea," this last remark with a knowing smile.

When he arrived at the cabin, FitzRoy was waiting for him at the door.

John Clements Wickham

"My friend Darwin, I must apologize for my most inappropriate behaviour." He showed Darwin in. "I believe my state of mind brought out the worst in me."

"I must also apologise for my lack of respect, Captain" said Darwin, "I have no right to raise my voice just because you do not share my views."

"However, more serene, I wanted to explain that my view on slavery is not so different from yours. I believe, as you do, that all men have been created equal and therefore no one has the right to own another person. But in certain countries, as in Brazil and southern United States, if the slaves were suddenly set free, the white population would not give them a chance to integrate in their community and they will be worse off than they are now."

"But do you really believe that the slaves in the plantation you visited did not want to be free?" asked Darwin.

"I do not doubt that from an absolute point of view they did. But I also know they understand that if the owner of the plantation were to free them, they would be hunted by the slavers and be enslaved again in worse conditions than today, or they and their families could be killed. I believe slavery should end, but it must be done gradually, so the former slaves can survive and be accepted as members of the community. In a country with two different races where the difference in their culture and education is so great, if the government does not have an active policy to protect the weaker group, they will be worse off than with slavery."

FitzRoy was being sincere.

"Captain what are the plans for the Fuegian Indians we have aboard?"

"We would want them to be no more and no less than a seed of civilization that may enable their people to be ready to face Argentina and Chile's expansionist pressure when the time comes. If they do not succeed, I am afraid they will disappear."

Unwittingly FitzRoy predicted what would actually happen in the future. Nearly fifty years later, another Englishman, Thomas Bridges, would try to protect these Indians, but no matter what, they would finally disappear.

"My good friend Darwin, again I beg your forgiveness. I believe I am responsible for the death of the three young men as a result of a fever they fall victim to when I sent them to the Macacu river, and that weighs on my conscience. As I said before, this brings out the worst in me. I fear that, and this I tell you in the most strict confidence, the weight of being responsible for the safety of over eighty people may one day plunge me into a depth of despair I may not be able to return from," said FitzRoy with the tone of one who knows he has been defeated.

Chapter 5

A Cemetery of Extinct Species

After rapidly passing through Montevideo and Buenos Aires, we first set foot on the "Wild Pampa" at a place called Bahía Blanca where there was a fort manned by a group of badly equipped soldiers who seemed to be more savage than the Indians they fought against.

The geography of this area is very complicated to sail in. The coast from here to the mouth of the 'Rio Negro' (Black River), many miles south, is plagued with islands, sand banks and channels that are very hard to plot because of the tides. There are many places along the coast that have the appearance of a safe port, which beckon the distressed ship as would the sirens in the Odyssey, to then lead it to disaster by running aground on a sand bank or be left stranded when the tide goes out, or, worse, hit an underwater rock.

So, due to this difficulty, Captain FitzRoy decided to spend whatever time was needed to survey the area properly. The size of the territory and the shallowness of the adjacent waters made it impossible to survey it with the *Beagle*, so the Captain decided to lease two smaller vessels from a Mr. Harris, and Englishman who lived in the area. One would be in Wickham's command and the other in mine. It was the first time I had command of a ship.

While we were outfitting these vessels, Mr. Darwin seized the opportunity to explore the area.

Darwin invested most of his time in hunting local animals to augment his collection. In this part of the Pampa, in spite of there being plenty of water, the vegetation was scarce, mainly grasslands and a few bushes; the animal life was abundant and varied: ñandu (rhea), guanacos, foxes, pumas, deer and several varieties of armadillos.

On the 22nd September the *Beagle* was anchored in an inlet called Pozo de Belgrano, that was one of the few places where there was deep water for ships to lay. The shore had a low cliff about twenty feet high, the highest point being known as Punta Alta (High Point). From the face of this cliff, where Darwin dug, he found several bones of unknown animals. After working hard all day to unearth them, he hauled them back to the ship.

Wickham watched, appalled, as Darwin unloaded these enormous bones covered in dirt and gravel, littering his pristine deck.

"Mr. Darwin, what is all this garbage doing on my ship?"

"These are fossils, not garbage, and I have put them here to clean, catalogue and later put them away. It took me all day to unearth them."

"It took my crew all day, too, to clean the deck and you have littered it in half a minute."

At that moment FitzRoy, in the company of Harris, turned up. They stared at the results of Darwin's work in astonishment.

"Any discovery Mr. Darwin?" asked FitzRoy.

"Fossils, Captain."

"Of what animals, if I may ask?"

"You may ask, but I cannot answer you, because I frankly don't know."

As he spoke, Darwin brought a bucket of water, and with a brush started cleaning the bones. FitzRoy picked up what seemed to be a stone imbedded with many shells. "What interest do these oysters have, my friend? The place is full of these animals."

"That is correct, Captain, but what makes them interesting is that I did not find them at sea level, but at the top of the cliff. There shouldn't be oysters there, unless the sea was at that level many years ago. Either the land was pushed up or the sea dropped to its current level. The latter is probably not the case, since we would have noticed that all over the world."

"I agree with you on that, the land must have been pushed up. Look what I have found." FitzRoy showed Darwin a piece of pumice stone.

"Mr. Harris says there are many in the area. Probably Sierra de la Ventana (Window Range) conceals a volcano that pushed all this area up."

"I doubt it, Captain," said Darwin as he examined the stone. "In Sierra de la Ventana there is no volcano. The rocks are either granite or quartz, none of these are volcanic. But what you found is definitely volcanic, so they must have come from some other volcano."

"The nearest one is in the Andes," said Harris.

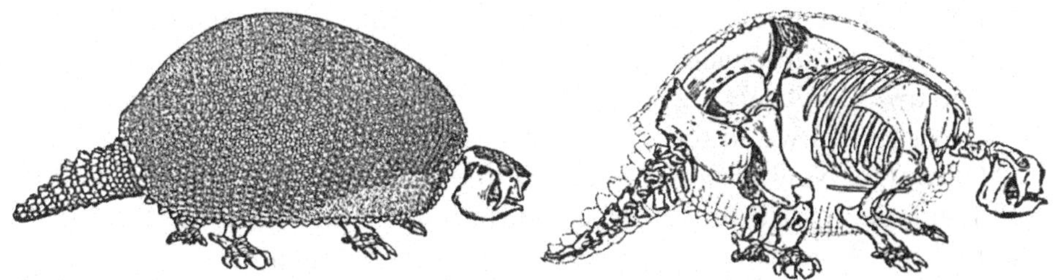

Glyptodon or giant armadillo

"That is over three hundred miles from here! It must have been a tremendous explosion to throw rocks this far, maybe the same explosion that killed all these strange animals." FitzRoy said this as he looked at what seemed to be a large skull, "what do you make of this, Darwin?"

"It seems to have been an animal similar to a rhinoceros. They might have lived here, as they do today in Asia and Africa, and perished due to a great cataclysm, as you say. But look at this one," and he showed him a shell that seemed to be of a giant armadillo, almost three feet across.

"Amazing!" said FitzRoy, "Mr. Harris, have you knowledge of the existence of an armadillo this size?"

"No, Captain, I am as astounded as you are. I have never seen animals like the ones Mr. Darwin has found."

"I must still study and catalogue them, Captain, but I must declare that what is surprising is that I did not find bones of any present-day animals."

"And what does that mean?"

"Just imagine, if a great cataclysm killed these animals, it should have killed guanacos or pumas. Why is it that I only find bones of animals that are extinct?"

"Well thought, but a difficult question, Mr. Darwin. One possibility would be that the incident, an eruption, maybe, was selective, killing the plants that these animals ate, causing their death, while the guanacos were able to eat other plants and were able to survive."

"It could be, Captain, but I think it is not likely that the ash would affect only one type of plant and that these animals only ate that type of plant. I would suggest a different alternative. Maybe these were the only animals that lived in this region, and as the eruption killed them all, later the guanacos, foxes and pumas and other animals we know today moved in."

"But Darwin, in that case these animals should still exist in areas not affected by the cataclysm."

"You are absolutely right, Captain. Let me clean, study and catalogue these fossils and we can work out an answer to this enigma later."

"Of course! Now we have a subject to talk about for several breakfasts and meals in my cabin. But let me point out: Today, 22nd September, In Punta Alta, Argentina, you, Charles Darwin, have made a discovery of fossils of extinct animals which will be remembered. Maybe, many years from now, they will build a museum here in your name. Congratulations," and he shook Darwin's hand. Harris nodded in awe.

"I would be satisfied with a lot less," said Darwin with a broad smile, accepting the compliment.

FitzRoy walked off along the deck with Harris and he was overheard saying "I knew I had made the right choice when I asked him to be our naturalist on this voyage."

A few days later the *Beagle* was sailing close to the shore about thirty miles east of Punta Alta. The Captain had decided to build a stone landmark at a place known as Monte Hermoso. The shores of the flat Pampas do not have prominent features that can be used as natural landmarks that would give sailors a reference point. Monte Hermoso was the highest point on the coastal cliffs, so a landmark in this place would give sailors a reference point which would help them find the access channel to the deep-water port called Pozo de Belgrano.

A fairly large group, led by FitzRoy, landed in four boats. This group included Stokes, who would take readings and establish the coordinates, and Darwin.

The Captain, with the main group, got down to the construction of the landmark. As had been done with previous landmarks, to build it they started by digging a hole about four feet deep. There they would first place a ceramic plaque that had an inscription which indicated that it had been built by the crew of the *Beagle* in 1832. Over this plaque small stones would be arranged in layers, which increased in rock size as it grew. Once it reached ground level they would use the largest and flattest rocks they could find, which would be piled one on the other until it reached a height of at least six feet. One of these flat rocks that the crew had reserved to build the landmark caught Darwin's eye. It was not strictly a rock but rather sediment that had petrified over a long period of time. What had caught his eye was that on one of its sides you could clearly see a ñandú (rhea) footprint. He asked the seamen where they had found it, and they answered that in certain parts of the beach, under the sand, there was a very hard rocklike sheet which they had broken with their hammers to use them for the landmark.

"Captain, if you don't mind I'll just go down the beach to have a look at the rock-like sheet under the sand."

"I don't mind at all, but don't go alone, this is Indian territory. Mr. King!" shouted FitzRoy, "please escort Mr. Darwin, maybe you will witness some great discovery. Go armed."

"We will hurry because I believe there is a storm looming, but we have to wait until midday anyway for Mr. Stokes to be able take his readings and calculate the coordinates, so you have about four hours."

Darwin and young King walked along the beach. Every so often they would stop and dig up the sand a little until they reached the hard rock sheet below. Every time they found footprints of guanacos and pumas and ñandú and several types of birds.

"How strange," said Darwin.

"What is strange? They are all animals that are quite common in the area."

"Yes, but these animals are rarely seen on the beach. On the other hand, there are no traces of animals that are on the beaches, like shellfish. I would not have been surprised if I had found these inland, but here, on the beach ... it is very strange."

"And how do you explain it, Mr. Darwin?"

"I believe that when these prints were left this was not near the sea at all. Maybe at that time the sea was several miles further away. That would mean that either the sea raised or the land dropped. I would even venture to say that it was very far from the sea and that the sheet was the bottom of some shallow fresh water pond. The reason for the amount of footprints is that these animals would come to the pond to drink and left their prints in the muddy bottom. It later dried up and turned into this rock we see today. Finally the sea rose and the waves cleared part of these rocks."

King was impressed by the amount of deductions Darwin could make by just looking at a stone anyone else would not even give a second glance to.

The wind had started to blow harder and clouds were obscuring the sky. It was still two hours to midday, so there was still time. They continued walking and soon dug up another piece of rock sheet, but this one surprised both of them. They stared at it in disbelief and then went on to clear a larger area and it confirmed their incredible finding.

These were several footprints three or four times larger than a human one. From the print that had been left in that ancient lagoon, these feet seemed to possess a very large toe which must have ended with a large and powerful nail or claw. The sequence of the footprints indicated that this animal walked on two legs, but it must have been much larger than a human being. King instinctively took his hand to his waist and felt more at ease when he found he had his pistol with him.

"What is this, Mr. Darwin?"

"I don't know. I am as lost as you are. I have never seen anything like it."

A stiff southeast wind was blowing. Darwin and King hurried back to place where they had left the main group, only to find that only two boats remained on the beach. Stokes told them that as the weather had deteriorated so much, the Captain was concerned that they might not be able to return to the *Beagle*, which was undermanned and with few officers. So he decided to return with two of the boats since he believed the storm would warrant his presence on board. The rest of the group would wait until Stokes finished his midday readings and calculations.

When those two boats left, the sea was so rough already that they just managed to get passed the breakers. By midday it was not possible to return to the *Beagle*. Stokes, being the highest-ranking officer, decided to ration their food since he did not know when they would be able to return to the ship. An hour later the storm unleashed: thunder, lightning, squalls and pouring rain. The temperature dropped dramatically.

They managed to pull the boats to safety above the high-water mark, and turning them on their side, with the sails put together a makeshift shelter, but they were soaked none the less. Darkness came, but the rain prevented them from building a fire. They ate the remaining food.

"I am not sure the *Beagle* can remain anchored with this wind," said Stokes, "maybe the Captain will decide to take it out to sea."

"And what is the advantage of doing that?" asked Darwin-

"With this sort of wind the ship puts a great strain on the anchor. It could tear loose, which means the ship would be adrift and could run aground before the crew manages to steer it, or, worse, the chain could break which would leave the ship in the same predicament, but minus an anchor."

"How many anchors does the *Beagle* have?"

"We carry three, which we will need when we get to Tierra del Fuego, where our lives may depend on a good anchor. And in this part of the world, Mr. Darwin, a good anchor is hard to come by."

"So why is the *Beagle* still at anchor there?"

"To protect us. We probably will not be able to return tomorrow either and would be defenceless if the Indians decided to attack us. In that case the *Beagle* could defend us with its cannon."

"What will the Captain do?"

"He will stay as long as he can."

They both looked into the darkness to seaward and were comforted by the dim lights of the *Beagle*.

They suffered a cold, wet, sleepless night. By morning the wind still howled and it was very cold, but it had stopped raining. The sea was fierce and the waves beat at the cliff with fury.

They managed to start a fire to warm up a bit, and split in two groups to try and find something to eat. All they could find were two birds that had been killed by the storm which were quickly turned into breakfast.

The *Beagle* rocked furiously in the waves, but it was still there, watching over them.

At noon they saw that a boat was lowered from the *Beagle* and started off towards them. It was the Captain who was risking heavy seas with a few seamen to try and get some food to them. They would not be able to get passed the breakers, so Stokes sent two seamen, with life jackets, to swim towards the boats. From far out, FitzRoy managed to toss the provisions in their direction and returned to the *Beagle*. Lunch was much better than breakfast and there was still enough left over for the evening.

That afternoon the wind subsided, but the seas were still fierce, so they could not return yet. Night came and although it was cold, a good fire helped them sleep warm and dry. The clear starry sky promised good weather and the prospect of returning to the comfort of their quarters on board.

A hand shook Darwin. "Mr. Darwin, wake up! Come and see a fantastic sight!" It was Stokes. Darwin followed him up the sand dunes to the place where the landmark had been built. Looking out to sea from this vantage point they could see the *Beagle* tossing in the rough seas.

"The other way," said Stokes. Darwin turned to look inland. From there they could see the Sierra de la Ventana mountain range white-topped from an overnight snow-storm. Just as the Teide, in Tenerife, the

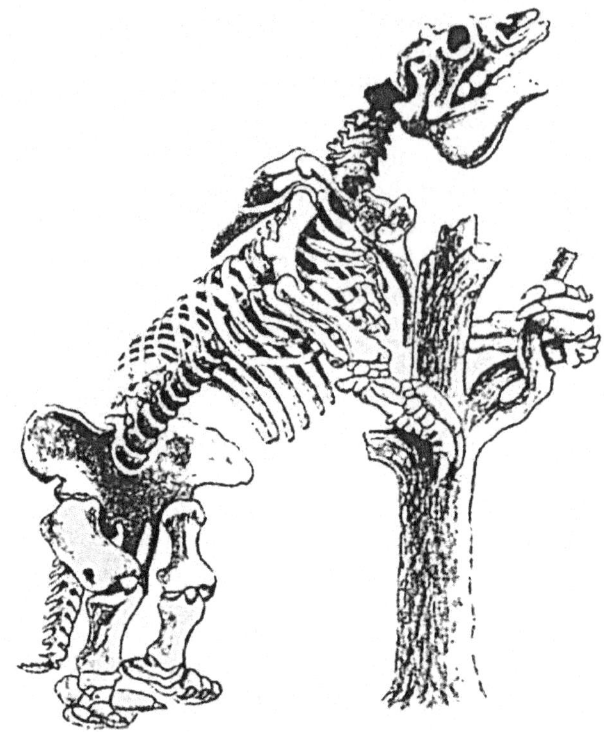

Mylodon, extinct ten thousand years ago

morning sun made them glow triumphant in orange glory. The Greeks must have been inspired by a similar view when they thought their Gods lived on the Olympus.

"The Captain will be coming to fetch us soon, but until then, please tell me about your observations and deductions. What is this about a giant footprint?"

"Exactly that, a giant footprint of an animal that walked on its hind legs, probably in the same way as bears do at times."

"How large would this animal be?"

"It is hard to say. There is a footprint comparative method based on the fact that in the same terrain the area of a footprint is proportional to the animal's weight. According to this theory, an animal that is double the weight of another would leave a footprint double the size. I compared this footprint with that of a guanaco on the same rock sheet and it is twenty times its size. This animal is biped, so it rests one foot at a time while the guanaco, being a quadruped, rests two at a time, so the ratio is ten to one. I would say it weighed about eight times a human being and probably was twice as tall."

"Could it be a giant human?"

"The footprint is completely different to a human one; it is from an extinct species."

"Amazing. And has it disappeared lately?"

"I don't think so. These footprints are very old, at least several thousand years. I did not find any marine animals on these rocks, which means that this was not near the sea, probably several miles from it, because this must have been a fresh water pond where animals came to drink."

The men could see that two boats were being lowered from the *Beagle*. The Captain would be coming to verify the landmark that had been built, and Darwin would take him to see his discovery.

"There is another thing that transpires. The sea was far from here, so this process must have been a lot slower than in a volcanic region, so I have come to the conclusion that the Creation occurred at least a million years ago."

"I see ... maybe Lyell is right and the Bible is not as precise as most people believe. Some problem! What does the Captain think of this?"

"FitzRoy wants to have a clearer picture before jumping to conclusions. But he is as excited as I am with the way the observations are taking us."

The boats from the *Beagle* had almost reached the beach.

"Tell me, Mr. Darwin, what are those bags full of stones you are carrying"

"Fossils I found on the cliff face."

"How many fossils and how easily they appear, do they not?"

"That is true, Mr. Stokes. The Pampa seems to be a cemetery of extinct animals."

The boats had already arrived at the beach. Darwin and Stokes started down from Monte Hermoso (Beautiful Hill), but first they gave the Sierra de la Ventana one last look. The landmark, built of stones with mysterious footprints, would be the only witness of their passing.

Two days later Darwin was having lunch with FitzRoy. He had his notes with him since the Captain wanted to be kept up to date regarding the scientific side of the expedition. FitzRoy considered himself a scientist. His mentor had been Admiral Beaufort, a seaman who had developed a wind force scale[1] that had proven to be very useful to sailors. FitzRoy wanted to study storms and find a way of predicting them. He permanently measured atmospheric pressure, temperature, relative humidity and wind direction and kept a log of this data, and endeavoured to find a correlation between the data collected before each storm.

The Captain was open-minded and had a sharp intellect so their conversations were always stimulating.

"So then, Mr. Darwin, it seems you have found a great deal of remains of extinct animals and also volcanic rocks that must have come from some explosion hundreds of miles from here."

"I have been studying these fossils and I have found that many of these extinct species are relative to present day animals."

"Let me add another thought, Darwin, these animals were much larger than today's. What can that mean?"

"Maybe before the cataclysm there was more food here. Maybe later when everything was covered with ashes food was scarce. Only small animals can survive on little food."

"Then, as you suggested before, the large animals died and smaller ones moved in from other territories."

"It could be, Captain, but I have come up with bolder idea."

"Go ahead, my friend. What is this idea?"

"Maybe they did not all die. Some may have changed over several generations to adapt to the new circumstances. Some might have changed their habits and others simply grew smaller. That was surely the case of the armadillo, of which I found the fossilized armour, that must have weighed fifteen times that of the largest you can find today."

"In truth, Darwin, it is very bold but also very interesting. And let me add something that I believe supports your idea. Some years ago I visited a friend of mine who breeds race horses. He told me that he only used the fastest stallions to mate with his mares and as a result today's horses are much faster than the ones that raced a century ago. It means that he chooses the fastest to breed so each generation is faster than the previous one."

"Excellent example, Captain! In this case it is the breeder who selects which horses will be bred. I am not sure what the mechanism would be in wild animals."

"In that case the selection could be natural. A female armadillo would have several offspring of different sizes. The larger ones would not sur-

1. The Beaufort Wind Force Scale.

vive for lack of food but the smaller ones would thrive and reproduce. Naturally this system would not be quick enough to survive a volcanic eruption."

"Maybe not, in that case they would all die without offspring. But the mechanism you described would account for the way some animals adapt to slower changes that are nevertheless very important."

"What changes do you mean, Darwin?"

"The sea seems to have advanced and retreated several times, which would have produced severe changes in the climate. Only a few animals could adapt to such great climate changes."

They had finished their meal a long time before, but were so taken up with their conversation that they would not get up.

"But, Captain, all this has some unexpected effects."

"Of one we have already spoken, my friend, that the Bible may not be exact when the Book of Genesis narrates the Creation. That I will leave to you, since you intend to be a minister you must have better knowledge in that area."

"Captain, I do not intend to be a minister! But in any case, the effect I refer to is that not only have some species disappeared, but others have changed, creating, I believe, new species."

"I see it as perfectly logical. More so, I am sure the natural process must be similar to the one used by my friend the horse breeder."

Two men in a small cabin in a ship rocked by waves near a muddy beach somewhere in South America were making inroads in science as no one had ever made before.

Little did they know, at the time, that these same ideas they were developing together, would one day pull them apart for the rest of their lives.

Chapter 6

Danger at Woolya

I have wondered many a time when and where did Captain FitzRoy start losing confidence in his command and in himself, and I have come to the conclusion that it must have been at Woolya. Perhaps it was there that he started to have doubts about himself, perhaps it was there that he started to think that things would not always turn out for the best and slowly started to be obsessed by the idea that he may fail, not only in this voyage, but in life itself. Certainly this would, almost two years later, lead to a crisis that would affect us all.

During the month of December 1832 the *Beagle* sailed in and around the channels and inlets of Tierra del Fuego. The purpose was, apart from surveying the area, to find a suitable location to set up the first Anglican mission in the extreme south of the continent. This mission would consist of the three Fuegians aboard (Jemmy, Fuegia and York Minster) and Reverend Richard Matthews.

During the process of surveying these difficult shores, they often had to land to take readings and calculate coordinates. On several of these landings they came across Fuegian Indians who always seemed anxious to meet the Europeans. Their curiosity was colossal, only surpassed by their desire to own the crew's possessions. It usually started with the Fuegians asking for things, shoes, buttons, bottles, hats, handkerchiefs ... anything at all. They would repeat "yammerschooner", which the Englishmen believed meant "give me", over and over while pointing at the object they wanted. It did not matter if they had been given presents, they would continue demanding in an increasingly emphatic manner. When they realized they would not be given anything else, they started to propose bartering; a sealskin for a belt or blubber for a candle. One even offered one of his daughters in exchange for a knife. When they came to the conclusion that this did not work either, they simply stole whatever they fancied.

Darwin did not believe the civilizing and evangelizing effort would succeed, but FitzRoy was optimistic. He proudly pointed out the enormous differences between the savage Fuegians and the civilized ones they had on board. This proved, according to the Captain, that with an effort, many others could be civilized. "See how they ask for things. It means they want what civilization can give them. Once they see that at the mission many of these things are produced, they will surely join it."

It was strange to observe the reaction of the 'civilized' Fuegians when they met up with the savage ones. At first they tried to pass for Europeans. An elder of one of the tribes recognized York Minster, who started to laugh as if the thought of him being a Fuegian was ridiculous. He then showed the old man his clothes as if saying: "Can't you see I'm wearing clothes? I'm from the ship."

Jemmy, when in the company of seamen, would laugh at his own people, "ha, ha, look at them, they're almost naked!" or "they look like animals!"

Fuegia, the Fuegian girl, now around twelve, refused to leave the *Beagle* and meet the other Indians.

Darwin asked Jemmy if he wanted to stay in Tierra del Fuego or if he would rather return to England. Jemmy answered:

"No place for me in England, Mr. Darwin. Like it or not, this my place. Jemmy must live here."

Almost a year later, FitzRoy would ask him the same question.

After enduring a terrible storm on Christmas day just off Cape Horn, Captain FitzRoy decided to find a safe harbour for the *Beagle* and take four boats to look for a good spot for the colony in the vicinity of Navarino Island.

On 19th January 1833 a group of twenty-eight people, including the Captain, Darwin the Fuegians and Reverend Matthews, left the *Beagle*. Three days later they found a place they thought was ideal and named it Woolya. The Captain instructed the crew to start the construction of cabins and to prepare the site where the vegetable garden would be; it was the beginning of what promised to be grand project.

A few hours later Indians started to arrive in their canoes. At first they just watched the white men's work with some curiosity, then started "yammerschooning". By the end of the day there were close to 200 Indians, the men watched the white men's activity while the women set up camp and collected food.

Fuegian Indian, by Conrad Martens

Jemmy helped Darwin collect specimens of certain strange plants which only he knew where to find. They were both with their backs toward the sea when suddenly Jemmy said, "My brother comes." Darwin turned and saw several canoes approaching in the distance.

"How do you know, Jemmy?" he asked.

"Me hear him," and then pointed at one of the canoes furthest away, "and now see him."

Darwin, and the rest of the *Beagle*'s crew, had learned to trust in the Fuegians extraordinary sight and hearing. They usually could see things that the Europeans could hardly see with the aid of a telescope. Both their sense of sight and hearing were greatly developed compared to a white man; this was probably a necessary element for their survival. Darwin couldn't help wondering if this was not proof that human beings also changed to adapt to their environment.

"In canoe behind, my mother."

"How did you hear your brother? I didn't hear him shout."

"He not shout. He told mother that he see me next man from ship, you Mr. Darwin."

"Clearly his sight is as good as yours, Jemmy, since you were not only far away but you had your back to him. Go on down to the shore and greet them."

"I don't care to say hello Mr. Darwin. They believe I traitor. They not want me now."

"But you must explain that you were taken to England by force, that you did not want to go!"

"Will not work, Mr. Darwin. I wear sailor clothes, they think I prefer to be sailor, not Fuegian."

"Then dress like they do." Darwin was always amazed not only by Jemmy's sharp mind, but by a matureness far beyond his fifteen years, quite the opposite to York Minster, who, at twenty eight, was exactly what he appeared to be: an extremely coarse man.

"Me no want to dress as Fuegian for sailors to make fun of me. Me no want to be like them," he pointed at some of the Indians who were watching the proceedings, "Me want to be Fuegian of British colony in Woolya; that is why I dress like Englishman."

Jemmy acknowledged, with the resignation usually found in older men, that he did not belong to any of the worlds he knew. He did not consider himself an Indian any longer, but he wasn't British either. He felt that the only way to find a place for himself was to be part of a successful colony at Woolya. Darwin did not have much confidence in the success of the colony, but did not want to burden Jemmy with his pessimism. He was very worried by the way the Fuegians rejected Jemmy. If the colony did not succeed he would be in trouble.

As the building of the little hamlet advanced, the Indians escalated from "yammerschooning" to more vocal and aggressive demands, including threats, although they never got to act on them. FitzRoy had a rope fence put around the compound where the cabins and the crew's camp site were, and had made the Fuegians understand that they were

Jemmy Button dressed as an Englishman, by Robert FitzRoy

not allowed to cross it. Many of them, as defiant children would, stood next to the fence, touching the rope, as if saying, "Ha! I can be here!" Then one afternoon a spade went missing.

At night FitzRoy set up a five man watch to guard the perimeter. But on the third night there was an unsettling incident. One of the Fuegians, who until then had accepted the fence as a barrier, attempted to cross at the point of entry. Naturally, there was a sentry there, but the Indian shoved him, trying to push past him. The sentry, who was of a larger build than the Fuegian, pushed back and the Indian was sent sprawling. He went into hysterics and, looking the sentry in the eye, made signs to the effect that he would cut his throat and eat his heart.

Worried by this act of aggression, FitzRoy decided that a show of force was in order, to convince the Fuegians to keep their distance. So he organized a shooting practice. They picked targets that would show the destructive power of bullets. The Indians were astounded. When, after about an hour of shooting, the practice was declared over, the Indians went off muttering to each other. Surprisingly, about two hours later the canoes started to leave and by mid-afternoon there were no Indians left in Woolya.

FitzRoy's confidence in his project returned. He decided that, since there were no aggressive Indians in the vicinity, it would be a good idea to leave the three Fuegians and Reverend Matthews to have a first night on their own. The Captain, Darwin and the rest of the crew left on the boats to camp at some other site out of reach. His idea was to return the next day to see if everything was going well. It would be the Woolya Colony's maiden night.

That night FitzRoy could not sleep, worried by what could be going on at the colony. He woke everybody up earlier than usual and gave instructions to break camp and leave immediately. "If everything is all right, we will breakfast at Woolya." The twenty minutes it took them to reach Woolya seemed to FitzRoy the longest of his life. When they sailed round a point and saw Woolya straight ahead, he felt a wave of relief: the three cabins were standing and there were no Fuegians in sight.

As soon as the boats reached the beach, Fit Roy jumped out. Matthews came out of one of the cabins smiling, proving everything was well.

"Captain, you must not worry about us. No one will bother us, they know we are peaceful, that we won't harm them. They will eventually learn who God is and that He protects us."

"So, no canoe came near?"

"No, Captain, and they won't. Only York Minster thinks that they did not appear because they knew you were near and that they will return the moment you are not around anymore. But I am sure he is mistaken."

FitzRoy and Darwin exchanged glances. They were already very much a team and they both had the same thought: that York Minster was right. But what could they do? The colony had to operate on its own. The *Beagle* would not be around to protect them forever. It had to find its own destiny, whatever that may be.

The Captain took a cautious decision. He sent two of the boats back to the *Beagle* to let Sullivan know they were all well (Wickham had remained surveying the area around the Rio Negro with the two boats FitzRoy had leased). The Captain, with the other two boats would continue surveying the channels and would return to Woolya in about a week to see how things were working out.

They boarded the boats and shoved off at midday. As they sailed away, FitzRoy kept looking at the receding cabins. Darwin could read worry in his eyes, he felt responsible for the four people he was leaving behind. Would he see them again?

The survey of the channels and islands south of Tierra del Fuego was both fascinating and dangerous. The risk of being caught in a sudden, fierce storm was always there. The one they had gone through near Cape

Horn after Christmas was in everyone's mind. On the other hand the dense forests, the white frosty waterfalls and the misty mountainsides gave the place an eerie and mysterious atmosphere.

Glaciers flowed down to the sea in several places and the pieces that broke off them crowded the water around them with ice floes of a deep sky-blue. They decided to set up camp at one end of a small cove across from a glacier that reached down to the sea. While they cooked their meal they admired the colours of the ice and were enthralled by the rumble and crack of the ice that sometimes resembled thunder.

They ate their dinner sitting around the fire, chatting happily and content. Suddenly a loud explosion made them turn towards the glacier in time to see a great mass of ice hit the water creating a great wave that rushed in their direction.

"The boats! They will be destroyed!" shouted Darwin who jumped up and sprinted to where the boats had been beached. Several men followed him and they managed to hold on to the ropes before the wave hit them. It washed over the men and lifted the boats, but they managed to hold fast and saved them from destruction.

The whole incident lasted just a few minutes. When the rest of the men arrived it was over. FitzRoy said approvingly:

"Mr. Darwin, your speed has saved us from being stranded on this beach. You are the hero of the day!"

"In that case I deserve a reward. An extra glass of rum, perhaps?"

"Much more than that, tomorrow you will see."

Next morning they started out early to continue the survey. The mist was dispersing, so, as they left the cove, they saw that behind it towered a mountain.

FitzRoy stood up and pointing at it said, "gentlemen, I give you Mount Darwin! Congratulations, Mr. Darwin. Now your name will be on all the maps of Tierra del Fuego."

"Thank you, Captain. I am touched; I don't know what to say ..."

"It is the highest peak in the area, close to six thousand feet. You deserve it, thanks to you we can sail out of here today."

After a few days they set sail back to Woolya. Their tension and anxiety grew with every mile they advanced as they worried about how the colony was faring. When they sailed into the channel that would take them there they saw several canoes leaving. FitzRoy frowned. That was not a god sign.

"I am afraid, Darwin, that something has happened that is not good. Those Fuegians are leaving Woolya beach because they saw us coming. They have surely been up to mischief and fear our reaction."

As they drew closer they could see that two of the cabins had been destroyed and the third one was in very bad shape. When the boats grounded on the beach, Reverend Matthews rushed out of the remaining cabin with terror written on his face and in a terrible state.

"Captain, Captain! Your arrival has saved my life!"

Behind him the three 'civilized' Fuegians came out of the cabins. Although they did not look very well, their faces showed no fear; Matthews' did. When FitzRoy saw them he was relieved. "Matthews, you must tell me what happened, from the very beginning." The men started a fire and cooked some food. When they were all settled round the fire, Matthews started his tale.

The first day after the British had left things where quiet. No Indians turned up. The next day around thirty turned up in several canoes; while the women got down to setting up camp, the men watched what was going on at the colony without saying a word or even asking for anything. Now Matthews understood that they were not sure if the ship would return or not. As time went by more canoes arrived with more Indians. The minister would have liked to believe they came out of curiosity, but he feared they were preparing the last assault.

By then there were a great deal of people crowding around the colony. Sensing that the British ship had left and would not return, they got progressively bolder. They did not ask for anything, but whatever was left on the floor they would snatch and run away. They also started to shout at them. According to Jemmy, they shouted "white man's friends!" in a way that meant "traitors". But they shouted different words at Matthews. Jemmy had not wanted to translate for Matthews, but now that FitzRoy was there with them he said that what they shouted was "we will eat your heart!"

On the fourth day, when Jemmy took a bucket to go and fetch water, another Indian, who had a larger build pushed him to the ground and snatched the bucket from him. Seeing this, Matthews ran after him, and taking advantage of his size snatched the bucket back from the Indian, but immediately two other Indians grabbed him, threw him down and pinned him to the floor. The put their faces next to his and gnashed their teeth as if saying "we will chew you up". They took the bucket and walked away squabbling over it. Neither Jemmy nor York attempted to

Fuegian Basket, by Robert FitzRoy

defend Mathews. "Bad Fuegians, could kill everyone," said Jemmy in his defence.

The next day widespread plundering broke out. Evidently the Indians had come to the conclusion that the British would not be returning and decided to take everything they wanted. Matthews and the three Fuegians shut themselves up in one of the cabins from where they could hear the Indians shouting. They were pillaging and carrying away everything: clothes, spades, rope, pots, nails, seeds ... nothing was left out. The voracity with which they went for everything often started quarrels amongst them over who would keep a certain item. From their cabin, Matthews watched and wondered when they would try to break in. Fortunately darkness came and some rain dampened their spirits a little, but they could hear their raving shrieks. Jemmy and York said nothing; they knew the worst was yet to come.

In the morning three of the men tried to break into the cabin. Matthews tried to prevent them but they managed to open the door. So Matthews confronted them, which was a dumb thing to do. He applied his knowledge of boxing, British rules, and felled two of them who sprawled with bloody noses. At this, about twenty other Indians ran in, howling, and took hold of Matthews. They threw him down pummelled and kicked him and started to drag him by his hair towards the sea.

Suddenly a shout was heard from one of the canoes. They were all petrified for a moment, and then, in unison, they all rushed off to undo their camp, leaving Matthews face down in the water. Jemmy and York ran to help him. The minister spat blood, and maybe a tooth, and was helped back to the cabin. Meanwhile the Indians hurriedly loaded their belongings on the canoes and took off paddling furiously. The beach was deserted in under five minutes. "They saw Captain coming, that is why they leave," said Jemmy with a smile.

"And that was how your arrival saved my life."

"What were they going to do to him, Jemmy?"

"They take him to other island, kill him and eat his heart. Reverend shouldn't hit bad Indians. They many. Not smart thing to do."

"Clearly you cannot stay here, Matthews."

"But what will happen to the colony?" though his tone was of relief rather than worry.

"That depends on our three friends, here," said FitzRoy looking at Jemmy, Fuegia and York. "What do you want to do? Return to the *Beagle*? Set up a colony somewhere else or stay here?"

"Fuegia and me stay here. She be my woman," said York. Fuegia obediently nodded her approval

"And you, Jemmy?"

"I stay here. It be my place, I must accept it."

"But aren't you afraid of staying among such violent people? Not even your family will defend you!" Darwin could not believe that such a bright young man could prefer such a bleak future.

"Jemmy only afraid of being Jemmy no more," he said with sadness in his voice. The part of him that liked to dress with gloves and top hat and ride in a carriage around London would have to be forgotten.

"That is not so, Jemmy," said FitzRoy forcefully, "This does not mean you must forget the colony. The three of you should continue with the vegetable garden, fix the cabins ... I shall bring you more tools from the *Beagle*. You must continue the civilizing effort in this land and educate other Fuegians who want to join." FitzRoy did not really believe his own words, so he added, "but Jemmy, if you believe that to survive you must cease to be the Jemmy we know, we will understand and wish you the best."

"I will make effort to continue colony, Captain"

With that FitzRoy ended the conversation. They loaded the boats with the few things they would take back to the *Beagle*. The Captain told the Fuegians that he would return in two or three days with tools and seeds for the colony. They manned the boats and started their way back to the *Beagle*.

York Minster, by Robert FitzRoy

The sea was rough so Darwin was a bit seasick. FitzRoy was quiet, his gaze fixed on the horizon.

"All those who helped and supported my plan for a colony in Tierra del Fuego will be very disappointed by this failure." FitzRoy was assimilating what he understood as the first failure of his career. He would never have the same self-confidence again.

"It is not a failure yet, Captain. The colony can still survive with our three Fuegians." But FitzRoy was not listening.

"I introduced Fuegia to the Queen. She showed great interest in this project and helped to secure subscriptions and contributions. The Church of England was excited by the project and appointed a minister for the mission. Even though it may not sound as much, there was a great deal of effort and work behind it, Darwin, much hope. When I return to England I shall have to explain to all those involved how this project, that took two years to be put together, collapsed in just five days ... a disaster."

Only the waves that lapped at the boat seemed to answer the Captain. They seemed to say that he was right, it was a failure. He went on:

"On the other hand what I did to our Fuegians was wrong. I snatched them from their world and burdened them with the responsibility of a venture they did not want. Now they are neither here nor there. I ruined them."

"I do not agree with you on that, Captain. York and Fuegia will adapt and form a family. And Jemmy ... I believe he will always be grateful for having seen the world. That young man is one of the most intelligent people I have met. I think that having seen England and been in contact with our civilization has been a blessing for him."

"You may be right there, Darwin. For Jemmy it might have been a parenthesis in his life that allowed him to get to know a world he would never have seen otherwise. Yes, Jemmy appreciated that experience ... Jemmy appreciated it ..."

Five days later, FitzRoy returned from Woolya feeling a little more optimistic about the future of the colony. The Indians had not caused any trouble. They had been hanging around in the vicinity but had not bothered. They possibly had accepted the presence of the colony and were content with getting rid of the minister. Fuegia, York and Jemmy were working at the vegetable garden. They had repaired one of the cabins and seemed to be making an effort to create an island of civilization in this hostile land.

"What bothers me is that they are not wearing their clothes any longer," said FitzRoy, "they are wearing skins like the rest of the Indians."

Darwin knew what that meant.

"We will visit them in a year's time, when we return on our way to survey the shores on the Pacific. I am sure I will see Jemmy again then," said FitzRoy almost to himself as if he were speaking of his younger brother.

It was true, he would see him, but not in the circumstances he thought he would.

Chapter 7

A British Soldier's Duty

There were two episodes that can completely explain different aspects of the personalities of both Darwin and FitzRoy that would eventually trigger a deep and tragic conflict between them. On the one hand, Mr. Darwin was becoming more and more adventurous and bold and on the other FitzRoy was starting to feel the burden of his duty as Captain and soldier, which was summarized in Admiral Nelson's famous words, mentioned before: "England expects every man to do his duty."

After leaving the Fuegians at Woolya, the *Beagle* set sail for the Malvinas (Falkland to the British) Islands. There had been a skirmish between a British ship and the small Argentine colony on the islands a short while before, but that was not the reason for the *Beagle*'s presence there. The object was to survey the islands to map the shores and find and map possible deep-water harbours that would offer shelter to ships damaged or in distress after crossing over from the Pacific. In this sense the Malvinas (Falklands) had great strategic value since their shores offered several natural harbours that were sheltered by the hills around them.

While in Malvinas (Falklands) FitzRoy purchased a schooner. The master of this ship, an American sealer, after a most unproductive year, was almost bankrupt and needed to sell it. FitzRoy renamed it *Adventure* after the ship that accompanied the *Beagle* on its first voyage and also after Captain Cook's ship on his legendary voyage in the Pacific.

In spite of being warned by Sullivan that these expenses required Admiralty clearance, the Captain went ahead, saying that he had no doubts that they would be authorized, since the use of this ship would shorten the trip and improve the quality of the maps. In any case, if for some reason the funds were not approved, he would cover the cost with his own assets. Several months later the Admiralty's answer would hit him like a sledgehammer.

Meanwhile, Darwin explored the islands and wrote his findings in his travel notebook: "No reptiles? ... the Falkland fox is different to the Patagonian one, why? How did it get here?"

As soon as the *Adventure* was outfitted, both ships headed for the mouth of the Negro river, where they met the two small survey boats that had been leased and were in the command of Wickham and Stokes. Their next destination was Bahía Blanca, though it would take some time since they had to continue their survey up the coast, and then to Buenos Aires.

During dinner on a quiet evening, while they were anchored at the mouth of the Rio Negro, Darwin asked FitzRoy for permission to undertake the trip to Buenos Aires by land.

"Impossible, Mr. Darwin. You cannot go on such a trip without the protection of the *Beagle*'s crew. It would be a dangerous trip through hostile territory which is disputed by Indians and bands of government soldiers. You are a Naturalist, not an adventurer."

"I believe, Captain, that I am becoming something of an adventurer. Remember why there is a mountain named after me."

"I could never forget that. Your commendable act saved us that evening."

"Exactly, a commendable act! It is not typical of a Naturalist. Maybe a year and a half on this adventure has hardened me. I deserve the chance."

FitzRoy was pensive and grave. Darwin was certainly not the inexperienced young man that had left England, but the trip across the pampa was truly dangerous.

"So Captain, what do you think?"

FitzRoy was certain that his problem was not whether to give Darwin permission to go or not, but rather what to do to minimize the risk. Darwin had shown his worth and he knew he could be trusted to act sensibly.

"Very well, Darwin my friend, I will allow you to make this trip, but with certain conditions."

"What conditions?"

"In the first place, you will make it in two stages. The first one from here to Bahía Blanca, where you will meet us, and if all is well, the second one from there to Buenos Aires."

"I think that is very reasonable, and what else?"

"Second you will be escorted by Mr. Harris, who knows the land, the people and the language, at least as far as Bahía Blanca."

"That seems very satisfactory. More so, since Mr. Harris happens to be good company."

"He will engage a group of gauchos to aid and protect you in the event of being attacked by Indians."

"I am not entirely in agreement with that, since I think the gauchos are as dangerous as the Indians, but I will accept your decision."

"Mr. Stokes will take you ashore on one of the smaller boats, up the Rio Negro to El Carmen[1], and will escort you inland for a day. He will then decide if it is all right for you to continue."

"Mr. Stokes will accompany us? Excellent! Is that all?"

"Just one more thing. You will go straight to the camp of the Argentine Army chief who is in charge of the war with the Indians in this part of the country. His name is Juan Manuel de Rosas. You will explain your plan and request a safe-conduct from him. I will write a letter to him immediately; my signature and stamp as Captain of the Admiralty will give it the desired importance."

"Thank you, Captain, for your trust."

"You have earned it. A new Darwin has been born, bold and fearless, whom, I hope, I have contributed to create. From now on I shall call you Filos."

"Filos? Friend in Greek."

"Correct. Not only are you my friend, you have the wisdom of a Greek philosopher," he added making funny face – it was half serious half in jest. "Very well, Filos, raise your glass and we shall toast your little adventure and the discoveries you shall make."

On 7th August the group, which consisted of Darwin, Harris and seven gauchos, left El Carmen on their voyage north to where Rosas had his camp on the Colorado river. Stokes escorted them until noon and seeing that all was well, bid them farewell and returned to his boat which was anchored off El Carmen.

The party advanced uneventfully through a territory Darwin found uninteresting. He tried to strike up a conversation with some of the gauchos to no avail. The language was not the problem; even with Harris translating he could hardly get a word or two out of any of them. They were terribly curt. One day they spotted a flock of ostrich and two of the gauchos took off at a gallop, managing to catch one with their

1. "El Carmen" was the name of the town that is called Carmen de Patagones today.

Carmen de Patagones, by D´Orbigny

boleadoras[2]. When the rest of the group arrived at where they were slaughtering the bird, Harris told Darwin, in English, "Here they call these ostrich ñandú (rhea – South American ostrich)." One of the gauchos understood the word ñandú and said:

"This is not a ñandú, mister. This is little ñandú, it is called choique, it is smaller than the ñandú."

"But what is the difference with the ñandú?" asked Darwin in halting Spanish, his curiosity tickled by what he had heard, "two ñandúes have smaller offspring that you call choique?"

"No mister, ñandúes have ñandúes and choiques have choiques. The ñandú and the choique never cross."

Darwin was intrigued. The fact that they did not cross made it clear that they were different species, although very closely related.

"Do the choiques and ñandúes live in the same area?"

"No mister. South of the Rio Negro there are only choiques. North of the Rio Colorado there are only ñandúes. Here, in between, there are both."

"Why aren't there any ñandúes further south?

"I don't know, mister. But further south there is less to eat, not easy for a large animal."

2. Indian weapon, also used by gauchos, consisting of three rounded stones connected by leather strands which were thrown at the animal (or person) to twine it round the legs and cause it to fall.

"Yes," thought Darwin, "that must be the best explanation. If there is less to eat a small animal is more likely to survive. Perhaps that was why they split into two species, each better adapted to their territory. The opposite must have happened to the Malvinas (Falklands) fox that is larger than the one on the continent. After arriving on the islands, with no competition from other predators they had more food and developed into a larger animal."

In the late afternoon they stopped to set up camp and unsaddled the horses. The gauchos told them they would use the saddles as pillows that night. Then they hobbled the horses and let them loose. "They can feed, but they will not wander very far."

They built a fire and roasted the choique and heated water for mate. When the meat was ready they ate with their hands. Once the meal was over Darwin collected all the bones and put them in a bag. He saw them staring at him in astonishment, so he said:

"As I am a naturalist, I will keep these bones so I can study them later."

One of the gauchos whispered to the one next to him as he handed him a mate, "rather strange, this Englishman."

A couple of days later they saw a solitary tree in the distance. Darwin overheard the gauchos repeating the word Gualichu. "Gualichu is the name of the Indians' god," explained Harris, "but I don't know what connection it has with that tree."

The gauchos insisted on making a detour to pass by the tree, in spite of the extra time it would take. When they got there they found that strands of string hung from the branches, and an otter skin was attached to one of them. One of the gauchos rode up to it, snatched it and galloped off at full speed. The rest of the gauchos took off after him. Darwin and Harris, seeing that they were left alone, followed suit. When after a lengthy gallop they finally stopped, they asked the gauchos why they had done that.

"The otter skin was an Indian's offering to his god. We stole it, that's why we hurried away. If any Indian had seen us, he would surely have killed us, even if he was a friendly one."

On 13th August they arrived at Rosas' camp. It was a large square enclosed by wagons. Within this square a few mud shacks had been built with a rough plank fence around the perimeter in an attempt to give some protection against an eventual Indian attack. The troops – if they could be called that – performed their military duties within the square. The river was only five hundred feet away, so water would not be lacking. It seemed to be an ideal place to set up an outpost.

They were received by a mixed-race soldier who had more teeth missing than he had left. "The general is not here but he will be arriving soon. Wait for him here, he knows that you were coming."

"How could he know we were coming?" Darwin asked Harris.

"Rosas probably has lookouts spread out over the territory who keep him informed of everything that happens. We must have been spotted."

"It looks like Rosas is good at his job."

They turned to look west and saw, less than a quarter of a mile away, five riders approaching at a break-neck speed. One of the horses broke ahead of the rest and came directly at them. The rider seemed to have no intention of stopping and they were in their path. As they approached Darwin was about to jump aside when Harris held his arm and said "keep still!" When horse and rider were just twelve feet from them, the rider checked the reins and the horse, evidently very well trained, practically stopped dead just a few feet from them. The rider showing great control and superb horsemanship easily dismounted in one fluid movement before the horse had fully stopped.

"Sergeant Sosa, I beat you again!" he shouted at the man that came behind him. He turned back to the Englishmen and said, "Juan Manuel Ortiz de Rosas, although everybody calls me Rosas," and he shook their hands.

Darwin, still a bit shaken from the close call, noticed that Rosas did not look like he expected him to. He was tall, with a heavy build, brown hair, blue eyes and a penetrating gaze. His uniform, although better than the ones of his subordinates, was faded by the sun and rain.

"I am Charles Darwin, Naturalist on the HMS *Beagle*, and this is Mr. Harris, an Englishman who lives in Bahía Blanca."

"Ah, yes, I've seen Harris a couple of times," Rosas' memory was legendary, "and you, my friend, everyone around here call you The English Naturalist." At Darwin's inquisitive look he added, "ever since your ship and Captain FitzRoy arrived in the area we have received reports on every move of your crew and we know the names of all your officers. There are also innumerable anecdotes about you."

Darwin hardly spoke Spanish, and Rosas had no English, but as they both spoke a little French Harris was not called upon to translate.

"Follow me to my headquarters and let's have some mate."

On the way Rosas kept giving orders to his subordinates.

"Any clue on the whereabouts of the Mapuche malón[3], General?" asked one of his lieutenants.

"No Castro, none. One would think the earth swallowed up those filthy, murderous Indians. Mind you, I galloped out for over ten leagues and nothing, not a trace."

The headquarters was just a mud shack guarded by a few famished dogs that slunk away as soon as they saw Rosas approaching, "Segundo, brew some mate and get some food for our guests, here!" They sat outside the shack on three-legged stools with cowhide seats.

"What brings you to these lands, Mr. Darwin? Are you planning to join us in our war against the Indians?" he asked on a humorous note.

"Wars are not my thing, General. I specialize in Nature and I have always wanted to travel across the famous pampas."

"Well, if you are looking for pampa, this is the right place. There is plenty of pampa, leagues and leagues of it. I can't imagine what you could find interesting in it."

"One never knows where you can bump into something interesting. Just a few days ago I discovered that there are two species of ñandú, and in Europe no one knew about it. A previously unknown plant or animal may turn up anywhere, or one could find the remains of extinct animals like the ones I discovered near Bahía Blanca. I am also interested in describing the people and customs of the countries we visit."

"If you are interested in describing these savage Indians, you had better hurry, because at the rate the war is going there will be none left in a few years."

"Captain FitzRoy believes that the indigenous people who do not adapt to modern times will eventually disappear because they will always be defeated in a conflict."

"Your Captain is right. I am supposedly the evil one around here, but this is war. The Indians attack the estancias[4], killing all the men. The women, they kidnap the younger ones and kill the rest. The only way to stop that is to fight back."

Rosas handed the mate gourd to Darwin, who had already got used to drinking it. He did not specially care for it – he found it rather insipid – but he found it helped to keep a conversation going. He also knew that to turn it down was a breach of etiquette.

3. Indian raiding party.

4. Ranch – large estate.

"And what do you do, General, when you find an Indian camp?"

"Well, at a toldería[5] what we do is not too different to what they do at our estancias. We kill the men and take the women and children to work as labourers or servants in estancias further north. This is a war of extermination."

The topic was not one that appealed to Darwin, so he changed the subject.

"On our way we went by a tree where the Indians leave offerings. What sort of place is that?"

"The tree is an algarrobo[6], and it is known as Gualichu's Altar. This place has a religious significance for the Indians who dwell south of the Colorado river."

"I noticed that it is not a tree native to this region."

"True, the algarrobo grows naturally further north. This one must have been planted over a hundred years ago, probably to mark the place. For the Indian travelling from the south it is the place from where you can see the Sierra de la Ventana for the first time, and this range has a special magical symbolism for them."

"But you cannot see the Sierra de la Ventana from there; it is over a hundred miles away. I did not see anything from that place!"

"In the first place, my friend, you can only see it if you stand on your horse, something I doubt you could do because only the Indians' horses are trained for that. Perhaps the Indians planted that tree before they had horses, so they could climb the tree and see the Ventana from there. On the other hand white man does not have the eyesight the Indians have. I cannot see the range from there either, unless I use a telescope." He took a sip of mate and continued, "You see, this place is very important to them. They take great risks bringing their offerings, and do so even knowing that we may be in the vicinity. We keep the place watched at all times. They are very brave, these Indians ... very brave, and superb riders."

Darwin detected admiration in Rosas' tone, which reminded him of Julius Caesar's writings on the Gallic wars, in which he described the Gauls' courage with admiration.

"They are brave and do not know that they are going to die, right, General? Have you read Julius Caesar?"

5. Indian camp.

6. Carob tree.

"I believe, my naturalist friend, that I have read that book over twenty times."

"And don't you feel a bit like Julius Caesar, fighting in your own Gaul?"

Rosas smiled, as if admitting that Darwin had read his mind.

"You are an intelligent man. Maybe, as Julius Caesar, after defeating the barbarians I will be crowned Emperor, ha, ha!"

"Perhaps, General. I recall that when Julius Caesar returned in triumph he received an order from Rome not to cross the Rubicon, or he would be held in contempt. Caesar crossed it anyway, his enemies fled, and he was crowned Emperor." Darwin let that sink in a bit before asking, "is there a Rubicon in the pampas?"

"O course, my friend. The Salado river separates the Province of Buenos Aires from Indian territory … we'll see if I cross the Salado with my army … another mate, my friend Harris?"

Harris, overwhelmed by the political impact of what he had just heard answered hurriedly, "certainly, General!"

"But returning to your business here, how can I help you, gentlemen?"

"Well, General, we would need you to tell us which is the safest way to travel from here to Bahía Blanca and then from there to Buenos Aires."

"Very well, my friends, the best way is for you to use the trail, sleeping over at the postas[7] I have set up all the way to Buenos Aires."

"And what are these postas, General?"

"To be able to communicate with Buenos Aires, I set up a line of small forts every ten or twelve leagues, so you can travel from one to the next in one day. Each fort has a garrison, which gives them some protection if attacked by Indians. I will personally write and give you a letter which you will have to exhibit at each posta, for them to treat you as a guest."

"Thank you very much, General. I hope I will someday return this favour in England."

"I hope it won't be necessary. Because if it were, it would mean that I crossed my Rubicon and something went wrong, ha, ha!"

"The Rubicon is dangerous, General. Just see what happened to Julius Caesar, betrayed by his protégé."

They bid each other a warm farewell. Little did they know that thirty years later they would meet again, in England, under very different

7. Post where one could change horses and/or rest.

Indian camp, by Landseer and Parker King

circumstances. Rosas' destiny would be similar to Caesar's; he would also be betrayed by his protégé, but would manage to escape death and flee, leaving behind a country divided by hate, hate he had contributed to create.

At Bahía Blanca Darwin came on board the *Beagle*. But this time FitzRoy was convinced that he would have no problem in continuing his voyage by land, so he gave him permission to continue by his own means. Once the *Beagle* arrived in Buenos Aires a very active social life commenced.

In spite of being used to the arrival of foreign ships, the *Beagle*, or rather its crew, caused a great sensation in the upper echelons of Buenos Aires society. FitzRoy was the only person related to the British Royal Family who had ever set foot in Buenos Aires, so he received all sorts of invitations where his presence, that of his Officers and the pipers on board, were required at the events organized by the ladies.

At one of these events, organized by María Sanchez, married to an English tradesman, Thompson, and recently widowed, there were some tense moments where FitzRoy did not know what to do.

The evening started with some piano music, then someone sang a few local and Spanish songs. Then it was the Scottish pipers turn, who delighted the porteños, who were not used to that type of music. The Captain went on to explain that the colours and design of the tartans of each kilt were related to the clan of the person who wore them, and that the clans could be explained as the traditional families of Scotland and Ireland.

They continued to chat in a most friendly manner, but the topic of the British invasions of Buenos Aires in 1806 and 1807, could not be avoided since many of those present had lived through them and, for better or for worse, they had a lasting effect on the country's future. Most of the porteños believed that they had been a good thing since it had given the local population the confidence to shake off Spanish dominance. There was no animosity against the British, so much so that one of the ladies told them how one of her best friends had married a British soldier.

"My friend Carola married Jimmy O'Connor thanks to the Cut-Throats."

"What do you mean, 'thanks to the Cut-Throats'?" asked FitzRoy, intrigued.

"Well, Captain, in the second invasion the British troops were attempting to reach the Plaza Mayor marching up the streets. The inhabitants threw all kinds of things at them: stones, boiling water and boiling oil from the roof-tops, and shot at them from windows. The closer they got to the Plaza, the harder they found it to advance, until they were finally pinned down, unable to advance or retreat. Many of the soldiers that had been recruited to defend the city were gauchos from the interior who were used to fighting Indians. They never took prisoners, they cut their throats. That is why when British troops surrendered many were killed by the Cut-Throats."

Lieutenant Johnson and three privates had been separated from their platoon. They were only four blocks from the Plaza Mayor. From their position they could see the Santo Domingo church towers where two British soldiers had been killed by cannon shot from the fort. Their bodies were sprawled in the church forecourt.

Johnson and his men were in a desperate situation. They could not advance. From one of the street corners several sharp-shooters were keeping them pinned down.

Church of Santo Domingo, Buenos Aires, by M. Iglesias.
On the left tower shrapnel dating from the English Invasions of 1807 can be seen

He decided to go into one of the houses and resist there until help came. The ships would surely start bombarding the city to weaken their resolve. But until then they had to survive this inferno.

They chose one house and started to force the door open while Jones covered them. After some pushing and shooting the lock they managed to open it. "Jones, get in here," ordered the lieutenant, but Jones lay sprawled, shot in the chest. They got in and blocked the door as best they could. It was the sitting room of one of the elegant families of Buenos Aires, the Larrazábals. They took up positions at the windows to cover the door. In the next room, Carola Larrazábal, only fifteen years old, her mother, Doña Angélica, and their slave Aurora were hiding. Carola, quite bold, opened the door a crack and saw the British soldiers firing. Then she saw two gauchos come in the door from the patio – they had dropped into the patio from the roof top – and in horror saw how they jumped on Johnson and cut his throat. They then went for the next soldier. "In here!" she shouted at the soldier nearest to her, who, seeing the door open dived in to escape certain death. "Carola, what do you think you are doing?" asked Doña Angélica as her daughter closed the door and locked it. The soldier dropped his gun, surrendering. His life depended on these women. "Save him, mother, they will kill him." On the other side, the gauchos were trying to open the door to get at the only soldier that had got away. When they finally opened it and came in they were confronted by Doña Angélica who, holding the rifle levelled at them said, "this man has surrendered. Go and get the ones that still fight." The gauchos tried to mumble an objection, but seeing Doña Angélica's determination they decided to leave.

"And that was how Carola Larrazábal saved Jimmy O'Connor's life," said their hostess. "They were married a week later. But, how strange destiny is ... almost a year later, at the Larrazábal's estate, Jimmy was killed when he fell off a horse and knocked his head on a rock. He never saw the child Carola was carrying – Santiaguito - who is a grown man now. He is as handsome as his father was."

Everyone present, barring the *Beagle*'s officers, knew the story. Carola O'Connor had never remarried and, even though she was still young and pretty, did not care for social events and had not attended this one either.

A man made a comment on the fact that although it was true that the gauchos were bloodthirsty, the British were no less cruel. FitzRoy, himself a British Officer, took it personally and asked the man what he meant.

"An English officer will treat an English soldier better than a Scots or Welsh one, and an Irish one the worst." FitzRoy did not speak much Spanish, but he noticed that this man spoke the language with a foreign accent. The porteños knew well where he was from.

"I believe you are mistaken, sir," said FitzRoy, conciliatory, yet firm, "Wellington, who defeated Napoleon at Waterloo, was himself an Irishman."

"I must disagree, Captain, Wellington was born in Ireland, but he is Protestant, not Catholic. He always made it clear that he was not Irish. He would say that being born in Ireland does not make him Irish in the same way that if he had been born in a stable he would not be a horse.

The same applies to Beresford, who was in command during the first invasion."

"It is true that Wellington is Protestant, but neither he nor any other British officer will treat their subordinates different on account of their religious beliefs."

"Let me tell you a brief story. When the British invaded Buenos Aires the first time, in 1806, they governed for forty days. Several Irish soldiers escaped and joined the resistance rather than fight against other Catholics."

"Deserters from His Majesty's Army," said FitzRoy who was starting to feel uncomfortable.

"True Irishmen do not feel they are the subjects of a king who has invaded and occupied their country. But that has no bearing on this story. The thing is that Beresford got word that the resistance were training at a villa in San Isidro; not all the local population were in favour of evicting the British, so someone leaked this information. Beresford left the fort early in the morning and by forced march reached San Isidro and engaged and defeated the inexperienced native soldiers, and took one of the Irish soldiers prisoner."

"According to the British martial law he would be sentenced to death," interrupted FitzRoy, who could picture a brief court martial.

"That is correct, but it was not enough for Beresford. His disdain for the Irish was such that he had poor Sean Fitzpatrick lashed to the mouth of a cannon and ordered it to be shot, so his body was blown in all directions to, in his own words, 'feed the vultures'."

"My dear sir, I refuse to believe that was done because the man was Irish. Something else must have happened. One would have had to be there to know the facts."

"Captain, I was there. I know exactly what happened."

"But Beresford did not do the same to you."

"Simply because he didn't catch me."

"What do you mean by that?" demanded FitzRoy in a rage.

María Sanchez tried to appease them, "Mr. Thwaite, please say no more, "

"You see, Captain, I was one of the Irish soldiers you called deserters."

Thwaite immediately turned, walked to the door, retrieved his hat and cane and left. FitzRoy, flushed with rage, turned to Wickham and said, in English:

"Wickham, we must seize this man. He is a deserter and must be tried as such."

Wickham approached FitzRoy and tried to calm things down by saying, in a low voice:

"Captain, I beg you to reconsider. We are in a foreign country and cannot take one of their citizens prisoner. At least not if we want live."

"Wickham! Our duty as British soldiers is to make sure that martial law is observed!"

"Yes Captain, but your duty is also to take the *Beagle* and its crew safely back to England. Thwaite is an honourable member of the local society, and I don't believe they will allow a group of Protestants to harm a fellow Catholic who fought with them against their enemy."

FitzRoy calmed down; he could see everybody watching him, waiting to see his reaction. Wickham was right. He might be ready to die in the line of duty, but he could not expect the same from the rest of the crew. Duty had limits dictated by rationality. Wickham had managed to get Fitz in control over Roy.

"Madam," said the Captain, addressing their hostess, "let us not allow this little conflict to affect the wonderful evening you have offered us. Please delight us with another song."

I know that the story of the "cut-throats" deeply impressed Captain FitzRoy and I am sure that he had it in mind that very last day of his life.

Chapter 8

"God is my Right"

The closer Darwin was to completing his thoughts about the Creation the more FitzRoy understood its consequences; so he started to feel responsible for what these could trigger. Slowly two separate loyalties grew within FitzRoy which he would not be able to satisfy simultaneously: his King and science. An inner conflict that would tear him apart.

December 1833, the *Beagle* was sailing on its way from Montevideo to Puerto Deseado (Port Desire), in Patagonia. As usual, FitzRoy shared his meals with Darwin, using these moments to discuss ideas. During this particular breakfast the Captain seemed to be absent, he did not seem to be paying much attention to Darwin. At one point FitzRoy interrupted Darwin:

"My dear Filos, last night I had a most disturbing dream, which has made me ponder a great deal."

"Tell me about it, Captain."

"You see, it went something like this ... I was strolling in downtown London, when I suddenly saw a mob who were shouting 'death to the king!' Our King was being forcefully taken to a gallows which had been set up across from Westminster Abbey. The rabble continued shouting, in a frenzy. The King, impassive, looked down at them, and spotted me in the crowd (you are aware that I know him personally and that we are not too distant cousins). Suddenly the crowd fell quiet and he said, loudly, while looking at me, 'God was my right.' The executioner made him kneel and with one stroke of his axe, cut off his head."

"A scene similar to the way Louis XVI was killed in the French Revolution."

"Yes, my friend, and also very much like Charles I execution in 1648. Although Charles I died due to religion during the fighting between Catholics and Protestants, while Louis XVI was killed by reason, since the French revolutionaries did not believe in God."

Dieu et mon Droit in the Royal coat of arms of the United Kingdom

Darwin could still not understand what was bothering FitzRoy so much.

"This morning I awoke alarmed, wondering why the king was looking at me and why he had said 'God was my right,' and that was when I recalled the Royal Coat of Arms." FitzRoy opened a book that was on his desk, "take a look at this Coat of Arms."

"Dieu et mon Droit, which is French for 'God and my Right."

"That phrase, Filos, was uttered by King Richard I, The Lion Hearted, at the battle of Gisors in 1190. As you surely know at the time the English nobility spoke ancient French. This phrase, in modern French would be Dieu est mon Droit, which correctly translated would be 'God is my Right.' This is what is called Divine Right and means that the King reigns by the grace of God."

"And why, in your dream, would the king say this to you?"

"My interpretation is that the king blames me for his death because it was I who took the news that God does not exist to England."

"What do you mean, Captain?"

The Captain poured Darwin some tea and then another for himself. This breakfast was going to be longer than usual. Sullivan could supervise the changing of the watch.

"To explain this I propose we go over your theories and their implications first. Please give me a summary, Filos."

"In a nutshell, Captain I would say that my observations take me to believe that the world is not static, but is in a state of constant change. The seas rise and fall at certain times and over long periods mountains, islands and valleys are formed, perhaps even continents."

"But there something else with animals, Filos. Animals are modified. Yesterday you showed me the way you, and other naturalists, are classifying them. Tell me some more about that."

Darwin could not yet find the connection between this and a king having his head cut off, but he continued anyway.

"Well, Captain, each animal is given a scientific name which is made up of two words. The first one is the genus, that is the 'family' of similar animals, and the other is the name of the actual species."

"So see this example, Filos.! People have names and surnames. Two who have the same surname belong to the same family, so what do they have in common?"

"A common ancestor."

"Exactly! So, Darwin, if we establish that animals change over several generations, could we then conclude that if two animals have the same 'surname' then they had a common ancestor?"

"That is correct, Captain."

"But then, Filos, one could also group different 'surnames' that have something else in common and give them yet another name. Equivalent to finding out someone's mother's surname and then come to the conclusion that they too are related through a common ancestor, only older. Where would we be then?

"You tell me, Captain."

"We would have a 'family tree', the story of how the evolutionary road was developed for each animal.

"Yes Captain. And each time we find the fossil of an extinct animal we find one of those ancestors. Where are you taking us, Captain?"

"Man ... I am trying to see where man is in all this classifying and so see what ancestry man has."

Fits Roy's answer took Darwin completely by surprise. The issue of man's origins was something he had not spoken to anyone about.

"You see Captain ..." It was not an easy decision to let everything out, "if we consider man as just another animal ... so far nobody has found a close relative. That is, just as a lion is 'related' to the tiger or the leopard, man has no species close to him."

"I see ... " the Captain was thoughtful, "so we could say that, so far, your theory does not contradict the biblical version that man is not just an animal, but was created in His image. But, there always is a but, you said that there is no close relative, which means that there might be a distant one."

They were getting to the heart of the matter and Darwin was pleased to see that FitzRoy had a positive attitude in the quest or truth. He continued:

"Yes, there seem to be 'distant relatives', animals with which we share some common ancestor."

"And which would these animals be?"

"These could be the gorilla or the chimpanzee or maybe another Asian monkey, the orangutan." Darwin looked at FitzRoy, trying to assess his reaction. On seeing none, he realized that FitzRoy had followed the same line of reasoning and come to that same conclusion.

"Then, Filos, what would this common ancestor look like?"

"Doubtless some sort of monkey, Captain."

"Right. I would venture large hairy monkeys, who communicate by grunts and sit around picking lice off each other. What do you think the Archbishop of Canterbury would have to say if we came to him with this conclusion?" he asked mockingly.

Darwin almost choked with laughter.

"Captain, I do not think he would be amused. But I still do not understand what relation this has with your dream."

"It is very simple. If your theory is correct the very existence of God would be in doubt. If there is no God, then the divine right ceases to exist. Therefore the king would have no right to be king ... and so, there goes the mob to overthrow the lying king. Reason is the new religion," FitzRoy paused, "that is why in my dream he looks at me and blames me, God was my Right, he says. And I stress the word 'was', because if God does not exist, then he has no right to be king. And in my dream it was I who brought the news that triggered fury."

"But Captain, none of this would actually happen. They would not behead him as they used to two hundred years ago."

"In France this madness occurred just forty years ago, which is not very far back ... In any case what matters is the symbolism of the dream. I do not think that our king's life would be in danger, but I am sure there will be a bitter debate over the matter and society will be split in two. And you and I, Darwin, my friend, will be in the middle of this upheaval which will do our careers no good. In my case, the Admiralty will not take kindly to the notion that, as a result of my exploratory voyage, the very foundation on which the British Empire is built should be undermined. My military career will probably end and my family and friends will strongly disapprove of me. You, my friend, will probably have to deal with a violent confrontation with the Church, and do not expect much sympathy from your colleagues since they will want to avoid your fate."

Darwin was not used to dwell on his career. He acted as if the voyage would never end. He had not the faintest idea of what he would do when he returned to England. But now he believed that FitzRoy was right, that he would be the target of vicious criticism. Without Henslow's backing he did not think he could cope.

As Darwin remained silent, the Captain tried to give him a more optimistic view.

"In any case, you would not be the first scientist to question the Church's beliefs, Galileo and Newton did so before."

"You say this because they both came to the conclusion that the planets and the other heavenly bodies rotate and move without divine intervention. Galileo very nearly lost his life in the hands of the Inquisition, but I did not know that Newton had any trouble with the Church."

"Exacltly, Filos! They each chose different approaches to confront those who believe the Bible should be taken literally. Galileo, a stubborn man, no doubt, decided on the direct confrontation, was tried by the Inquisition and finally had to back down to avoid being burned at the stake."

"And what did Newton do?"

"Newton left room for God in his discoveries."

"How is that? Newton discovered the laws that govern the gravitational movement of the heavenly bodies. The planets rotate around the sun in a way that can be easily determined by using the correct formulae according to the universal gravitational constant. Where did he leave room for God?"

"Newton said that the planets moved on their own, without divine intervention, just like clockwork. But just as a clock needs a clockmaker to make it, so did God create the universe and as a proud clockmaker, observes the final result with satisfaction. Newton left room for God as the Great Clockmaker ... And was rewarded with knighthood."

Darwin could not get himself to believe that one would have to think of how to present a discovery or a theory. He had always thought that all you had to do was tell the truth as it was, without having to think of a 'releasing' strategy. But FitzRoy had a point. The experiences of Galileo and Newton proved how important it was to minimize the impact of 'bad' news for the Church.

"So, Filos, the moment you decide to publish your theory leave room for the Great Clockmaker," said FitzRoy ironically. He knew how to move in the world of politics and intrigue.

"But Captain, do you think that everything we have found on the way the world, animals and even man have been transformed over thousands of years should be kept secret?"

FitzRoy poured himself another cup of tea. They were arriving at the point he had intended to get to.

"My dear Darwin, I shall use the same example you said you used with Rosas, Caesar and the Rubicon. Julius Caesar knew he would prevail."

"Julius Caesar would not have crossed if he were not sure that he would win. Is that it?"

"Exactly, and we must not cross our Rubicon until we are sure we will succeed. When the *Beagle* arrives back in England we must decide what to do, that will be our Rubicon. Until then we must be cautious. Not a word about it."

"So what must we do until then?"

"We must prepare our guns, Filos."

"And what are our guns?"

"Irrefutable proof. If you have proof that will justify your theory, it will prevail when confronted."

Darwin thought it over. He liked the plan. During what was left of the voyage he would have to accumulate evidence to uphold his theory. That was a job he liked.

The Captain declared the lengthy breakfast over, but when Darwin got up to leave he said:

"Darwin, I hope you understand that my fate is tied to yours. If your theory is made public without proper foundation it will mean the end of your career, and it will also be the end of mine." FitzRoy was grave as he looked Darwin in the eye, "My future is in your hands, Filos. I hope you will act responsibly."

"Do not worry, Captain. We will decide on the crossing of the Rubicon together."

"Until then, not a word."

Chapter 9

Dangerous Tides

A minor accident gave us the opportunity to start a thrilling voyage to one of the most mysterious places on earth: The Terra Incognita in the heart of Patagonia. In this expedition FitzRoy proved he was capable of organising and managing the group in such a way as to carry out the exploration under very special circumstances.

In one of the natural harbours on the Patagonian coast, Puerto Deseado (Port Desire), the *Beagle* hit a submerged rock. The Captain was sure that it had done some damage below the water line. As the water was very clear some of the bolder seamen dived in to inspect the hull.

"The keel, Captain!" shouted one of the men as he surfaced in the freezing water.

"Is it split?" asked a worried FitzRoy.

"It doesn't seem to be, but at one-point half is missing."

"Make sure that it has not split!" ordered FitzRoy and the seaman went under again.

The keel is a wooden beam that runs down the middle of the ship from bow to stern. Its function is two-fold. On the one hand it gives the ship directional stability, especially when affected by side winds, on the other, and this was what worried the Captain, it is the backbone of the ship – it is built around it. If the keel is split the ship will probably break in half and sink. When this happens the crew rarely survives.

"No Captain, it has not split, but it is quite badly damaged."

"Well done, Clarke! You may come aboard now. Sullivan! Double ration for him tonight! Stokes, come over here!"

FitzRoy and Stokes went to the bridge.

"Mr. Stokes, we cannot risk being caught in a storm with the keel in this state. We must find a place where our carpenter, Mr May, can repair it. You surveyed this area, where do you suggest we do this?"

Bivouac in Port Desire, by Conrad Martens

Stokes thought for a few minutes.

"I would say that the estuary of the Santa Cruz River is the perfect place. It is well sheltered from wind and heavy seas. The tide is extreme there, so if we take advantage of high tide we can run the *Beagle* aground and when the tide goes out it will be left high and dry, ideal for the repairs."

"Excellent idea! Besides it is close by so we would not have to sail very far in these conditions."

"The access to the estuary is rather complicated, but our previous Captain, Pringle Stokes[1], surveyed it and the charts and instructions have been published."

"Well, now we have the opportunity to test Pringle Stoke's work, and also to add detail to the charts. We shall also be able to ... "

"Captain!"

It was Darwin climbing the steps that led to the bridge.

"Is the damage serious, Captain?"

"It is not, my dear Darwin. I could add that it is a lucky mishap."

"And why is that?"

"Because this little accident will give us the time we need to embark on an expedition I very much wanted to make. While the *Beagle* is being repaired we can travel up the mysterious Santa Cruz River and perhaps go as far as the Andes."

1. Even though he had the same surname, Pringle Stokes was no relation to John Lort Stokes.

Darwin could almost hear bells ringing in his head. To cross the Patagonian steppe and reach the mythical mountains was more than he had ever hoped for.

"Sullivan, set sail to the Santa Cruz River mouth immediately," FitzRoy was not losing time. "Darwin, come with me to the map room. Let us see what we have on the area."

Once in the map room, FitzRoy took out a thick roll of maps and lay them out on the large table. He picked one out and rolled up the rest and put them away. "This is the chart of the area." While Darwin studied it FitzRoy went to one end of the room and returned with a wooden box, which he placed on the table. From it he took a large handwritten book. "This is the log of the *Beagle*'s previous voyage. Captain Stokes surveyed the estuary; I want to see what comments he made."

There was a moment's silence while the Captain studied the log and Darwin the map. Finally the Captain spoke:

"It seems the Santa Cruz is no ordinary river. Only the estuary has been explored. No one has ever gone upriver, so no one knows where the headwaters are or where its water comes from. From the Plata to the Straits of Magellan it is the by the far the fastest flowing river. It has an amazingly strong current, between six and eight knots[2]. What do you think of that?"

"That the slope it runs down is very steep, which suggests that its headwaters could be in the mountains. But listen to this, according to this map the Andes are around 160 miles from the Atlantic. That means that it runs across nearly the whole continent."

"With that speed, if the river were straight the water would take just one day to reach the Atlantic. If its course is winding it may take two, so it should still be very cold, if as I believe, it is melt water."

FitzRoy continued reading Pringle Stokes' notes in a low voice.

"Listen to this, Filos, 'the water is of a light blue or turquoise colour and not transparent but rather milky'."

"It carries sediment, but that colour ... how strange."

"And why so unlike the Deseado river that is of a murky brown colour?"

They both pondered for a while.

2. Six to eight knots is equivalent to 7 to 9 miles per hour (10 to 15 Kilometres per hour).

Mount Saint Michael, Cornwall, England

"Eureka!" said Darwin, "the Deseado does not bring water from the Andes, it drains rainwater from the Patagonian steppe. It carries silt. The water of most plains rivers is brown because they carry silt. I am sure that the Deseado does not have its headwaters in the Andes. On the other hand the Santa Cruz has cleaner water because it is from the ice melt, but it is not transparent either."

"It is sky blue, the colour of the glaciers! The water in the Santa Cruz River comes from glaciers in the Andes!"

"But look at this map, Captain. The only other river that seems to come from the Andes is the Chubut, and it is several hundred miles north of here.

"But then where does the water from the thawing of almost five hundred miles of snow-capped mountains go?"

"That is a good question. It can only drain through the Santa Cruz, that is why it has such a volume of water. Nearly five hundred miles of thawing ice and snow flowing out through a single river. The Santa Cruz must connect several lakes at the foot of the Andes."

FitzRoy picked a book from the bookcase. "Over a hundred years ago a Spanish explorer ventured into Patagonia, his name was Viedma. He reached a great lake at the foot of the mountains that had an intense sky-blue hue. But this lake is quite a spell north of the mouth of the Santa Cruz."

"This lake must be its headwaters. It is well worth being explored."

"There we will go."

A few days later the *Beagle* floated, stately, in the estuary of the Santa Cruz, an ideal natural harbour. Most of the crew was detailed to unload the ship. Not only the baggage, but everything on board, including guns and ammunition, since they needed to make it lighter to prepare it for the repairs.

The shore consisted of a steep bank at the foot of which was a beach of shingle and coarse sand. The site chosen to camp at was at the top of the bank where it was safely above the high-water mark of the terrific tides where the sea level rose almost forty feet. John Stokes set up the observatory near the camp site. From there he would take the readings to establish coordinates, and the height and speed of the tide.

"Captain, for the charts, what name should we give this place?" asked Stokes.

"We shall call it ... Keel Point, since it is here we will repair it."

"Aye, Captain."

"Stokes, take your readings and calculate at what time we will have the tide at its maximum level. We will need it to run the *Beagle* aground as high up the beach as possible."

Once the *Beagle* was completely unloaded, they tied ropes to several points on the side of the hull and masts and waited for the tide. When it started to come in it did so at an incredible speed. It seemed as if the river's current had reversed and the sea was rushing towards the mountains.

"How long to high tide, Mr. Stokes?" asked FitzRoy.

"Fifty-six minutes, Captain."

"Sullivan, have the men keep pulling at the ropes to ease the ship closer as the water rises."

The speed of the incoming tide had subdued and the water had risen to an incredible level.

"I have never seen such extreme tides," said Darwin, "I understand they are greater than the ones at Mont Saint-Michel, in France, here depending on the tide the Benedictine abbey is on an island or a peninsula."

"I was never in Saint-Michel," said FitzRoy, "but I have been to Mount

St. Michael, in England, which is similar. It was also originally a Benedictine abbey that was an island or a peninsula according to the tide. I recall that to get there I walked along a sandy path. But when I wanted to return, five hours later, I had to do so by boat because the water had risen fifteen feet. Really impressive and dangerous."

"Why dangerous?"

"Where there are tides of great magnitude the water level will raise in a very short time. So a person who has decided to take a rest near the sea might be caught by the rising tide before they can get to a safe place. Many pilgrims have died this way both at Saint-Michel as at St. Michael."

"How right you are, Captain, look over there," said Darwin pointing north. "Four hours ago that was a plain where I had intended to go to find sea shells. Thank goodness I did not go because now it is completely under water."

"Every seaman must beware of extreme tides," and turning to look at the young man with the sextant, "did you hear that, Stokes? Remember to pay attention to the tides when you are in charge of an expedition."

"Aye, Captain," answered Stokes, who did not think it possible that he would ever be in charge of an expedition like FitzRoy's. But this piece of advice would save his life and that of five of his men when in command of the exploratory voyage to Australia six years later.

"And you, my friend Darwin, will now be able to study a collection of shellfish and snails."

"And who has that collection, Captain?"

"The *Beagle*, Filos."

"The *Beagle*? Where?"

"On its hull. Before fitting it for this voyage the *Beagle* had its hull scraped and cleaned. But when in the water, snails and shellfish stick to the hull. So we must have specimens from Plymouth, the Canaries, Brazil, the Plata and every other place we visited. Mr. May will remove them to improve the ship's handling, but I have instructed him to keep them for you to study."

"Thank you very much, Captain, it is very interesting."

"Fifteen minutes to high tide," said Stokes.

"Very well, everyone down to pull on the ropes. We need everybody's help to pull the *Beagle* aground."

They went down the slope and joined the men at the ropes. FitzRoy gave instructions. They all tugged until the *Beagle* was on the beach with

The *Beagle* stranded on Keel Point, by Conrad Martens

her hull touching the shingle. Then FitzRoy started shouting in a steady rhythm to get everyone to heave in unison. On each shout the ship was dragged a few inches up the beach. After a few minutes the current reversed and the water level started dropping. The *Beagle* remained aground and leaning on one side. The master carpenter, May, put several props to avoid it from toppling over further.

"Mr. May, I would like a report on the state of the hull as soon as you inspect it."

"Aye, aye, sir."

"Mr. Martens!" FitzRoy called for the artist on board the *Beagle*, "please make a painting of the *Beagle* aground on the shores of Patagonia. It will be and exotic image the Admiralty might find interesting."

"I think it is a splendid idea, Captain."

"One more thing, Martens."

"Yes?"

"Get ready to come with us on our expedition up the Santa Cruz. I believe we will find stunning images which will be well worth capturing."

"I love the idea of painting landscapes that have never been seen by white man. I shall bring my sketch-book."

"Darwin, Stokes! Come, let us go and plan our little expedition to the Andes. We shall leave tomorrow with the incoming tide."

"I see, Captain, that you are making the most of the tide," quipped Darwin.

"As would need be. As far as I know, this is the most extreme tide on Earth."

Three whalers that carried FitzRoy, Darwin, Stokes, Martens and several seamen and marines, in total 25 souls, shoved off westward with the morning tide of 18th April, 1834 up the estuary of the Santa Cruz River. Both the tide and the wind were favourable, so they advanced at a good pace.

As they sailed a seal swam past them. Darwin was intrigued to see these salt water animals so many miles from the sea. The seal was on its way to one of the islands within the estuary. With a telescope Darwin could see several seals on the beach of this island, so he asked FitzRoy to make a small detour to sail close to the island and so be able to watch the colony. FitzRoy blew his whistle to attract the attention of the other boats and signalled them to sail towards the island.

When they got near the island they were able to see that there was a very large colony of sea lions with their offspring, and they also saw a couple of sea elephants. It is quite common to find these two species sharing the same beaches. Darwin put his hand in the water. "Salty," he said, "they get into the water when the incoming tide brings seawater in."

"Why would they make this colony inside the estuary when they could use the outer beaches?" asked FitzRoy.

"I would imagine that here their offspring are safe from their main enemy, the killer whale. I do not think these would venture this far from the sea; these are dangerous waters for them."

"Dangerous? In what way?"

"They are in danger of being run aground when the tide goes out. These tides are dangerous for man when they rise, but they are dangerous for whales when they go out."

"Very smart animals, these. Stokes! Mark this island as 'Sea Lion Island' on the charts."

They continued sailing west but, slowly, the current started to lose strength. The wind also started changing and by early afternoon it was blowing steadily from the west. The only way to continue against the wind and current was rowing, and so they did and continued to advance but at a much slower pace and with a great effort.

By mid-afternoon the current was so strong that they could hardly advance at all. They rowed harder. The estuary narrowed and it seemed to finally turn into the river. The water was still sky blue and milky. Further ahead they could see some thickly wooded islands. FitzRoy decided they would make an extra effort to try and camp on one of them. They arrived exhausted.

"Filos, this is as far as Pringle Stokes got on the *Beagle*'s previous voyage. Look that way."

"What is there?"

"Over there, Darwin, is all Terra Incognita. We shall explore land that white man has never tread on before. We shall try to reveal its secrets."

Chapter 10

Terra Incognita

Our expedition along the River Santa Cruz was most enlightening to me. There I came to know something that I shouldn't have known. On those endless walks Darwin taught me to read Nature as if it were a book, and from its pages a story emerged that differed greatly from the one we believed in when we left England.

In the evening the temperature dropped dramatically. The men huddled around the fire, and a bottle of gin made the rounds in an effort to keep warm. The Captain had calculated the supplies for a three-week journey, and as he considered that the men needed to indulge every so often, he had included some spirits, chocolate and tea.

In the clear sky the stars shone with an intensity that the first seamen from the northern hemisphere had found disturbing, but the *Beagle*'s crew were veterans of these latitudes and knew these constellations better than the ones that could be seen in London or Edinburgh.

"The Southern Cross, Filos, a real symbol of this part of the world."

"It is curious, Captain, as we are Christians, we see a cross in the sky, I wonder what the Indians see."

"I understand they do not see figures in the sky. The Yamana's consider them guides, because they help them to get their bearings and find their way at sea."

"Similar to our North Star[1], which even the Vikings used to get their bearings."

"Yes Filos, the stars are used by most aborigine peoples to find their way. The people of the Pacific Islands can sail for weeks on the open sea

1. The North Star can only be seen in the northern hemisphere. It is directly above the North Pole which is why from ancient times it was used as a compass.

with no land in sight, but they know exactly where they are and where they are headed."

"But how do they do it in the southern hemisphere where there is no star to mark the South Pole?"

"So let's return to our Southern Cross. You see, Filos, if you project the longer axis in its same direction two and a half times, you will find the exact position of the South Pole; almost as if it were a Polar star."

"You obviously know more about these things than I do, Captain."

Stokes approached with the bottle of gin in his hand.

"It is almost empty, Captain."

FitzRoy took the bottle and drank the last tot. It was a naval tradition that the last swallow was for the Captain.

"Stokes, put a message in the bottle, close it tightly and bury it under a visible landmark. We must leave a message for posterity. We are the first to explore this land."

"What message should I write?"

"The usual, Stokes, today's date, all our names and that we intend to get as far as the Andes by going up this river."

"Aye, sir," said Stokes, and left.

"Do you think that someday someone will find all these messages we have been leaving during our voyage?"

"Of course, my friend. I have found several of previous explorers; Bougainville, for example. Furthermore, someone someday will actually look for them, because we are making history, don't you think?" said FitzRoy, smiling.

Darwin remained pensive. After a few minutes FitzRoy retired to sleep and the rest followed suit. The next day promised to be a hard one.

When Darwin woke the next morning, there was a strong westerly wind. FitzRoy and Stokes were talking on the river bank. He joined them to hear what the situation was.

"Six knots, Captain," stokes was saying, "and it is steady."

"Rowing is out of the question with this current. And I do not think it will be any slower up river."

"So how do you intend to go up river?"

"As long as the wind continues from the west we cannot use sails, so the only alternative is to haul them from the shore using ropes."

"But Captain, it is almost one hundred and forty miles to the Andes. How can we cover that distance towing three boats?" asked Darwin.

"We simply will, Filos. That is why I brought supplies for three weeks." FitzRoy was dead serious. When he took a decision there was no turning back. "Very well, friends, let us start immediately. The sooner we start, the sooner we will return."

Darwin returned to his tent to fetch his duffel bag and take it to the boat. Stokes continued with FitzRoy.

"Captain, here's your sextant. I took the readings with it last night, and I must confess I have never come across such an exact instrument."

"Thank you for your compliment, Mr. Stokes. I purchased it in London because I believe the ones furnished by the Royal Navy are not quite good enough. Furthermore, as we need your measurements to be of the greatest precision, I will give it to you, since from now on you will be the only one responsible for drawing charts."

"Captain, I am speechless! I don't know how to thank you."

"You can thank me by making good use of it, and producing exact coordinates. Let's do it, then."

Stokes put the sextant away in its wood and leather case. Many years later it would be exhibited at the Royal Naval Museum, and the caption in the glass cabinet would say that it had belonged to Admiral Stokes, famous explorer of Australia and the south Pacific.

FitzRoy split the party into three groups that would take turns towing the boats upriver. Everyone except Darwin and Stokes were included. The exceptions were because Stokes was to take readings very frequently to draw maps as accurate as possible, and Darwin was to collect as many fossils, geologic and animal samples as possible.

Whenever one of them had to stray further afield in their activities, FitzRoy had a rifleman escort them. Even though they had not seen any Indians, they had seen evidence of their presence. One night they had heard horses close by, but in the darkness the watch could not tell their number. They came across evidence of their presence constantly: arrow heads, boleadora stones, abandoned campfires, etc.

On one occasion they saw two columns of white smoke, one on each side of the river. It was an Indian custom to announce their whereabouts by burning bushes, which, if green, let off abundant white smoke that can be seen from very far. When they finally arrived at the spot where the bushes had been burnt, it turned out to be a ford where the Indians crossed the river. The bushes were still smouldering, but the Indians were nowhere in sight. The trail, still damp, on the other side of the river proved that a rather large party had crossed the fast-flowing river. It was quite amazing that these Indians, without boats or rafts, could ford such a fast-flowing river with their children, elders and all their belongings, but somehow these amazing people managed to do it.

Days went by and the river was ever more winding which almost doubled the distance the boats had to be towed.

The river ran along a valley, but what seemed to be mountains at the edge of the valley were in fact the sides of a canyon that cut through the Patagonian steppe. After climbing what seemed to be a mountain one reached a plain. The endless Patagonian tableau was only interrupted by the river that meandered in a canyon almost three miles wide.

Stokes was permanently along these heights, taking readings with his instruments and drawing the landscapes of the meandering river in the canyon from jutting rocks from where magnificent views could be seen. Darwin could be found sometimes at the top of the cliffs or others along the river banks examining some stone or hitting the cliff side with his geologist's hammer in search of fossils.

He was busily at this activity when he heard shouts from far ahead. He looked up to see Stokes, who from the top of the cliff was shouting and waving his arms. Darwin could not understand what he was shouting, so straining and putting his hand to his ear to help listen, he thought he heard a faint "daar..wiin!"; he listened harder and, sure enough, Stokes was calling him. He put his hammer away in his rucksack and started the long climb to the tableau. It would take him fifteen or twenty minutes to get there. "It better be worth it, Stokes," he thought as he started to sweat.

Stokes came down a bit to meet Darwin. Between his excitement and Darwin's panting they could not understand each other.

"A hand, Mr. Darwin!"

"What's that? A hand?"

"Didn't you hear what I was shouting from the top?"

"I couldn't hear it properly. What is this about a hand?"

"I found a hand in one of the caves. It seems to be a child's hand and it is protruding from some rocks against one of the walls of the cave."

"Let's go!" said Darwin and made an extra effort to hurry up the cliff.

As they approached the cave Stokes was pointing at, Darwin saw a group of stones that were piled up in a unnatural manner. "A cairn," he thought. He had seen several of these in San Julian and Deseado. They usually marked the place where an Indian had been buried, and it seemed fitting for one to be near a child's grave.

Basalt Glenn, near the valley of the Santa Cruz River, by Conrad Martens

"That is the entrance to the cave," said Stokes pointing at an entrance about three feet high amongst some rocks.

They went in. The cave was small, just seven or eight feet deep. They had to get used to the gloom, so it took Darwin a few seconds before he could see what Stokes wanted to show him. From between some stones on one of the walls of the cave some articulated bones stuck out that seemed to be the hand of a two-year-old child. Only four fingers could be seen. Probably the thumb was out of sight due to the position the hand was in. When Darwin looked closer, there was something that didn't quite fit.

"I wonder if it is very old," said Stokes. "Poor Indian boy, must have been a chief's son to have been buried in this place."

Darwin carefully pulled the bones from where they were held and took them outside to examine them thoroughly by daylight.

"It's a hare."

"What!?"

"Your Indian boy's hand, (son of a chief, no less), is actually a hare's foot. A mara, the Patagonian hare, to be precise," said Darwin with irony. It took Stokes a few seconds to get it. "You see, only four fingers; there is no thumb, because maras do not have one."

"Oh, how disappointing! I am truly sorry, I really believed it was a human hand. I regret I made you come up in haste."

"Don't worry, my friend. I really like it here; we have a magnificent view of the river."

Far below the rest of the group form the *Beagle* advanced slowly, towing the boats against the current. They could see that they were in for quite an effort since further ahead the river had so many curves that the actual distance west would not be great.

They both sat down to rest while making funny remarks about the mistaken hand. Darwin decided to accompany Stokes while he took readings for his coordinate calculations on the plateau above the river. They took turns carrying the heavy theodolite, sextant and a chronometer. They chatted cheerfully as they walked and enjoyed the wonderful view of the river below.

"Tell me, Mr. Darwin, what did the Captain mean, yesterday, when he said 'this was not made in forty days'?"

"It's a long story, but in a nutshell that this valley could not have been shaped by the rain that fell during the Flood that lasted forty days."

"I don't see how he could be sure."

"Look around you, Mr. Stokes. We are walking along a plateau that is a thousand feet above sea level. To our left, however, it falls abruptly to around four hundred feet over sea level, and then on the other side of the valley it returns to be a plateau a thousand feet above sea level. So all this part of the Patagonia is a plateau except for this enormous channel, so to speak, along which the river runs. But how was this valley formed?"

"Well, I am not a geologist, but I suppose that this was just a great plateau and the current of river carved the valley."

"Possibly, but how long would that take?"

"I don´t know, but now I see. It must have been much longer than forty days, as FitzRoy said."

"I have made some calculations. Let's suppose that the headwaters are in the mountains; that would mean that the length of the valley is of roughly 140 miles. It has an average width of about two and a half miles and, although the depth increases as we near the sea, we could say that on average it is a quarter of a mile deep. A simple calculation shows us that the amount of material missing is just under ninety cubic miles."

"And what is the purpose of these calculations?"

"Because now I know how much soil was carried away by the river, and if I can measure how much soil the river carries now, I can calculate roughly how long this process took."

"And did you measure this?"

"Yes. I left a tumbler of river water to rest all night and in the morning I measured the amount of solids that had precipitated. If I can measure the volume that flows I can calculate the total amount of solids the river carries. So then if I divide the ninety cubic miles by the amount of solids carried I can deduce how many years ago this process started."

"Darwin, my friend, you lost me. But let me guess. You calculated this and you came up with a number close to the one you calculated at the Canary Islands, about one million years, correct?"

"No, Mr. Stokes, this time the result was a lot more disturbing."

"How much?"

"One and a half billion years."

"WHAT?! What did you just say?"

"That it would take the river one thousand five hundred million years to carve this valley."

Stokes was stricken dumb. The number was so great he couldn't grasp the enormity of it.

"But that is not all."

"What more can there be?"

"You know well that the Bible says that God created the world, then He created the animals and finally Man. But you must recall that a few days ago I found some animal fossils at the bottom of a deep ravine."

"Of course I do, there were also some petrified wood."

"Yes. By the layers I found them in I can conclude that they were deposited there before this valley was formed. The river, on eating away as it formed the valley finally exposed them."

"Does that mean, Mr. Darwin, that these animals existed before the river, that is, over one thousand five hundred million years ago? Then God did not create the world and later the animals?"

"It would seem that the world was not created directly as we know it today, that it is in continuous change, like a never-ending task. The world must be very different from what it was when those animals lived. All these changes must have been gradual. Some animals must have adapted, and those that didn't, perished."

"You have left me speechless, Darwin. Animals one thousand five hundred million years ago! ..."

"Strictly speaking, Mr. Stokes, I am not sure it took that long. What I am saying is that at the current rate of erosion, that is how long it would take."

"It doesn't make much difference, Mr. Darwin. Supposing that the rate of erosion was ten times what it is now, it would have taken ten times less: one hundred and fifty million years! It is still a formidable number that completely changes the current beliefs on Creation and the history of the world."

"Nevertheless, there is another explanation which is just as interesting and revolutionary."

"What is it? You keep telling me things piecemeal, as in a mystery story."

"Ha, ha! There is a bit of that, no doubt. It is all a grand mystery ... Just before leaving Keel Point, where the *Beagle* is being repaired, I discovered an enormous, solitary rock which must weigh fifty tons or so. This rock is of a type that does not belong there. None of the mountains or strata are of this type, so it can only have come from the Andes."

"So the river washed it there?"

"That is what I thought at first, but according to my calculations, the slope of the river is not steep enough, so the current could not move a rock that size, let alone push it one hundred and forty miles."

"Then how did it get there?"

"As far as I know, Mr. Stokes, only ice can do that."

"Ice? Down to the sea? You mean to say that there was a glacier that spanned the continent all the way down to the sea?"

"Not only that, the glacier may still be there," he pointed west, "It may have retreated but still exists in the mountains ... If that is so it must be one of the most magnificent glaciers in the world."

"Fantastic! We must get to see this glacier. But tell me, Mr. Darwin, what about the other rivers and estuaries in Patagonia, were they formed by glaciers too?"

"From my observations at the Chico, Deseado and Gallegos rivers, those valleys could not have been formed by the effect of the current since they are almost trickles, so I would venture that several glaciers crossed the continent from the Andes down to the sea. Perhaps even the Straits of Magellan were the result of glacial activity. I recall seeing large solitary rocks on the beach at the bay of San Sebastián, so I believe that enormous glaciers crossed the island of Tierra del Fuego."

It was near noon, so Stokes started to set up his instruments to make readings and record the coordinates. He set up the theodolite and with its level-gauge he slowly coaxed it into a perfectly horizontal position. While he did this Darwin kept on talking:

"So, Mr. Stokes, about a million years ago this land was totally different from what it is today. Everything changed very slowly and the animals adapted to this change. To do so they also changed, in some cases they changed so much that they turned into different animals; new species."

"So then, Mr. Darwin," said Stokes while he kept his eye on the bubble of the theodolite's level-gauge, "what are we doing in this God forsaken part of the planet? Looking for the Holy Grail or some such?"

"Ha, ha! It could be ... some such, indeed!"

"Mr. Darwin, what is that all important thing that we can discover?"

"Well, maybe I shouldn't talk about this until I am more certain of it, since so far it is mere speculation."

"Come on! Let it out!"

"All right ... we are after something more important than the Holy Grail ... we are trying to discover the origin of Man."

"And what would the origin of Man be, Mr. Darwin?"

"It would seem that Man evolved from some inferior animal instead of being created by God."

"So what did God do?"

"I do not know. Perhaps God does not exist. It would seem that God is not necessary for the world and us to exist."

"My, my, Mr. Darwin. That is revolutionary. I find it hard to believe, but I will make an effort to understand it." As he said this he took out the notebook where he registered the readings. He recorded the data of each observation point on a different page and had taken the habit of giving each observation point a name. He chose 'No God' for this one and wrote it down. "And what does the Captain make of all this?"

"The Captain agrees with me on these theories but believes that nothing must be said until we are absolutely convinced of it and have conclusive proof. FitzRoy believes that these conclusions will create quite an upheaval."

"I am sure they will! But then you shouldn't have told me any of this, should you?"

"Well ... you are part of the crew ... I do not know if you should know this or not, but just in case, act as if you know nothing."

"Not a word," said Stokes as he aimed the viewfinder west, set the magnifying at its greatest and "Oh my God! I must tell the Captain right away!"

He ran to the edge of the plateau, blew his whistle as hard as he could and waved his arms desperately to call the attention of the men toiling at the boats.

"Captain! Captain!"

To make sure they heard him he took his pistol, which he carried loaded at all times, and fired into the air.

"Captain! Captain!" he turned to Darwin and said, "The Captain must know about this."

Darwin, white as paper, could not understand what was going on.

On the valley floor the crew heard the shot and saw that Stokes was calling their attention. The signals they had agreed upon beforehand indicated that FitzRoy's presence was required. So, escorted by two armed midshipmen, he started the ascent to the plateau. It would take him half an hour to get there.

Stokes noticed that Darwin did not understand what was going on.

"The mountains! After nearly two weeks we can finally see the mountains." He ushered the naturalist to the theodolite and told him to look through the instrument's telescope. Darwin's heart stopped racing. For a moment he thought that Stokes would give away his little breach of trust.

"I cannot see anything, Mr. Stokes, just clouds."

"There are clouds, and below them snowy peaks. The thing is that you do not have a trained eye. Just look for a few minutes and you will see the clouds move and what is behind and under them are the mountains."

"I hope you are right, because if you have made the Captain come up to find it was a false alarm, as you did with me, he might not be amused."

"Don't worry. I may not know much about bones, but I have quite a long experience at observing mountains. Those are the Andes."

While they waited for the Captain, Stokes started to take some readings with the sextant although it still was several minutes to midday when he would take the exact reading for his coordinate calculation. Darwin looked through the instrument again and this time he could tell that Stokes was indeed right, they were mountains.

Suddenly FitzRoy appeared. He had climbed a lot faster than expected.

"What is up, Stokes? Why were you calling?" he asked, breathless after the long ascent.

"The Andes, sir. For the first time the Andes can be seen."

View of the Santa Cruz River with the Andes in the background, by Conrad Martens

"Very well, let us see." FitzRoy moved up to the theodolite and looked through it, a grave look on his face. Several seconds went by and his silence prompted Darwin to think that he believed they were not mountains after all.

The Captain stood up, and still with a grave look on his face said, "Fantastic! Who saw the Andes first?"

"Mr Stokes, Captain," said Darwin.

FitzRoy walked up to Stokes and shook his hand. "Congratulations, Stokes, you have just earned a mountain!"

"Beg your pardon, sir?" said the young man in disbelief.

"I said that you have earned a mountain. Come, bring your notebook." They went up to the theodolite again. FitzRoy looked through it again.

"Mr. Stokes, I want you to make a sketch of the profile of the mountains as seen from this point. But take note, we shall name some of them. There due north, 303 degrees there is a mountain that looks as if it had a fortress on it, name it Castle Hill[2]. Further south at 291 degrees there is a triangular shaped mountain with its peak leaning slightly left, call this one Hobbler Hill. Then you will see several lower mountains, but a bit further south, at 262 degrees there are several higher peaks. One of them must be the highest of the lot, I will let you measure their heights. The highest one will be named Mount Stokes."

FitzRoy shook his hand again, "congratulations again, Mr. Stokes, you now have a mountain. Your family will be proud of you." And before

2. Castle Hill translates to Spanish as "Cerro Castillo", which continues to be its name today.

starting back down to the river and the boats he added, "continue your work, gentlemen, I'll see you this evening."

During the almost three weeks that they towed the boats up that incredibly winding river they did not come across Indians again. The snowy peaks of the ever-closer Andes seemed to be the only witnesses of their slow and gruelling progress west.

The night before they had camped at a place that showed signs that it was one of the sites chosen by the Indians to ford the river. But that evening, 3rd May, would be the last camp before they started their return. Stokes took the readings, calculated the coordinates and named it Last Bivouac in his notebook.

As they were already running short of supplies, Captain FitzRoy decided that next day they would push forward in one last effort to reach the headwaters which they believed to be a lake. As the headway towing the boats was so slow, and as the river took a sweeping curve south, he decided that the boats would be left at the camp with just over half the men to stand guard over them while the rest would continue west on foot as far as possible. At noon they would take the readings and record the coordinates of the western limit of their exploratory adventure. The Captain had written the message they would leave in a bottle at a landmark for future explorers to find.

They turned in early so as to start at dawn and so take advantage of as many hours as possible in their quest for reaching the headwaters of the mysterious Santa Cruz.

They had been walking now for several hours along a plain that Stokes had named Mystery Plain because he supposed that at the end of it they would finally discover the headwaters of the Santa Cruz River. Both Darwin and FitzRoy were certain that it was a lake which should not be very far, but midday was near and the plain seemed never-ending. Only a few bushes every eight or ten feet broke the flat monotony of the plain.

Suddenly a Patagonic hare (mara) dashed out from behind a thicket.

"Stokes, look!" cried Darwin, "there goes another Indian boy's hand! Ha, ha!"

"Very funny. It seems you will not forget that incident, my friend. I shall return the favour as soon as I get a chance."

They continued walking side by side along the most uninteresting landscape.

"Tell me, Mr. Darwin, now that I see this desolate landscape, I recall you mentioned something about this land being cursed by sterility. How can the earth be so dry so close to such a large river?"

"I used the word 'curse´ because anywhere else a river like the Santa Cruz would cause everything near it to be green and fertile. An example is the Nile which flows through one of the largest deserts on earth, the Sahara, but its waters spread life on its shores. All along its course the land close to it, and up to a mile from its banks is green and fertile, full of life."

"And why doesn't the same happen here?"

"Here is the answer," Darwin bent down and picked up a handful of dirt, opened his hand and showed it to Stokes, "the topsoil is just sand and shingle. It is so coarse that it cannot hold water, it filters through, as if through a strainer, and does not stop until checked by a layer of waterproof material."

"You mean that there is water under this desert?"

"Yes, a real curse of barrenness."

"Stokes!" called FitzRoy, "How long till midday?"

"Stokes glanced at his chronometer, "one hour and twenty six minutes, Captain."

"Very well, then we shall continue until yonder elevation where we will take the coordinates and leave our token."

"We evidently will not reach any lake, is that not so, Captain?" said Darwin.

"I am afraid not, Filos, but perhaps we can see it from there." The small hill was nearly a mile ahead of them and around one hundred feet higher than the surrounding 'Mystery Plain'. If there was a lake to see, then they would see it from there, because the walls of the valley, that widened noticeably, were seven miles away on either side of them.

FitzRoy was the first one to reach the top of the hill. When Darwin caught up with him he could see that he was disappointed. All that could be seen was the plain that continued west with a gentle slope until it finally dropped away and disappeared. The wind blew hard from the distant mountains as if to discourage any attempt to continue.

"I could go on while the rest of you set up your instruments and take the readings to calculate the coordinates, Captain."

"And what do you expect to see from there, my friend? Another hill you will want to climb, and then another and another. Look here, the

View from Western Station, by Conrad Martens

mountains are at least thirty miles from here and the landscape must be the same all the way to the foot of them. It's useless, this is as far as we'll go."

They did not imagine that only four miles ahead, about one hour brisk walk, was the shore of a magnificent lake that would be discovered forty years later by an American gold prospector.

"Mr. Stokes, while we wait for noon we will use the theodolite's viewfinder to draw the profile of the mountains. Mr. Martens will do that since his artist's hand will make sure that the shapes are accurate."

"Very well, sir. Once he is finished I will use the theodolite to measure the heights" he turned to look at Darwin, "I will prove that Mount Stokes is higher than Mount Darwin."

"Impossible! Mount Darwin is over six thousand feet."

"Maybe so, but I, Stokes, will be measuring Mount Stokes, so ... anything is possible, ha, ha."

The two young men laughed heartily. It was not often that one could tell that, in spite of being hardened by vast experience, they were only in their early twenties.

Stokes took out his telescope and peered at the mountains. "Look at that!" He handed Darwin the telescope, "there, to the right of Mount Stokes you can see snowy peaks. I believe there are more, but anyway they seem to be very white. Perhaps they are capped with ice, that's where our friend must be."

"Yes, I see them, but what friend are you talking about?"

"The glacier that made all this. You see, Mr. Darwin, if we could see it we could name it the Darwin Glacier."

"Oh thank you, Mr. Stokes! And what prompted such kindness?"

"That the glacier would flow past at the foot of mount Stokes. A Darwin at my feet!"

"Very witty, but from here we cannot be sure there is any glacier, though I can almost feel its presence. I think we will miss seeing this wonder ... But talking of names ... we have our mountains, but the Captain does not have any."

"In the Navy it is not good etiquette for the Captain to name places after himself. It is considered bad taste."

The Captain was supervising the digging of the hole where the bottle with message to future explorers would be placed. It would then be covered with stones to form a cairn.

"If I ever have the fortune of leading an exploratory voyage I will name some important place 'FitzRoy' ... I shall not forget you either, my friend."

"Thank you, Mr. Stokes, but it seems so unfair that in this area that he explored there is nothing named after him."

"You could do something about that."

"Me? What could I do?"

"Are there not countless new species of plants and animals that must be classified and named? Make sure some of the ones you collected here are named after our Captain."

"That is a splendid idea ... but it is not I that selects the names," he thought of Henslow and other well known colleagues who were set on classifying all living species, "but I believe I could do something about it."

Years later, the impressive Andes variety of the Patagonian cypress (Alerce in Spanish) which the Mapuches called Lahuán, and whose trunk can grow up to 15 feet diameter over thousands of years, was given the scientific name Fitzroya cupressoides in FitzRoy's honour.

Finally, at noon Stokes was able to make the readings and record the coordinates of their station; and with the theodolite calculate the angles and distances to the visible landmarks. He named this last position as Western Station. The Captain instructed him to name the plain that lay before them, where they had hoped to find a lake, 'Disappointment Plain'. His state of mind at the time was thus immortalized on the charts.

Slowly they picked their way back to their camp, Last Bivouac. Stokes, burdened with the heavy theodolite, moved close to Darwin.

"I bear bad news."

"Oh? And what is it?"

"Mount Stokes."

"What about it?"

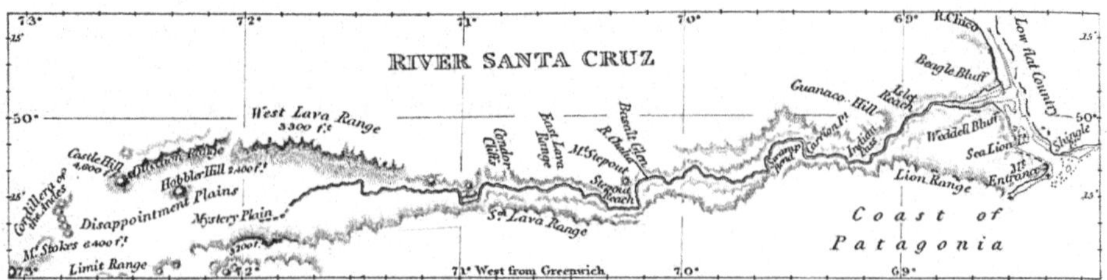

Original map of the Santa Cruz River expedition

"It is higher than Mount Darwin."

"Did you cheat?"

"I didn't have to. It is almost eight thousand feet high ... I'm sorry," he said with a smile.

"Mr. Stokes, I am sorry too," said Darwin pretending to be furious, "you have dilapidated your chance of some fantastic animal being named after you ... Thinking it over, however, I may call some new variety of sloth after you ... Slothus Stokeatus."

The return to the Atlantic coast was much easier, since they had both the current and the wind in their favour. It only took them two and a half days to return to the *Beagle*, which was waiting, ready to continue on its mission.

FitzRoy's plan was to try to find a small island which was marked on some old French charts, but which had never been seen again, and appeared to have been named L'Aigle (The Eagle). They would then make the hazardous crossing to the Pacific Ocean. Before that, however they would drop in to see a friend who had been left with the natives of Tierra del Fuego. FitzRoy was worried about Jemmy Button's fate.

Chapter 11

Three Forsaken Friends

The crossing from the Atlantic to the Pacific Ocean was, as expected, a very challenging experience. But it was not that that most affected our Captain, but to leave behind dearest friends. Once more his emotional balance was affected, which is something not easily tolerated from the Captain of a ship; and FitzRoy was his own most exacting critic.

The *Beagle* and the *Adventure* left the Atlantic and sailed west along the channel that bears the former's name to continue the survey of the labyrinthical shores of the south of Chile. Then would come the crossing of the Pacific Ocean and finally the return to England.

They were sailing near Navarino Island. The Captain had decided to make a detour to visit the site of the colony where they had left Jemmy Button, Fuegia and York Minster. He had a sense of foreboding as the *Beagle* approached Wollya Cove. They entered the cove at dusk, and what they could see was not encouraging; there was no trace of the cabins or the Fuegians. Stokes and Darwin wanted to go ashore and inspect the place, but FitzRoy did not allow it. In the dark it was dangerous, ideal for an ambush.

Next morning Darwin, as was his custom, went to have breakfast with the Captain, but on his way Sullivan informed him that the Captain had had breakfast before dawn and had gone on deck.

Darwin found him at the bow looking at the horizon through his telescope.

"Captain, let us go ashore and look for our Fuegians."

"It is useless. They are not here, there is nobody here. I have been inspecting the place with my telescope and no one can be seen. The only possibility is that they left. They will see the *Beagle* and come back."

Darwin could only answer "probably". Without uttering another word they both stood there, one trying to see something with his telescope, and the other immersed in his thoughts.

Fuegian Indians in Tierra del Fuego, by Conrad Martens

Darwin knew that the Captain felt responsible for what happened to "his Fuegians", as he called them. He had taken them to England without even asking their opinion, he had, in fact abducted them. He then educated them as Englishmen and returned them, totally changed, to a destiny that no one else wished to share with them. It had all been a grand experiment, overlooking the fact that they were human beings. Only an inveterate optimist as the young FitzRoy of 1829, only twenty four years old, could think the experiment had any chance of success. But now, although he was not yet thirty, FitzRoy was an optimist no more. Several years spent in solitude as Captain of a ship with eighty souls in his charge made him painfully aware that things can sometimes turn out for the worst, and when they do they were invariably his fault.

"Over there!" FitzRoy's shout startled Darwin.

"What is that, Captain?"

"There, there!" he said again, pointing southwest, "Three canoes approach. It must be them. Here, take the telescope, have a look."

True enough, Darwin could see three canoes approaching, he could not tell who they were, but was surprised yet again by how fragile looking the Fuegian canoes were. "I wonder how many people have perished in high seas," he thought. The canoes were short, squat and very unstable; in short they seemed to be totally unseaworthy. It did not seem likely that any human being could navigate these vessels, but the Fuegians did so in any sort of weather, no matter the size of the waves.

"One of them is waving ... it is Jemmy!" said the Captain animatedly, who had the telescope back, "see for yourself, Filos!"

It was him, all right, but now that they could see the rest of people in the canoes, they could tell that Fuegia and York Minster were not with him. That worried the Captain.

Once the canoes were alongside the *Beagle*, Jemmy shouted, "Presents, I brought presents, Captain." Once the canoe was fastened to the *Beagle*, Jemmy scrambled up the rope ladder, hurdled the railing and started greeting the crew that had assembled on deck to see him. Jemmy had always been well liked by everyone.

It was amazing how he had changed. Not only had he abandoned European dress, clearly he had returned to live with his people, his hair was tangled, he was growing a beard and had lost weight. But what most affected them was that his body was smeared with blubber and charcoal, which gave him a darker tone, but mainly a smell that was hard to ignore.

However, his mood was as jovial as ever. His smile contrasted with this dark and cold land.

"Captain, present for you." He gave FitzRoy two otter skins which, many years later he would hang in his study and show his visitors with pride. But at that time the Captain wanted to know something else.

"Thank you, Jemmy, but what happened to Fuegia and York Minster?," he asked, concerned.

"Oh, no worry, they be well."

"Where are they, Jemmy?" asked FitzRoy firmly.

"York bad Indian. After you leave, all Indians want to take things from us. York built canoe and take Fuegia and all he could from colony. Then he go that way," he said pointing west, "where his tribe lives."

The answer calmed FitzRoy. York's attitude seemed reasonable. If the other Indians would not allow the colony to exist it seemed logical that York would want to return to his own land, with his people. And it was also natural that he takes Fuegia with him, he had considered her his property for some time now.

"Look at me, Captain, Jemmy is dirty Indian again," said Jemmy in jest, but with a touch of shame.

"Not at all, Jemmy. You just adapted to your new way of life. It goes to show that you are very smart," said FitzRoy sternly, but showing he understood what Jemmy had been through. "Tell me Jemmy, do you wish to return to England with us?"

"No, thank you Captain. This Jemmy's place. This Jemmy's life and must live it now. Also Jemmy now has woman," he said pointing at a young girl that looked on in fear from the canoe, "and soon Jemmy will be father."

"Congratulations! You are a full-grown man now!" said the Captain smiling.

"Thank you. But Jemmy wants to ask favour from Captain."

"Whatever you want, Jemmy."

"I would like to spend day on the *Beagle*, just like good old days."

These words had a profound effect on FitzRoy, but he tried not to let it show.

"Of course," said FitzRoy half choking, "would you like to shave and dress as you did then?"

"Yes! I want that." And turning to Darwin he continued, "Mr. Darwin you smile, I have present for you too. Here," he gave him two chipped stones.

"Two arrowheads! Thank you, Jemmy."

"Not two arrowheads! One arrowhead, other spear head. Look, they different," said Jemmy, wondering how Darwin hadn't noticed the difference.

"Of course, how silly of me."

The girl started wailing from the canoe, which went on and on. Jemmy looked over the railing and shouted at her in an angry tone, but she did not stop.

"What is the matter with your woman, Jemmy?" asked FitzRoy.

"She afraid Jemmy leave. But I tell her I come back later."

"But apparently she did not believe you, because she is still crying."

"Oh, she understands. But she cries anyway until Jemmy returns ... all the time. Women the same all over the world, Captain."

"Very well, then let us go and get you dressed like the Jemmy of yore."

"Yes, Captain."

After dusk dinner was prepared, the last one for Jemmy on board the *Beagle*. It would be served in the officer's mess and the menu would be

Jemmy as a Fuegian, by FitzRoy

special. The cook had to break into his reserves to prepare what Jemmy wanted: lamb and mint sauce.

They all sat at the table with FitzRoy in the place of privilege, in the centre, and Jemmy on his right. Then Wickham, who had come over from the *Adventure*, Sullivan, Stokes Darwin, Martens and the rest of the officers. Darwin couldn't avoid comparing this scene with Leonardo Da Vinci's 'Last Supper'.

The meal started in very high spirits, with everyone remembering amusing anecdotes of the trip. Then Jemmy rendered a very amusing account of the city of London as seen by an Indian. The Captain recalled how quickly Jemmy had learned English, Martens told of Jemmy's surprise when he saw a painting for the first time; he had never imagined that reality could be reproduced so vividly. Jemmy loved to sit and watch Martens draw, admiring his bold and precise strokes, but no matter how he tried he was never able to draw even the most elementary figures. Stokes nearly choked with laughter when Wickham described Jemmy's face when he had his first beer and the effect it had on him later. Finally Darwin told them, almost as a scientific observation, of the amazing precision Jemmy had when throwing stones: he could easily hit a bottle at fifty feet.

But as the evening advanced, the mood turned from jovial to gloomy. Happy faces gave way to wistful expressions. Late in the evening there was one last toast, and as none of them were very much for farewells, without much ado Jemmy returned to his Indian dress. Once on deck, he shook every crew member's hand in silence. FitzRoy asked him one last time if he was sure he didn't want to return to England with them, but Jemmy's woman's wailing was his answer.

Jemmy jumped over the rail, nimbly climbed down to his canoe, paddled away into the darkness and was lost. For a while they all remained in silence looking into the darkness where he had gone.

An abandoned friend ... The end of a sad day. The next morning they would set sail to where another abandoned friend lay.

After many years I came to understand that that day Jemmy wasn't only saying goodbye to us but also to the 'European' Jemmy.

At Port Famine[1] FitzRoy feared that he might face the same tragic destiny as the deceased former Captain of the *Beagle*, Pringle Stokes, who after committing suicide was buried in this desolate place.

On 2nd July, 1834 the *Adventure* and the *Beagle* anchored at a dark harbour that had been given the ominous name of Port Famine in remembrance of what had happened to the ill-fated colony that had been founded there in 1584 by a Spaniard, Don Pedro de Sarmiento. Phillip II of Spain, who wanted to control the Straits of Magellan to prevent English and French pirates from crossing from one Ocean to the other to ransack the Spanish colonies on the Pacific, ordered that a fort be established on the Straits. Settlers were brought from Spain, and a fort and dwellings for them were built. They did not, however, survive the first year. Hunger proved to be worse than the poor settlers' stamina and they died, one after the other. In 1587 Thomas Cavendish, an Englishman, found the place deserted and just the remains of a few bodies that had been hanged, probably executed as a result of the looting that preceded the downfall.

Captain FitzRoy wanted to have a remembrance service for someone closer to the *Beagle*'s crew, its former Captain, Pringle Stokes, who had shot himself there and died after a rather lengthy agony. For the service they chose the site of his tomb and the entire crew of the *Beagle* and the *Adventure* were present.

1. Port Famine is very near what is now Fuerte Bulnes, about 70 km from the Chilean city of Punta Arenas on the Straits of Magellan.

The overcast skies, gusty wind and extreme cold did not deter them. The weather reminded them that it was a place of sorrow and despair. The Captain, standing at the head of the tomb, next to the cross, read the passage about Jonas being swallowed by a whale, a favourite amongst seamen, from his bible. The heavens waited until the Captain had finished to mark the end of the ceremony with a persistent drizzle that only strengthened the general feeling that this was truly a wretched place.

As the party slowly returned to where they had left the boats, FitzRoy approached Wickham.

"Mr. Wickham, you were close to Pringle Stokes at the time of his demise, what do you think drove him to such an extreme decision?"

Wickham was taken by surprise since FitzRoy had never shown any interest in the matter even though he had been promoted as a result of Stokes' death.

"Well, Captain ... it is not easy to determine a cause. About a month before taking his life he fell into a severe depression that he would never come out of. He was rather unsure of himself and was always haunted by doubts. He was aware that his surveying was not up to standard and that his own ineptness had prevented him from finishing the survey on time, which would oblige the *Beagle* and its crew to remain in this bleak land for yet another year. The prospect of going through another winter in this Godforsaken part of the Earth caused him to plunge into the depths of his inner hell."

"I suppose that the loss of a year of surveying must have weighed heavily on him. It was his responsibility after all," said FitzRoy, who seemed to have a good understanding of what Pringle Stokes had gone through.

"Exactly, Captain," said Wickham, "I recall he said once that the loss of a year by eighty souls was equivalent to one person losing eighty years; a lifetime."

"I see ... I can imagine he did not consider it fair that eighty souls should lose a year of their lives on account of him ... Somehow he must have thought that by taking his life he was paying for his sins and therefore releasing the rest of the crew."

"It could be, Captain ... I hadn't thought of it that way."

"Someday, Wickham, you will be in command of an expedition and you will experience the weight of being responsible for the lives of so many."

The wind blew at gale strength with gusts even stronger and the heavy drizzle wet them through. They had almost reached the boats that would take them back to their ships.

Port Famine, by Parker King

"Look here, Wickham ... I decided to purchase the *Adventure*, without waiting for a response from the Admiralty, because I could see that with the *Beagle* alone I would not be able to conclude the survey in the allotted time. I made the same calculation as Pringle Stokes: a year in the life of eighty souls is a lifetime."

"But instead of surrendering you took a positive attitude to solve the problem. You are very different from Pringle Stokes."

"Not really, Wickham ... we are not so different ..."

They had already arrived at the boats that were waiting for them, but FitzRoy changed his mind.

"You go, Wickham, and send a boat back to fetch me. I will bid farewell to Pringle Stokes again. I feel I am abandoning a friend."

It worried Wickham to see a distressed FitzRoy slowly picking his way back to the tomb.

The death of one of his closest officers was another hard blow that pushed FitzRoy towards a state of mind he would fall into later on and would make us fear the worst.

On the 27th June, 1834 George Rowlett died after his health had taken a turn for the worst.

Captain FitzRoy had tried desperately to sail the *Beagle* away from the Fuegian channels to a city on the Chilean coast where Rowlett could

Cape Horn, by W. Wilson

get the medical attention he needed. But in the fight against the storms Tierra del Fuego prevailed over the Captain and Rowlett died when they were only two days from San Carlos[2] on the island of Chiloé.

FitzRoy had spent several days at his bedside, trying to lift his spirit, promising him that he would get him out of there. But the storms did their utmost to prevent the *Beagle* from making any headway. Rowlett, soaked in sweat from the fever, thanked the Captain for his efforts, but by the roar of the wind he knew that it was a losing battle.

In a rare lucid moment he took a medal that hung around his neck and gave it to FitzRoy, asking him to hand to his daughter whom he had seen only as a new-born baby and would never see again. "What saddens me most is knowing she will grow without a father," he said.

The day after Rowlett died the storm subsided, as if, after claiming its prey, it lost interest in stopping the *Beagle* and let her go.

FitzRoy decided to give him a seaman's funeral since he did not want to abandon Rowlett at a solitary tomb like Pringle Stokes, so on the 28th, the whole crew assembled on deck in their dress uniforms for the occasion. The *Adventure* also sailed close by with its crew in dress uniforms assembled on deck to witness the sad procedure.

The Captain read the chapter of Jesus walking on water from the New Testament. After that he spoke of Rowlett's personality, his life and his family. Finally a volley from both ships cannon saluted the friend they were leaving behind and Rowlett's body, draped in the Union Jack, was dropped into the sea. The sound of the body hitting the water wrung the souls of those hardened seamen. So ended ten years' service of the senior member of the *Beagle*'s officer corps. FitzRoy felt he had failed him.

2. Today San Carlos is known as Ancud.

"I would rather it had been me," he told Darwin in a whisper.

"You did everything within your power to save him. There is nothing to blame yourself for."

"But it was not enough, Filos. In spite of our efforts, Rowlett died, and joined the ghosts of those in my expedition who lost their lives, and haunt me every night. None of them hold any grudge against me, but they are dead anyway. How many more will I say farewell to? Will I join them?"

Darwin could tell that the best he could do was to leave the Captain to his thoughts and let him mourn in peace.

Soon the death and destruction they would witness at Talcahuano would make them aware of how cruel Nature could be, and would also help them understand the real value of certain aspects of life.

Chapter 12

Killer Waves

In the middle of a scene of death and destruction my friend Darwin found a voice that would change the manner in which he viewed God.

While the *Beagle* was anchored in the port of Valdivia, a terrible earthquake hit the town, destroying dwellings and other buildings but, fortunately, there were few casualties.

Seconds before the earthquake, which lasted just a few minutes, Darwin noticed a large flock of very agitated birds circling the old Spanish fort of Niebla (built to defend Valdivia from English privateers). The naturalist made an entry in his notebook that it would be interesting to study the behaviour of animals before and during an earthquake, perhaps a method to predict them could be found.

Half an hour after the earthquake the sea level started rising, as if it were a freak tide. It rose to about 23 feet above the normal high-water mark, and fifteen minutes later it dropped as mysteriously as it had risen.

Darwin wrote in his notebook. "Can an earthquake displace large volumes of water? Was the epicentre somewhere at sea?"

Shortly after, the crew was made aware that the earthquake had made the anchor shift and it was now stuck in such a way that it could not be hoisted. All that could be done was to cut it loose and lose it. They only had one anchor left. The Captain decided to suspend the last leg of the survey that had been planned and sail to Valparaiso in a week, where they would purchase two new anchors.

Ships coming south brought news of how Concepción, and its port, Talcahuano, were utterly destroyed by the earthquake and were then hit by several gigantic waves that killed hundreds. Talcahuano was precisely the next stop the *Beagle* had planned on its way to Valparaiso, so FitzRoy decided to sail there immediately.

When they arrived, some of the officers went ashore, but Darwin preferred to be taken to the nearby island of Quiriquina where he wanted to study the geological effects of the earthquake. Once on the island he hired a guide to show him the places where the earthquake was felt the most. Some rocks near the pier had risen fifteen feet in a matter of minutes. The dry kelp and rotting mussels were proof that they had been below sea level a few days earlier. In another part of the island the earth and rocks had shifted and there were great crevices that crossed the island north to south where the land had shifted sideways ten or twelve feet. In short, Darwin was convinced that earthquakes could modify the face of the earth dramatically in a very short time, in a way that could never be achieved by the slow effect of erosion. The conclusion was that in many places on Earth the landscape had been fashioned by great cataclysms and not by the slow effect of the elements.

On the beach that faced the mainland a great amount of debris could be seen strewn all over it, including wood, furniture and even books.

"It was the killer waves, when they retreated after flooding Talcahuano," said the guide to an astonished Darwin, and went on, "if you had come here four days ago you would have seen the bodies of the ill-fated who were dragged away by the waves; most of them were children."

Shaken by what he had heard, on his return to the *Beagle* he met Stokes who had just returned from Concepción and Talcahuano on the mainland. He was appalled by what he had seen: death and destruction.

"A scene that I shall never forget," said Stokes, "was a wagon that came into the town with a morbid load: the bodies of children that the sea had thrown back at a neighbouring beach after drowning them without mercy. The anguished screams of mothers as they recognized their children amongst the little bodies were heart-wrenching. No matter how I try, Mr. Darwin, there is no way I could prepare you for what you will see when you go ashore"

People said that, although the earthquake had caused widespread destruction, there had been few casualties. Most people rushed out of their houses after the first shock, so when the buildings collapsed they were empty. As they stood dazed, bemoaning the loss of their homes, they did not notice that the sea had withdrawn hundreds of feet. It was then that three successive waves over 25 feet high hit Talcahuano as if Nature had come to fetch the souls the earthquake had spared. Torrents rushed through the crowded streets. The strongest and nimbler were able to scramble onto the debris or hang on to stout trees, but the weaker, mostly children, were dragged away by the angry torrent which, as it retreated, carried them away to a certain death at the bottom of the sea.

The survivors could only amble along the now deserted streets blaming themselves for not having tried to save that that was more valuable than their own lives: the lives of their children. After two days of relentless mourning, the town priest, an indefatigable Spaniard, started to coax the population into snapping out of their distress and start to rebuild, not only their homes, but their lives, giving them a reason to live and finding a meaning in tragedy.

The day after being briefed on what had happened, Darwin visited what was left of Talcahuano. Once landed, he understood what Stokes had said. One thing is to be told about destruction, but seeing it was quite another thing. Nothing could have prepared him for this.

All the buildings had collapsed, except for the church belfry, which stood at such an awkward angle that it would probably fall if not buttressed.

To see a religious symbol still standing infuriated him. "How can anyone believe in God? What sort of wicked God would allow such horror?" thought Darwin.

He walked towards the church at a lively pace. Barring the belfry, nothing was left of it. At the bottom of the garden stood a makeshift hut with a hurriedly thatched roof that had been turned into a temporary church. To get to it he had to pick his way across the small cemetery. Many of the tombs were recent and the size of them made his heart bleed. Toys and children's clothes hung from the crosses; it was the way many parents found to remember their children by. Close by an old priest spoke earnestly to a woman with despair written all over her face.

After a few minutes, once the woman had left and the priest was alone, Darwin approached him and addressed him angrily in his broken Spanish:

"How do you dare speak to these people, who have lost everything, about God? How do you explain why He did such a thing?"

The priest ignored the attack and held out his hand saying, "José Iñiguez, Rector of Talcahuano Parish."

In spite of his rage, Darwin could not refuse the proffered hand.

"Charles Darwin, naturalist on the *Beagle*."

"Naturalist? Just what we need! Yesterday the officers from the *Beagle* helped us to buttress a wall that threatened to collapse, but today we need a naturalist."

The unexpected answer caught Darwin by surprise. Was it some kind of sick joke?

"I would love to be of use," he said, "but why do you need a naturalist?"

"You see, Mr. Darwin, I would imagine you have training in geology?" Darwin nodded, "one of the land shifts caused by the earthquake stopped up the spring that supplied fresh water to the town. We need to find another one. I believe your knowledge of geology would help us find a place where we could tap a new one. Can you help us?"

"Of course!" cried Darwin, happy to be able to help these people some way.

"Give me a minute so I can change into more appropriate clothes and I will take you to where the old well was."

The few words they had crossed caused him to change his opinion of the priest. He had been told that Father Iñiguez was quite a character, and his experience so far corroborated this.

"Here, take this," Father Iñiguez handed Darwin a pick and a shovel, "you are young, so you will find these easier to carry than I do. It's a 20-minute walk, follow me."

Darwin was still dumbfounded.

As they made their way up a mountain path, Darwin asked, "What made you think that a naturalist could help?"

"Many years ago I lived for a while near Quito. There I met a German who said he was a geologist. He studied volcanoes, but one of his pastimes was to find natural springs using his knowledge of geology, and he was very good at it."

"A German that studied volcanoes ... was it Alexander von Humboldt by any chance?"

"The same, he became well known after his book was published."

"Of course! It is my main reference book; I would almost say that I it was he who influenced me to go on this trip. What was he like?"

"There is nothing much to say. He was very intelligent and sure of himself, but was also arrogant and unpleasant."

"I learned so much from his book ..." he suddenly remembered his annoyance with the priest, "but going back to where I started, how can you believe in God after all this death and destruction? Haven't you given this any thought?"

"Of course I have thought about it, Mr. Darwin. I am as weak as the next man. Just like you I feel, think and doubt."

"And even then you believe in God?"

The destruction of Concepcion, Chile, by J. C. Wickham

"I believe in God in spite of everything."

"And how do you explain how God, if he exists, can allow such a calamity to happen?"

"You see, Mr. Darwin, my notion of what God is is special. I don't believe God is almighty. I would say that the forces of good and evil are pretty much balanced. Obviously, this tragedy was not the work of God. Goodness needs our help to prevail. Ignacio de Loyola, the founder of our order, the Jesuits, was a soldier before he decided to be a priest, and as a soldier he witnessed much misery and suffering, so he decided to become a soldier of Jesus. Jesus needs soldiers for good to prevail over evil. That is why we Jesuits consider ourselves soldiers of Christ," he stopped a moment to rest, "As one of my superiors, Father Iturri, used to say, 'If the good people on Earth allow the wicked to do evil, then the good are not good.'."

"That is an interesting way of thinking, but it does not prove that God exists."

"Does your science, Mr. Darwin, prove that God does not exist?"

"No."

"Then you should, at least, grant God the benefit of the doubt and not deny Him so categorically. Furthermore ... there is the miracle of life. Does science explain life on earth? Why we live? Why we die? Or what happiness and suffering really are?"

"I have no answer."

"Then your science cannot explain it all. There is a place for science and a place for God," he stopped to rest again. "Let me tell you of another miracle. The miracle of faith over despair. What would you tell a mother whose three children were dragged away by the angry sea?"

Darwin could only be silent.

"I believe I know," he went on, "you would tell her that they are dead, that their dreams have been lost, that their lives are over and there's nothing left to be done; a message of hopelessness. On the other hand, my friend, God's message is that her children are in heaven, with Jesus, in eternal happiness, that they can see her and she can speak to them in her prayers and that she will be reunited with them when the Lord calls her to his side ... Believe me, the message of faith is very powerful. It gives one the strength to continue after having lost everything. I have seen this miracle of faith happen over and over again."

Again he stopped to catch his breath, "not long to go, now," he mumbled and continued:

"You are still young and probably nothing really bad has happened to you yet. The moment you suffer a great loss, my friend, you will find that those who have faith will bear it with more fortitude. People that you believed to be frail will turn out to be stronger because they will have the strength of faith. God, Mr. Darwin, may not have been able to stop the tragedy from happening in Talcahuano, but He will make a miracle happen and I will help Him make it come true."

"What is that miracle, Father?"

"The miracle of life. In spite of all this death and destruction, if you return in five or six years you will see that the voice of children will be heard again, playing in the streets. Happiness will return," and looking up at the sky, "I only hope the Lord will grant me life enough, I am eighty-two, to be able to behold this miracle."

Darwin was dumbfounded by this way of seeing life and the world.

"Here we are at last!" said the priest, "over there you can see where the land shift covered the spring."

Darwin studied the little valley that ran down to the sea. Usually springs happen at the foot of the mountains. Rain water filters down the porous strata, earth or sand, and runs down following the slant of the land. But for water to sprout something else is needed, a layer of rock where water will accumulate and build pressure to be released.

Very often this stratum cannot be seen because it is hidden behind a layer of topsoil. In this case one must dig a hole to help release it.

Darwin searched for an outcropping of this layer of rock, but couldn't find it, so a hole would have to be dug. But where?

He walked to one of the sides of the little valley and furiously attacked the base of one hill with his pick. At first he just displaced loose earth and rocks, "Material deposited by superficial water," thought Darwin. He continued digging with the spade and after a while he began to find damp shingle. He was close! After a further fifteen minutes of labour a pool formed at the bottom of the hole. He tried some: it was fresh and pure.

"Victory! Fantastic Mr. Darwin! I knew I could count on you. Don't worry about enlarging the hole. I will send five or six men to enlarge it and direct the water to the town. "

Darwin sat down. He was happy, but he was soaked in sweat and short of breath from the exertion. The priest sat next to him and offered him a drink from his wineskin, "it's from Asturias, the real thing," he said.

"In one passage of the Bible," said the priest, "Moses took the Jewish people across the desert. They needed water desperately, so he hit a stone with his walking stick and water started to flow. Seeing you at work I would think that what Moses did must have been similar," and he added with a smile, "more geology than miracle ... but there is a lot of this in the Bible ..."

"Not long ago you would have been burnt at the stake for saying something like that," said Darwin amused.

"Probably, but we, the Jesuits, have always been in conflict with the Church." He took a swig from the wineskin, "The Church is an organisation made by men, not God, and as such it has the corresponding human defects and virtues. The Jesuits, as opposed to Calvin and Luther, chose to fight the Church's weaknesses from inside the organization. Rome has sometimes fought us, and even banned us from America. On other instances they tried to win our favour. They declared Ignacio de Loyola, our Iñaqui, a saint, as if they could determine who is a Saint and who is not! Precisely they who live in wealth and so far removed from Jesus' teachings!"

Iñiguez had got a bit excited. He took another swig and went on:

"The greatness of Ignacio de Loyola was not in his being a saint, or performing miracles or speaking to God. No! On the contrary, his greatness stems from having done all he did while being just an ordinary man, like you or me, with his defects and shortcomings, grudges and even doubts.

His teachings are fantastic in that goodness is available to anyone. You do not need saints or angels or Virgin sightings or miracles. None of that! Just the will to do it and the decision to make it happen. Our order fights for a more just world. That is why we help the poor by getting them organized so they can live in peace with dignity and without resentment. And on the other hand we try to educate the rich, from where our leaders will be formed, to instil in them the concept of a just world. The best schools and universities in America are run by Jesuits. America is the new world and this is where we are fighting for a better world."

"Father, you tell me that Jesuits make a vow of poverty, but I have seen, in several cities, that the Churches more richly decorated are precisely the Jesuit ones, how do you explain that?"

"A very shrewd observation. To answer you I will have to let you in on a little secret of our Order." He paused for a few seconds before continuing, "As I mentioned earlier, I lived for a few years in Quito. There the most beautiful and highly ornamented church belongs to the Jesuits. For over a hundred years the rich in Quito donated lavishly in cash, jewellery and other riches because they wanted their church to be the most fantastic one in America, to make them proud to be Quiteños. Our little secret is that not all the money went into the construction and decoration of the magnificent church. Most of the extra funds were siphoned to a fund to finance projects for the poor Indians, projects that, if it hadn't been for this little trick, would never have materialized, because the rich people never showed any interest in them. Now you will understand why we are not very popular in Rome." He adjusted his hat, "I think it is time to get back."

They took the path that led back to the town.

"Tell me, Mr. Darwin, what is the *Beagle* doing here?"

"Captain FitzRoy's task is to survey the South American coast so accurate maps can be drawn which will help to make the passage between the Atlantic and the Pacific oceans safer. In order to improve the accuracy of the calculations we must complete the circumnavigation of the Earth."

"Around the World? How interesting. I was born in Getaria, the same town where the first man to navigate around the World was born."

"Magellan?"

"Nooooo! Sebastian Elcano. Magellan was Portuguese and was in command of the Spanish expedition, but he died on the way and Elcano completed the trip."

"You are right, Magellan died before the trip was over, but I couldn't recall Elcano's name."

"Yes, and that was how Sabastian Elcano was the first man to circumnavigate the World. But if you are interested in the matter I can give you a little-known version of what really happened on that voyage."

"I am very interested. Please go ahead."

"In our town there was a rumour that before he died, Sebastian Elcano confided that during the voyage he discovered that Magellan was a spy for the King of Portugal. Amongst other things they found it strange that after discovering the strait that connected both oceans one ship had got lost and returned directly to Spain. On that ship was one of Magellan's closest aides, also Portuguese. That was how the Portuguese crown found out about the strait before the Spaniards. It would seem that while sailing across the Pacific, Elcano found secret instructions from the Portuguese crown amongst Magellan's belongings, intelligence which he shared with his fellow officers. They feared that, if their discovery had been leaked to the Portuguese crown, their lives would be in danger because they would soon be sailing along the busy Portuguese spice route round southern Africa. If they were discovered they would surely be killed. So the Spanish officers decided to kill Magellan, although the official version is that he was killed by savages in the Philippines."

"So Magellan was a Portuguese spy."

"So they say. But that is not all. There is a story that there was another Portuguese spy before him."

"And who was that?"

"None other than Christopher Columbus."

"Columbus a Portuguese spy? But he was from Genoa."

"That was what he told everyone so they would not suspect his foreign accent. Before convincing Isabel of Spain to back his project he had worked for the King of Portugal. They say he was really born near Bemfica."

"And in what way did he benefit Portugal?"

"Rumour has it that Portugal sent him to confuse Spain and make them embark in what they considered a wild goose chase trying to get to the Indies by an impossible route. Their plot backfired because he ended up discovering a new continent. Although for many years, by trickery he kept this knowledge from the Catholic Monarchs. Until Columbus' death Spain believed they had reached the Indies. In the meantime, Portugal, who had received the correct information from their spy, hastened to send ships to explore the new continent and thus discovered what today is Brazil, while Spain ignored that it was in effect a new continent."

"Very interesting," said Darwin, "this version would explain some facts that I have never found very reasonable. But why was this not known?"

"Because neither Portugal or Spain wanted it to be known, the former because they would be considered clever cheats and the latter because they were made fools of."

They were nearing the town by now.

"And tell me, Father Iñiguez, did you not ever want to return to your home town, Getaria?"

"No. I have the illusion that in America we are building a better World. Getaria, is full of hatred and bitterness, just like the rest of Spain and Europe. It pains me to realize that it will never change. The only one who I would have liked see again is Aitorcito."

"And who is Aitorcito?"

"Aitor is my younger brother. You see, Mr Darwin," he stopped to mop his brow with his handkerchief, "my parents had eight children, of whom only four of us made it to adulthood. My father was a fisherman and one day his boat did not return. My mother, who was still nursing Aitor, used to wait for him to return. I, instead, took control of the household even though I was only nineteen. When my other brothers grew enough to be able to work and support the house, I decided to leave the village and try my luck in America. The thought of being a priest never even crossed my mind. Aitorcito was six years old at the time and I was almost a father to him. He wept bitterly when I left-I can still feel his tears on my face. I went to Quito. Aitorcito would always write to me. He had great ideals, so when he grew up he decided to become a Jesuit and come to America. When he was twenty four they sent him to America."

"Then that was when you saw him."

"No, he never arrived. His ship disappeared. No one ever knew if it had been attacked by pirates or swallowed by a storm. For months on end I waited for him to turn up, but he never did. Losing my brother was the worst thing that ever happened to me. I hated religion and blamed God and the Jesuits for his death."

"So how was it that you finally became a Jesuit yourself?"

"I met Father Iturri. I got to understand the Jesuit's philosophy and I came to terms with God. I experienced the miracle of faith in the flesh. I believe that having become a Jesuit and doing what Aitor wanted to do makes me feel that my little brother still lives inside me."

They had arrived at the town. They bid each other farewell with a sincere and firm handshake, knowing too well that they would not meet again. But their conversation had made Darwin see the world from a different angle, and made him aware that he should be careful both in airing his beliefs as in judging the beliefs of others.

When Darwin came back on board the *Beagle* he told me that his visit had made him ponder deeply on the meaning of life. He summed it up as a true voyage to the origins of Man.

Chapter 13

The Deluge

Darwin had heard of fossilized seashells in the Andes, many thousands of feet above sea level. This could be part of the evidence he needed to support his idea that as the Earth was permanently changing, so did living creatures to adapt to these changes and sometimes new species were developed.

He was allowed to go on an excursion to the Andes while the *Beagle* returned to survey Chile's southern coast for two months. However, for very unfortunate reasons, the *Beagle* never left Valparaiso.

Thanks to the help of Alexander Caldcleugh, a British resident, Darwin hired one Mariano González, an expert guide who knew the mountains well, a mule driver and ten mules. They left Valparaiso on 18th March, 1835. His plan was to cross the Andes, through the El Portillo pass, to the Argentine city of Mendoza and then return to Chile by the longer, but safer, Pass of Uspallata. This route would take him across the Andes at one of its highest points and would skirt the highest mountain in the Andes, the Aconcagua, which means 'stone sentry' in Quechua[1].

The slow pace of the Mules was an invitation to indulge in conversation on light, but interesting topics. After three years in South America, Darwin's Spanish had improved and was more fluent, which helped him to integrate into local groups and befriend his guide.

"Mariano, do you know where the name Valparaiso comes from?"

"Sure, Don. When the Spaniards first arrived, they named this valley, which runs from the foothills all the way to the sea, Valle del Paraíso (Valley of Paradise). The name contracted over the years until it turned into Valparaiso."

1. Quechua or Quichua is a family of languages and dialects used across the Inca Empire, and still widely spoken in Ecuador, Peru, Bolivia and parts of Argentina and Chile.

"However, I do not see anything that would justify calling it 'Paradise'."

"At the time of the Colony there was no irrigation, so this valley was quite arid, except for a place called La Quillota, which is where we are headed now. This place is naturally humid and hence green and with lush vegetation. When they named the valley they were thinking of La Quillota, but later the port grew and kept the name."

They continued at a slow pace. The tinkling of the bell on one of the mules was the only indication that they were, in fact, moving.

"Tell me, Mariano, why does that mule have a bell hung around its neck?"

"It's the madrina[2], Don."

"What do you mean by madrina?"

"She is the leader of the drove. The rest of the mules follow her as if she were their mother. All they need is to hear the bell, which we call cencerro, and they know she is there and will keep close to her. Also, if one night we camp near other drovers and we let our mules loose to graze, in the morning all we have to do is fetch the madrina, and the rest of our mules will follow her while the ones of other droves continue grazing."

"What happens if she dies?"

"Then the drove sort of picks a new one and follows that one."

"Interesting ... " said Darwin as he wrote in his notebook.

"The same applies to horses, only they are less disciplined and occasionally one will escape or stray, while with mules that never happens."

Darwin continued writing. Then he looked back and could now see that as they climbed higher they could see the Chilean coast unfold like a map, while looking forward the mountains seemed to remind him that the great challenge of the crossing of the Andes had just begun.

That evening they did what most travellers did in this part of the world, request for lodging at an hacienda. The English naturalist was an oddity in this part of the World, so he was invited to dine with the landowner, Alvarez, and his family. During dinner Alvarez and his two pretty daughters, the señoritas, riddled Darwin with questions on the trip, the ship, and on the renowned, handsome and single Captain FitzRoy. Darwin's account of the trip and of life aboard the *Beagle* was engaging and had the hosts fascinated by it. Finally one of the Alvarez

2. Lead mare. The rest of the drove follows her.

girls asked Darwin why, if he was so learned and gentlemanly, he did not become a Catholic, which, she added, "is the true religion."

"The Anglican religion is not inferior to the Catholic religion," answered Darwin.

"How can you say that?" said her sister, "don't your priests and bishops marry? That is totally against God's will!"

Darwin avoided an argument, and changed the subject. He asked Mr. Alvarez what he thought the climate would be like for the next few days since the crossing of the Andes depended on it. When he was told that it would probably be fine for the next couple of days, he thanked him for the lodging, praised the food and retired early, apologizing for being so tired as a result of the long trip.

The next morning they started out bright and early. They had to take advantage of the available daylight so they could reach the highest point as soon as possible to reduce the possibility of being caught in foul weather. In March a storm could be dangerous since by the end of summer the cold could be intense at that altitude.

"To get to El Portillo pass we must first cross two ranges," said Mariano as their mules slowly climbed, "El Portillo is on the second one, which is also the highest. In between the land is pretty flat, but the altitude complicates everything. Getting caught in a storm there would be very dangerous because at that altitude the snow and cold can kill you, and there is no easy way down from there. It is not wise to try the El Portillo pass at this time of the year."

The guide was trying, one last time, to convince Darwin to take another route over the Andes. But he had chosen that pass for good reasons.

"I know, Mariano, but the purpose of this trip is that I want to find some fossils that I know are near El Portillo. We shall return by the other pass."

"The Uspallata, as you wish, Don."

The road took them across a great plain of white dust.

"This is the chalk valley, Don. It is all chalk."

Darwin stopped and dismounted to gather a sample. He then dug a hole to verify how deep this white layer was. The guide watched him impatiently. Clouds in the distance worried him, perhaps the weather would deteriorate. The hole was already four feet deep and still white. Darwin made an entry in his notebook, mounted his mule and they continued on their way. The climb to the top of the first range started.

As they went higher, the Englishman could feel his heartbeat accelerate. It was due to the altitude. He also noticed that every so often one of the mules would stop and rest before continuing.

"It is the apunamiento," the drover told him. But as Darwin did not understand what he meant, Mariano explained further:

"Apunamiento means that one is affected by the altitude. The word means that you feel as if you were in the Puna."

Darwin had heard of the Puna; a desert over fifteen thousand feet above sea level which covers a large area that spans the north of Chile, south of Perú and Bolivia. He knew that given enough time one could adapt to the altitude. In fact, Humboldt had climbed the Cotopaxi volcano, which is over eighteen thousand feet high, but first he had gone to Quito, ten thousand feet high, to adapt.

In the afternoon they arrived, after quite an effort, to the first range. Before crossing it, one last look regaled them with an unforgettable view of Chile. Below them some wispy clouds reminded them that they were at a great altitude. The deep blue Pacific disappeared into the haze while the valleys plunged down to the sea where waves pounded the shore.

"Let's go on!" Mariano's shout reminded him that the worst was still to come.

The plain between the ranges was very rough and the climate extremely dry. The only living things they saw were two condors, who, gliding slowly in circles, seemed to be waiting for the travellers to perish. Their patience must have often been rewarded.

Before dark they found a place to camp. They had to build a fire, which they found difficult to do since there were only bushes in the area.

"This place is haunted. You can't cook anything," said the drover when he saw Darwin put some potatoes on to boil.

"I don't believe in witchcraft," he answered, very sure of himself.

Mariano explained: "I don't either, Don, but for some reason water does not heat. I verified it several times, that is why we brought charque[3] to eat."

While they ate the charque and blood sausage with biscuit, the water started to boil. At Darwin's smile, the drover said: "But it is not hot."

The Englishman fetched his thermometer and tested the water's temperature. True enough, it was nowhere near 212 degrees Fahrenheit[4]. Then

3. Charque is dry salted meat. The salting was used to preserve it.

4. The Fahrenheit scale is still used in the U.S.A. and was used in the United Kingdom

Crossing the Andes, by T. Landseer

he remembered that at this altitude atmospheric pressure was lower than at sea level and therefore water boiled at a much lower temperature. The drover was right, you could not cook there.

"I will leave them on the fire all night and we shall have them for breakfast."

The two Chileans just shrugged their shoulders, meaning "as you wish, but you will see ..."

---

at least until the late 1970's. In this scale water boils at 212° and freezes at 32°.

When the sun went down the temperature dropped dramatically. Mariano was worried by some dark clouds that were gathering on the western sky and said, "If it snows during the night, we've had it."

Darwin wondered if he was losing the lucky streak that had been with him since they left England and had kept him from harm. This worry was increased on account of a terrible headache he was experiencing.

"It is the apunamiento," Mariano told him, "it will go away when we descend tomorrow."

They went to sleep.

"Mariano, wake up! It has clouded over!" Darwin shook his guide to wake him up.

"But there is no thunder, is there?" he asked, still drowsy.

"No."

"Then there is no danger of snow for the moment."

Finally, in spite of his headache and worries he managed to fall asleep, but two hours later ...

"Don! Wake up! Quick!" the Englishman was shaken awake by the guide, "we have to get out of here before it starts snowing."

The sun had not come out yet but a faint brightness in the east announced its imminence. The drover had already gathered the mules and was loading them. As fast as they could they made ready to get going and beat the white death.

Before leaving, Darwin couldn't help his curiosity and he examined the potatoes – they were still hard. "I told you so, Don, this place is bewitched," said the drover.

They started off at a forced march. The mules seemed to sense the danger because they walked at a faster pace than usual.

"I think we'll make it," the guide told him, "in an hour we will be up at El Portillo. But if it starts snowing before that, we will be in trouble."

Half an hour later, when it was already broad daylight, he saw El Portillo and understood why it had that name. The Spaniards called the highest part of a pass puerto (port) and it usually had the shape of a saddle. In the range ahead there could be seen an opening shaped like a "U". That was El Portillo, a small port and their salvation ... but there was something missing.

"Mariano, the place where we could find fossils was around here, was it not?"

"Yes, over there," said Mariano uneasily, "but we don't have time for that now, Don."

Darwin looked in the direction his guide pointed and saw that the terrain elevated steeply and he could see a strip that was lighter than the surrounding rocks. His geologist's eye told him that that was stratum containing marine fossils.

"Mariano, I must go there and collect some fossils. This was the whole purpose of this trip, if I don't do it the whole crossing will have been for nothing."

"But Don! It's going to start snowing any minute now ... " it was useless, Darwin had already started off, his geologist's hammer ready.

"This crazy gringo is going to get us killed," said the drover, breathing with difficulty, "and all for some shitty stones. What does he want them for, anyway?"

"He's a naturalist. He says there are dead animals converted to stone in them."

"Animals that turned into stone? Cruz Diablo! So the little gringo was doing sorcery. I knew there was something fishy about it all."

After a ten-minute climb Darwin reached the fossil-rich stratum. It was a strip about eight feet wide. The pressure of the surrounding terrain had incrusted the shells of sea snails and other marine animals. He was overwhelmed by the importance of this discovery. He gave it a whack with his hammer and a good-sized piece was dislodged, which he put away in his satchel.

He was about to start his descent when he noticed a huge oyster, over ten inches long, He started hammering carefully to dislodge it from the rest of the stone. It took him a few minutes but he succeeded, and put it in his satchel with the other sample. It was then that he noticed that he had been engulfed by a dense fog.

He could not see Mariano or the drover or the mules. All he could see was a milky white mist that hid the way back and goodness knows what dangers.

He went down carefully, feeling lost. He shouted, but the wind, that had increased its force, dampened it. When he started feeling snow on his face he feared things were turning for the worse. He willed himself not to panic and carefully continued his descent. He suddenly saw a dark patch in the whiteness; a mule. He was greatly relieved, and he soon found Mariano, bending over the drover who was lying on the ground.

"He's dying, he can't breathe," said the guide, fear in his voice.

Darwin, who had some medical training, put his ear to the man's chest and listened to his breathing.

"He has asthma," he said, feeling terribly guilty.

The cold, coupled with the altitude and anxiety had triggered a severe attack. To make matters worse it was snowing harder.

"Close by there is a cave we can take shelter in until the storm blows over," said Mariano.

"But that would mean waiting for an extra day."

"I would say two or three is more like it."

Darwin was aware that in his present condition the drover could not survive so long.

"What if we continue?" he asked.

"It is very risky. The snow will not let us see the trail and we could fall off a cliff or simply get lost".

"How long would it take?"

"Forty minutes to the top. On the other side the weather is probably better."

Darwin quickly evaluated the situation. He ground was covered in snow which turned into slippery mud when tread on. If they went to the cave, he and Mariano would be saved, but the drover would not survive. If they pushed on, the three of them might survive ... or perish.

"We must go on!" Darwin could not let the man die. It was all his fault. His conscience would give him no peace if it came to that.

Mariano, petrified with fear, did not question the order. He tightened the saddle straps on the mules. Between them they hoisted the drover on the tamest one. He could hardly hang on and his lips were already turning blue for lack of oxygen.

They started the hardest climb in their lives.

"I can't see a thing, I'm lost," said Mariano, white from cold and fear.

Meanwhile in the *Beagle* a letter from the Admiralty brought on a crisis. FitzRoy cancelled the remaining survey of Chile's southern coast. He reviewed the geodesic calculations that had been made so far and found something that infuriated him. He called Stokes and demanded an explanation; he heard him out and lapsed into a deep depression. He wrote out his resignation to the command of the expedition and delegated it to Wickham. The *Beagle* remained anchored in Valparaiso waiting for Darwin to return and give his account.

They had to move fast or the Andes would claim new victims.

They were in the middle of a thick fog; the snow fell in large flakes and had covered the ground with at least four inches.

"Which way should we go?" asked Darwin trying to keep calm.

"Towards the range, east, but I can't see which way that is."

The Englishman fished his compass out of his pocket, placed on the ground as horizontal as possible and waited for the needle to settle, pointing at the magnetic north. Mariano looked on with eyes wide. He had never seen a compass before.

"That way!" said Darwin pointing east.

The wind roared.

They got going in that direction. The slope got progressively steeper. It was a good sign ... but the drover was getting worse.

"Here! I found the trail!" shouted Mariano starting to recover his confidence.

As far as he could remember from having seen El Portillo from afar, Darwin believed they should be no more than six hundred feet away. At a good pace it would take them half an hour, but as they went higher it snowed harder. He took off his poncho and put it over the drover, who silently thanked him.

"Sir, your resignation makes no sense," Wickham was saying, "The instructions state that in that case we should return to England by the same route we came, that is the Atlantic ... going through the dangerous Strait of Magellan again ... and if we don't complete the circumnavigation we will not have exact coordinates."

"I have taken my decision, Wickham. My state of mind will not allow me to continue in command. When Darwin returns you will take us back to Plymouth." answered FitzRoy.

But Captain ... and your career in the Navy?"

"My career has been destroyed by the Admiralty with its decision and Darwin with his ideas."

Wickham could see that there was no use in continuing the conversation as long as FitzRoy was in this state of mind. He withdrew.

FitzRoy checked that his pistol was loaded and safe in the drawer of his desk. He hoped he would not have to use it, but it was comforting to know that if things got tough it would be there.

The trail got progressively steeper. He felt his head would split from the pain, and his heart beat at a terrific pace. The effect of the altitude was terrible, but Darwin didn't care. He was concentrating on going on. ... going on ... He was so immersed in it that he did not notice the change in the slope until the guide shouted:

"We're going down! We have passed El Portillo! We are saved!"

The relief was great, but it was no time to celebrate, it was still snowing furiously, and the drover's health was deteriorating rapidly. He needed warmth, thicker air and plenty of rest. They pushed on at a forced pace.

Ten minutes later they came out of the snow storm: the Argentine side was a lot dryer than the Chilean side. They continued their descent and finally came out of the clouds. They could see the mountains and gullies that sloped all the way down to the far away plain.

Mariano wanted to stop to rest and, build a fire, but the drover's state needed a more comfortable place, but mainly at a lower altitude.

"The first shelter is about three hours away," said the guide.

They went on.

On the sides here were patches of snow and ice, but in one area the snow was red.

"It is the red snow," said Mariano, "tradition has it that it is the blood of those who died in a storm ... fortunately it is not ours."

Darwin took a small bottle and put away a sample. He would send it to Henslow to have it analyzed. He was sure it was some type of seed or spore that gave the snow that colour.

He had already heard of red snow, but always in the Arctic, and he did not know that it also happened in the Andes. It seemed interesting to compare them ... They went on.

Hours later they were sitting before a blazing fire with the keeper of the outpost, Don David, who brewed some mate for them and heated a stew which he referred to as 'old rags'.

Darwin was enjoying sipping mate for two reasons: in the first place just a while ago he had been freezing, and also because it reminded him of when he was riding across the pampas with a group of gauchos.

Don David Hughes was the son of an Englishman who had been in the area prospecting for gold. "My mother fell in love with his green eyes," he said, "but this gringo, who was a bastard, just got her pregnant and bolted." A rancher felt sorry for her and made sure the child would never go wanting. When he came of age the rancher made him a foreman. Young

David married. He was doing well, but he liked to gamble. He played truco[5], taba[6] and bet on horse races, and ended up losing everything. His four children went to live elsewhere and his wife got tired of his bad temper and left him. Finally, already aged, he asked to be put in charge of one of the lonelier outposts, far away from everything and everyone. After several years loneliness mellowed him, he needed to talk.

"You were really lucky," said Don David, "Few survive a storm up there. The Aconcagua does not pardon the foolhardy very often."

"We were saved by a fantastic device that the boss here has," said Mariano, "show him."

Darwin rummaged in his pocket and fished out his compass. He set it on the floor so they could see it. The needle set and he made the 'N' coincide with it.

"And what's that good for?" asked Don David between angry and disappointed.

"It tells you where the road is," said the guide.

"How?"

"Well ... not exactly," explained Darwin, "the compass allows you to find the cardinal points."

"So?"

"For it to be really useful you need a map," Darwin spread a rather incomplete map of the area on the floor.

He made the map's north coincide with the compass.

"If you know where you are, with the map and the compass you can find the direction of your destination. You see? For example, I know that the city Mendoza is in that direction," he said pointing at one of the corners of the room.

Silence.

"Look here, young man," said Don David, "This may be good for birds that fly in a straight line, but for us it is useless. I can assure you that if you walk in that direction you will never get to Mendoza. To do so, first you have to go down into the valley, then follow the stream, and when you get to the plain, go on down. What you have there is gringo stuff. Maybe it's useful in your country, but here it is not worth shit. Without a guide you'll never make it to Mendoza."

5. Card game very popular in Argentina, played with Spanish cards.

6. Betting game in which each participant throws a knucklebone and bets on which side it will fall.

"You're right," said Mariano, who hadn't understood a word of what Darwin had explained, "It seemed better when we were caught in the fog."

Darwin did not care what Don David's opinion was, but Mariano's comment pained him, because if it hadn't been for the compass they would surely have perished.

"And why did you venture along this pass at this time of the year?" asked the outpost keeper.

"Mr. Darwin wanted to gather some marine fossils near El Portillo," said Mariano, who had lost all respect for the naturalist's skills.

"Fossils? And what is that?" asked Don David arrogantly.

"Fossils are animals or plants that died a long, long time ago and remained buried until they turned to stone. What I found were marine animals up there, in the mountains." He showed him what he had found, in which several types of sea shells could be clearly seen.

"I've seen loads of these stones. What are they good for?"

"With these I can prove that this was the ocean bed many years ago, that is why there are so many marine animals. Slowly, perhaps due to earthquakes, the sea bed was pushed up to what are now grand mountains. The fossils remained imbedded in the highest part of them."

"Look here, man, I sometimes add a little gin to my mate, but I think you´ve overdone it. Are you pissed? You believe that mountains grow? Come on! They are mountains, not trees!"

"So how did these fossils get there?" asked Darwin, defiant.

"Easy. The Bible says that the Flood covered the world, even these mountains; that´s how the shellfish got there."

"The water couldn't have risen this much in the forty days it lasted."

"But it did ... Some foolish notion ... mountains that grow ... come on now!"

Darwin decided not to answer and change the subject. His aunt used to say that to avoid conflicts, the best thing was to talk about the weather and one's health.

The weather had improved and so had the drover's health. After sleeping all afternoon, his features had regained some colour and he could now talk, although only in a whisper yet. They would be continuing their journey to Mendoza the following day, where he would feel much better since it was only two thousand feet above sea level.

Don David saw them off next morning. At one moment, when Darwin had moved away a bit, he told the guide and the drover:

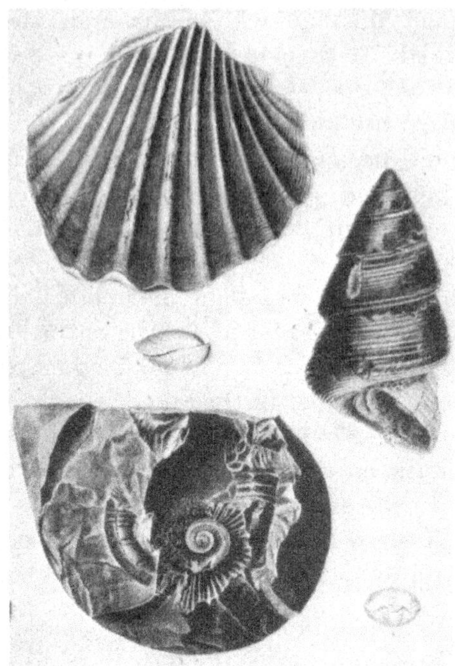

Marine fossils on the Andes

"Watch out with this gringo, he's a Goddamn nut."

The drover nodded in agreement.

The citizens of Mendoza were in a state of distress as the result of a swarm of locusts that had laid waste to the surrounding farmland. Darwin managed to collect a few specimens to send to Henslow. He also found, and collected, a strange insect. It flew, was about one inch long and survived by sucking blood, not only from animals, but also from human beings! This he had experienced himself. As it sucked its victim's blood it swelled to an enormous size. He was told that the local name was vinchuca.

After resting a few days, he decided to return to Chile, but this time by the pass of Uspallata, that was safer and busier.

During colonial rule, the Spanish government had built a series of shelters along the road. Travellers could get a permit and would be given the keys to these shelters and could then stay overnight or seek shelter from storms. They were kept stocked with firewood and basic provisions. After the wars of independence they had, as so many other things, been neglected and were now referred to as 'shacks'. But in spite of being neglected, these shacks were very useful when one needed to find shelter during a sudden storm. One of the guides main responsibilities was to know the exact location of every one of these shelters; it could mean the difference between life and death.

The way to Uspallata started across the plain close to the city of Mendoza. They followed the dry bed of a river and gradually approached the foothills of the Andes. As they got closer to the mountains the air got progressively more humid, and there even started to see puddles.

"Where does this road take us to?" asked Darwin.

"The first stop will be at Villa Vicencio."

Once they got there, Darwin felt the urge to imitate Humboldt and try to find springs. The geology of the place indicated that there had to be water on the mountain side. Just as he had done with father Iñiguez, he took a spade and started to dig. The guide and the drover glanced at each other. "Crazy gringo," murmured the drover.

With each shovelful the earth and shingle were damper. The hole got progressively deeper. Finally only shingle came out. He stopped. There was a lot of water.

"Mariano, could you hand me a cup?"

He scooped out some water and examined it. It was clear.

"It has small bubbles," said Mariano, looking over his shoulder.

"Yes, it is mildly gasified. Quite common with mineral waters," he took a sip, "it is good. But there is more to it," he put his hand in the water at the bottom of the hole.

"What?" asked Mariano.

"It is not cold, as spring water usually is, it is tepid. I'm sure that if I dug deeper it would be warmer. It is a thermal spring, which means that there is volcanic activity below, or rather geothermal activity,"

Darwin wrote in his notebook: 'The temperature of the water and the presence of gas in it suggests a rising pressure from far below, perhaps from magma. Will these mountains continue to rise?'

Mariano, who had not understood what Darwin had said added:

"At Puente del Inca there is a spring where the water is much hotter, but you cannot drink it. It is poisonous and ochre."

"It probably has sulphur, will we go past there?"

"Sure, but first we will go to a place close by you will find interesting, Hornillos."

"Look there!" said Mariano pointing.

"Fantastic!" shouted Darwin as he ran to where Mariano had pointed. "These are trunks of petrified trees. They must be ancient!"

They were prehistoric trees, petrified, that stuck out two or three feet above the ground that was white strata.

"Look at this, boss," said Mariano, pointing at some fossilized sea shells encrusted i the stratum.

"Of course! This was the bottom of the sea. Then it rose and the trees grew ... on the sea shore. I wonder what ocean it was. The Atlantic or the Pacific?"

The drover's expression was that of 'this guy is really nuts'.

"Fortunately Don David is not here to hear you, Don, he would kick up a row!"

Darwin made an entry in his notebook and they went on.

They crossed over to the Chilean side and descended along the valley of the Maipo river. They went straight to Valparaiso without stopping at Santiago. When they finally could see the port, he noticed that the *Beagle* was at anchor there. "How odd," he thought, "the survey they had planned should have lasted two months." In fact Darwin had thought he would have time to go on another trip, this time north to Copiapó and Coquimbo.

Once in Valparaiso he went directly to Alexander Caldcleugh's house, where he was boarding. He knocked on the door and one of the servants opened it.

"Mr. Darwin, they are expecting you," she said, secretive.

She led him to the library, where Caldcleugh was talking earnestly to a young man who had his back towards the door. When he saw him he exclaimed: "Darwin, at last!"

"Mr. Caldleugh, why such anxiety at my return?" and recognizing the young man, "Stokes! How nice to see you, but what are you doing here? Why is the *Beagle* here?"

"Mr. Darwin, you have to come aboard immediately. We are in trouble."

Chapter 14

The Promise at Valparaiso

Captain FitzRoy's emotional crisis had paralyzed the expedition. We knew not how to proceed without his leadership. Every one of us hoped he would review his decision to resign. The meeting we would have was precisely about that.

As the boat took them towards the *Beagle*, Stokes gave Darwin a thorough report of what had happened during his absence.

"What do you mean that the Captain resigned?" asked Darwin, not giving credit to his ears.

"That is exactly what happened. He resigned and delegated the command in Lieutenant Wickham. The instructions in the Admiralty's Manual for this occurrence plainly state that the survey must be interrupted and we must return to England along the route we came by."

"You mean we must sail south, through the Strait of Magellan and across the Atlantic to Great Britain?"

"That's right."

"But it is madness! We were so close to finishing the most exact survey ever made!"

"Exactly, and finishing the circumnavigation is of utmost importance to correct survey errors. Really, all for naught. I agree, it is madness."

"But what drove him to such a decision?"

"One the one hand, there was a short letter from the Admiralty informing him that the purchase of the *Adventure* was not approved and that its cost plus the expenditures incurred to outfit and man it were to be covered by FitzRoy's personal assets."

"With his assets? But it must be a fortune!"

"It will probably leave him close to bankruptcy."

"But there must be a mistake."

"No. Both Wickham and Sullivan received letters from friends in the Navy and it seems that the Admiralty´s rebuff of FitzRoy is all over London. There are certain details which are, at least, unusual. For instance, as you know, the *Adventure* was purchased over a year ago, how come they took so long to decide if it was correct or not?"

"Exactly. How could it be?"

"Apparently Admiral Beaufort, who is a close friend of the FitzRoy's, put in quite a struggle to try and get the Lords' Committee to alter its decision, but in the end he wasn't able to. The discussion dragged on for months and in the meantime the cost of the additional crew went adding up. In the end Beaufort unwittingly made things worse for the Captain."

"This must be interpreted as lack of trust," added Darwin.

"That was the Captain's understanding."

"Now I understand. He must be devastated. So he decided to answer the lack of trust by resigning."

"Something like that. But that was not the only reason that drove FitzRoy into a deep depression."

"And what was the other reason?"

"He found out something that concerns the two of us and that hit him like a sledgehammer."

"Something to do with you and me? What?"

"Remember our conversation on the Santa Cruz River?"

"Of course."

The boat had reached the *Beagle*.

"I can't tell you now," said Stokes, "we could be overheard."

FitzRoy's cabin was dimly lit. He and Wickham were discussing topics concerning the change of command.

"Mr. Figueroa has accepted our counter-offer of £ 14000 for the *Adventure*. That is about £ 100 more than you paid for it. Not bad."

"I'm very grateful for your efforts, Mr. Wickham, but even then it does not cover the costs of repairs and the extra crew members. That's almost £ 700, a small fortune, which will leave me in a most delicate financial situation."

"Sir, if instead of resigning you continue in command, our journey would last a further year. We could then simulate repairs and expenses on the *Beagle*, which would make it possible for you to recover most of the £ 665."

"We cannot do that! It is immoral to siphon the Admiralty's funds in that manner."

The Harbour of Valparaiso, by Alexander Caldcleugh

"It is also immoral that the Admiralty should take a full year to make a decision while costs accumulate and then they benefit from the reduction of our survey time that was the result of surveying with two ships instead of one."

"What you say is true, but nevertheless it does not change anything. My decision is final and is not motivated by economic factors but by my state of mind. The Admiralty's decision does not only affect my assets, but by not backing me they have withdrawn their confidence in me. So all I can do is to retire from the Navy ..." and looking out the small porthole at the sea, he added, "I have always prepared to spend my life in the Royal Navy ... they have not only withdrawn their confidence in me, but have taken my future too ... everything I had planned. Now I understand why my uncle did what he did."

FitzRoy's uncle had committed suicide a few years earlier. Wickham had heard this sort of talk before and was worried that FitzRoy might follow in the footsteps of the previous Captain, Pringle Stokes, and take his life. He was sure that that was why FitzRoy had shown such interest in Pringle Stokes' story. Wickham knew that FitzRoy kept a loaded gun in the top drawer of his desk.

There was a knock on the door.

"Come in," said FitzRoy.

The door opened a little Lieutenant Sullivan stepped in.

"Sir, Darwin and Stokes have just come aboard."

"Thank you, Sullivan, tell them to come," said FitzRoy, and turning to Wickham, "I can now address the other matter I have on hand."

"I'll fetch them," said Wickham, who had seen Sullivan make a sign.

He left the cabin and found Sullivan waiting for him.

"I didn't want to mention it inside, but the boat also brought the mail and this was in it." He showed him an envelope with the arms of the Admiralty, which was addressed in ornate handwriting: 'For the Commander of the *H.M.S. Beagle*.'

"I suppose we could say it is addressed to me, the new Commander," said Wickham putting it in his pocket.

"Aren't you going to open it now? It might be a message repealing the decision on the *Adventure*."

"Sullivan, the Admiralty never goes back on a decision that has already been taken, no matter how wrong this decision has proven to be ... you might say that persisting in error is their policy."

Wickham quickly walked over to the Mapping Room, where he found Darwin and Stokes.

"Welcome aboard, Mr. Darwin."

"Thank you, Mr. Wickham. I understand Captain FitzRoy wants to have a word with us immediately."

"That is correct. Let me say something while we go," they left the Map Room and slowly walked aft towards the Captain's quarters, "FitzRoy's state of mind is very serious. I have never seen him as depressed as he is now. I fear for his life."

"You believe he might commit suicide?"

"Yes."

"And what can we do to help?"

"Let us try to lighten his woes. Whatever he asks of you, do it. Any setback could make him take a drastic decision."

They continued walking in silence until they arrived at the cabin door.

"You go in first, I'll follow in a minute," said Wickham.

Once the door closed behind them, he put his hand in his pocket and took out the envelope. He opened it carefully, trying not to damage it. He took out the letter with the Admiralty letterhead, unfolded it and read it carefully; then he folded it and put it back in the envelope. He had a plan. He entered the cabin.

Darwin and Stokes had just sat down and had not spoken yet. When Wickham came in, FitzRoy turned and saw the Admiralty envelope in his hand; he gave him a quizzical look. "We had better read this later, Captain. Bad news can wait," said Wickham in a low voice, but loud enough for Darwin and Stokes to hear him and worry a little more.

"Mr. Darwin," FitzRoy spoke, "I trust you have been successful in your excursion to the Andes."

"Yes, Sir, it went very well, thank you for asking," said Darwin, tense.

"Have you made any discovery?"

"I don't know if to call it a discovery. I found marine fossils at an altitude of almost 12000 feet above sea level."

"Do you believe that this will help you prove your theories?"

Darwin did not want to argue with FitzRoy, but he found his tone irritating. His attitude had changed, fortunately Wickham took over.

"That was precisely what Captain FitzRoy wanted to talk to you about, Mr. Darwin. Rereading Mr. Stokes' calculation sheets we found something striking."

"Exactly," FitzRoy interrupted, "I found that one of the measuring stations from which Mr. Stokes took his readings was given the surprising name of No God," an awkward silence ensued. Stokes was white, "Do you not wonder, Mr. Darwin, why Mr. Stokes, who has always been a good Christian, would choose such a name?"

Fortunately Stokes had warned Darwin and he was ready for this.

"Mr. Stokes and I explored the steppe over the valley of the Santa Cruz River for several days, and that measuring station was in precisely that area. We had long conversations in which we discussed my theories and the possible effect they would have. Evidently Mr. Stokes was deeply impressed by the implications of certain discoveries and, probably unwittingly, chose that name. I must add that I find nothing wrong with it."

"Mr. Darwin, I believe that what you discussed with Mr. Stokes must have been similar to what we spoke about on several occasions," Darwin nodded. "As you will recall, in one of those conversations I explained that these theories would be a tremendous blow to British society, because the first conclusion it takes you to is that God does not exist. Mr. Stokes' reaction, giving this station that strange name, is proof of how deeply it hit."

"I have a clear recollection of our conversation. I agreed, and still do, with your view about the effect it would have on society. However, I cannot see why the name of a measuring station should be considered so serious as to have a meeting in these terms."

"Quite simple, Mr. Darwin, during one of those chats I explained that your future, and our careers, and in this I include all of the *Beagle*'s officers, would be seriously impaired if, as a result of this voyage, there were to be a debate that would undermine the very foundation of the British Empire. Do you remember what we agreed on then?"

Darwin hesitated. He knew he had been wrong, but did not believe it was serious.

"Yes, Captain, we agreed not to reveal the theory until we had proof. And I have done just that, I have not revealed it."

"Mr. Darwin, you explained your theory in detail to Mr. Stokes. Don't deny it"

"I don't, but Mr. Stokes is part of the *Beagle*'s crew. I would not call that revealing my theory."

"Perhaps you told someone else without my knowing."

"That is not true!" Darwin was convinced that FitzRoy was going too far. "I did not tell anyone else! I have not defaulted on our agreement!"

"Yes you have!" FitzRoy banged the table with his fist and stood up, his face flushed in anger, almost out of control.

There was a tense silence that filled the strained atmosphere in the cabin. The Captain sat down slowly. He knew he had overdone it.

"Ahem ... " Wickham cleared his throat and took over, "Captain, allow me to say something in Mr. Darwin's defence. He probably did not know exactly what you expected of him. I am sure he honestly believed that he was not incurring in a breach of trust by explaining his theory to Mr. Stokes. He would have explained it to me if I were interested in these matters. I am positive that Mr. Darwin acted in good faith and had no intention of deceit or going back on his word."

Darwin nodded, confirming Wickham's words. FitzRoy made a gesture acknowledging Wickham's move to calm things down.

"Furthermore," he went on, "I am sure that Mr. Darwin is aware of the damage the disclosure of his theory, without sufficient proof, can do to our careers, so he will surely commit to abstain from revealing it or even mention it to anyone until there is conclusive evidence."

Wickham now looked at Darwin reminding him with his expression of what he had asked of them before entering the cabin: not to oppose

FitzRoy. Everyone focused on Darwin, who knew that if he didn't act as expected, FitzRoy might plunge into a depression he would not come out of alive.

"Of course, of course!" said Darwin forced by the situation.

"So then, to sum it up," resumed Wickham, "Mr. Darwin, you hereby promise not to disclose your theory until you have conclusive proof. Do we have your word of honour?"

"Yes, you have my word."

FitzRoy, looking a lot calmer, stood up and held out his hand.

"Mr. Darwin, I should never have doubted your nobleness. I beg you to forgive my outburst and continue to regard me as your friend."

Darwin shook his hand vigorously, even though he was quite confused. He was aware that FitzRoy had no malice, but he found it very difficult to cope with such an unstable personality.

"Very well, gentlemen," Wickham was in complete control of the meeting, "what has been said here is strictly confidential and we must all take it upon ourselves that none of this must be mentioned to anyone but those of us present today." They all nodded their agreement. "Then we can consider this matter closed. Messrs. Darwin and Stokes," he said looking at each of them in turn, "we thank you for your time and you are now free to carry on with your duties. The Captain and I will continue our meeting for we must decide on certain aspects of the future of our expedition."

The Admiralty's envelope lying on the table reminded him that there were still problems to overcome. Stokes and Darwin thanked them, stood up and headed for the door. Just before stepping out, Darwin turned and asked:

"How will we decide if the proof is conclusive?"

"That will be easy," said Wickham, who had it all thought out, "as soon as you are sure that you have enough evidence, you shall give it to Captain FitzRoy to evaluate. His intelligence and scientific training are of a calibre that will allow him to test your evidence with equanimity. Once you agree that the evidence is conclusive, you can publish your theories."

Darwin walked away crestfallen. He had just been handed his sentence. He would be FitzRoy's prisoner until the day his twisted mind decided to set him free ... a prisoner confined to a cell made of his own ideas.

"Very well, let's see the confounded letter," said FitzRoy.

"Oh yes, the letter!" Wickham pretended to open the letter, which was really already open. He read it carefully, rising his eyebrows as he did so, in a perfect performance. "I believe, Captain, Sir, that you should read it first yourself."

FitzRoy took the letter from him. He had been prepared for the worst, but not at all for what he read. "A promotion!" he exclaimed.

"Congratulations, Captain!" Wickham shook his hand, "the Admiralty is evidently ratifying their trust in you." FitzRoy's head was reeling; he had not yet realized the change this implied. "I suppose you will review your decision to resign, right?"

"Well, I don't know ... " FitzRoy hesitated, "It certainly changes the situation, but I don't know if it will change my decision."

"Let me review the situation," Said Wickham, always meticulous, "until this morning you were faced with three problems. Bankruptcy as a result of having to take on the costs incurred with the purchase of the *Adventure*; social disfavour for being involved in a theory that questions the very foundation of our Empire, the Church and our King; and finally the Admiralty's withdrawal of their trust in you, which meant an end to your career in the Royal Navy. All this has changed for the better in the batting of an eye. On the one hand, the sale of the *Adventure* and some 'repairs' on the *Beagle* will practically offset the effect on your assets; Mr. Darwin's pledge has put the disclosure of his theory in your hands and, finally, the promotion proves that your star still shines in the Admiralty. What reason do you have to resign?"

"True ... looking at it from that angle, it makes no sense."

"Then ... you will continue in command of the expedition?"

"Yes, I will continue."

"Bravo! This deserves a toast. I keep an old bottle of Irish whisky in my cabin for these grand occasions. I will go and fetch it."

He walked off quickly towards the door.

"Mr Wickham! You are a sly fox! I do not know how you did it, but you controlled the whole proceedings. You are a sly fox, and I thank you for it."

"I don't know what you are talking about, Sir. I just do my duty."

"What you did, you did against your own interests, because my resignation would automatically place you in command. Your loyalty, Mr. Wickham, is truly great. I am very grateful to you and I will make sure, once we return to England, that you are assigned the command of your own ship."

"Captain, I am deeply grateful." He stepped out and closed the door.

Outside, Sullivan was waiting, anxious to know the result of the meeting.

"Mr. Sullivan, please give the order to weigh anchor. We leave Valparaiso today," said Wickham feigning sadness.

"Aye, Sir. Which will be our next stop on our way to the Strait of Magellan? Talcahuano? Valdivia?"

"No, Mr. Sullivan, Lima, because our destination is Galapagos," said Wickham smiling.

"Galapagos!? Then we are not returning to England? The Captain has not resigned?"

"No. The *Beagle* is the *Beagle* again."

For the *Beagle*'s crew everything was back to normal, except Darwin, who would find his commitment a ever heavier burden.

We all thought that the meeting had healed the wounds, but we were very wrong. The visit to Galapagos would give the motive for many things to cease to be as they were.

Chapter 15

The Mysterious Animals of the Galapagos

My friend Darwin had placed great expectations on the Galapagos Islands. He was certainly not disappointed by what he found, but the true value that this visit had for his theory would only be appreciated several years later.

"Land ahoy!"

James Door shouted these famous words, just as explorers had done a century before when discovering new islands and continents.

FitzRoy had sent him up to the crow's nest at the top of the main mast to scan the horizon in search of the Galapagos. The choppy seas had prevented them from calculating their position with precision and the Captain knew that there were strong currents in this part of the Pacific which could have driven them off course. He feared they might have gone past them as they sailed west, so Door's shout brought him relief.

"In what direction?" he shouted back from the deck.

"Over there!" Door pointed north by northwest.

The Captain took a telescope and looked in that direction. "I cannot see anything," he told Wickham who was standing next to him. He walked to the mizzen mast and climbed it. At the top the view was spectacular, but the ship's movement was amplified, which terrified those who tried it the first time, and very few, no matter how experienced, could resist more than five minutes before feeling seasick.

This time he saw, through the telescope, what seemed to be a volcano´s crater. The lower part of the island was hidden by the Earth's curvature.

"Congratulations Mr. Door," Said FitzRoy before going down. Once on deck he took a map and studied the Islands' topography. "I believe that

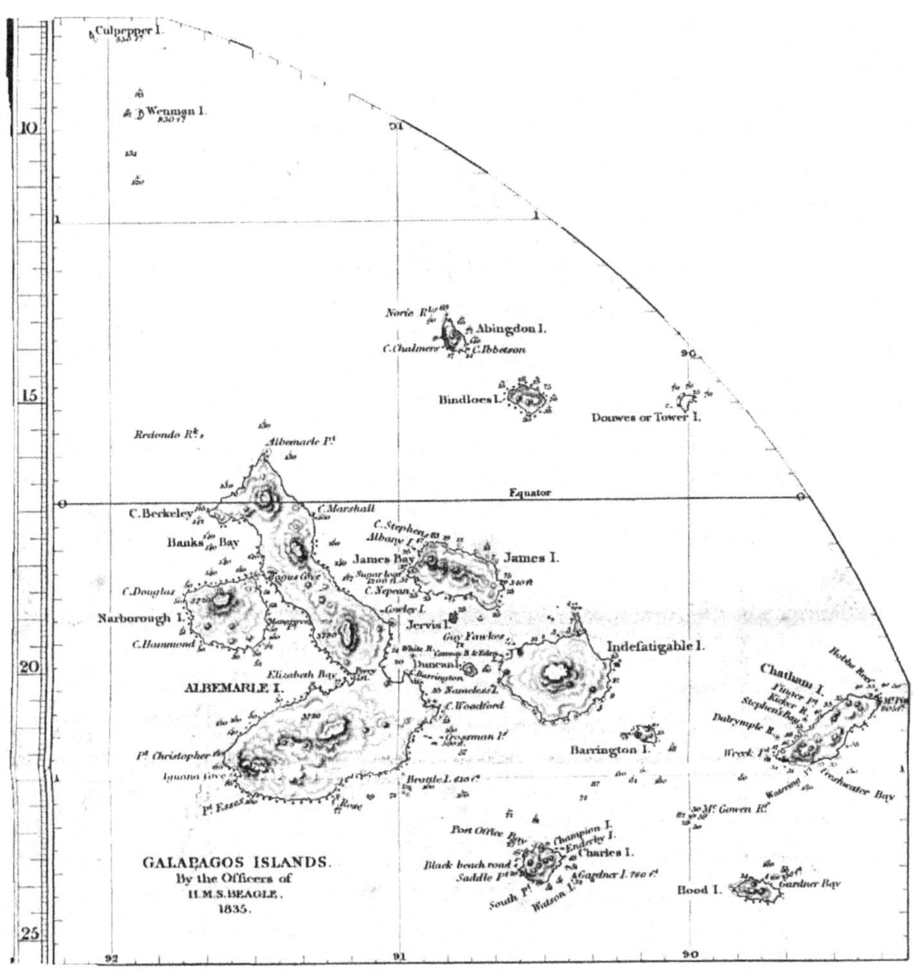

Map of Galapagos Islands, by the officers of HMS *Beagle*

what can be seen is this, Mount Pitt, the highest point of Chatham[1]. It must be almost twenty miles away. We almost missed it," he told Wickham, "Mr. Chaffers, set a course at three hundred and thirty degrees. I think we are here," he placed his finger on the map, "The currents have thrown us further off course than I had calculated."

"Very well, sir. If the wind stays as it is, we will be there in under two hours."

1. Chatham Island is known today as San Cristóbal.

"Perfect. Messrs. Wickham, Sullivan, Stokes and Darwin, let us all go to the Map Room so we can plan the survey of these islands."

The five men stood around the table where an old map of the islands had been laid out.

"Gentlemen, as you well know, the Galapagos are extremely important since they are the last place where a ship can stock up with food and water before starting on the long stretch across the Pacific. Our mission is to establish the exact position of each island, which means precise coordinates, and identify and mark natural harbours and where fresh water and food can be found. Mr. Stokes, why don't you give us a quick run through of the time needed to survey and map them?"

"Aye, sir," he said, and pointing at the map he continued, "The archipelago is formed by five large islands in the middle, three medium-sized islands removed to the north, and two removed to the south. There are also a great number of smaller islands and islets, but they do not need to be surveyed and their coordinates can be calculated from the larger islands."

"Tell us about the timing, Mr. Stokes," said FitzRoy, hurrying him up.

"The largest, Albermarle[2], requires at least five points with exact coordinates and five or six views from high ground to draw the outline, so I estimate ten days for this survey. The other four islands require two coordinate points and one or two views, which means three days each. The smaller islands only one coordinate point and one view so one day each."

"So then," said FitzRoy, "we need twenty-seven net days of surveying. To this time we must add cloudy days where readings are not possible, say ... six days. That makes thirty-three. We must also consider sailing from one island to the other. Mr. Sullivan, how many days do you estimate for that?"

"Well, one should determine the actual course, but with fair winds no less than eight days."

"Let's say ten days, then, which makes a total of forty-three days." He looked at them all, "I do not want to stay here more than four or at most five weeks. So I have come to the conclusion that we must split the work in two or three groups. The central islands, which are more protected, can be surveyed by groups using the boats we carry on board, while the ones further out by the *Beagle*. With two groups and the *Beagle* I believe we can do it all and save ten days. Any question or objections?"

---

2. Today known as Isabela.

"What about me, Captain?" asked Darwin.

"You can choose between staying aboard the *Beagle* or joining one of the smaller groups. "With us you will have a superficial view of all the islands, while with one of the smaller groups you will be restricted to less terrain, but surely in more detail."

"I would like to do a bit of both. That is, see as many of the islands as possible, but I would like to camp for a few days on a couple of them."

"Very well, Messrs. Sullivan and Stokes will do the planning, so you can then choose when and where to camp." Then addressing everybody, "Gentlemen, we must be close, let us go on deck to see what the first of the Galapagos looks like."

Even close up the islands did not lose their mystery. The rough seas and hidden rocks forced the *Beagle* to sail at some distance.

Stokes and Darwin, leaning on the railing, took turns looking at the island through a telescope, trying to make out the details.

"Tell me, Mr. Darwin, what do you know about these islands?"

"Not much, really. They are volcanic ... look over there," he handed Stokes the telescope, "those conical formations are craters."

"So, according to your theory, they rose from the bottom of the sea as a result of the eruptions?"

"Yes. As several islands we have already visited. I would say that the Galapagos are still in the process of rising, about half way between the Canaries or Cape Verd islands, which have very high mountains, and St. Paul's Rocks that hardly emerge from the sea."

"So what do you expect to find, regarding animals?"

"Less than at Cape Verd and more than on St. Paul's."

"Well ... that is not much; there were only two types of birds there."

"I understand there is not a great variety of animals ... but we must not jump to conclusions. It is not good to entertain preconceptions. One should always have an open mind."

Stokes could already see some detail with the help of the telescope.

"Take a look. There seem to be small trees or bushes, but they are leafless. I wonder if they were burned or if they lose their leaves at this time of the year."

Darwin studied the island through the telescope before answering.

"I don't think they were burned because they are not black. They seem to be brown, although the mist does not allow me to distinguish colours well. They have thin branches, if they had burnt only the thicker ones

Lowland tortoise, Galapagos Islands, courtesy of Roger Hall (www.inkart.net)

would remain. I don't think they have lost their leaves either, since being so near the equator the temperature does not vary enough; there are no seasons."

"Conclusion?"

"The conclusion is that we have a mystery to unravel: The Mystery of the Leafless Trees of the Galapagos."

"Another question: Why do we find penguins and sea lions on these islands if we are so near the equator? Aren't these animals from cold climates?"

"There is a current from the south of Chile that brings very cold water to these latitudes, and probably also the penguins and sea lions, which would account for their presence. We would have to verify if they are the same species as those in southern Chile."

"So cold water, eh? ... Well, if it comes from Chile it makes sense; the water there is terribly cold."

"Changing the subject, Mr. Stokes, you have just finished the sailing plan for the islands. What do we do now?"

"The Captain has not approved it yet, but our plan is to sail directly to Hood[3] island where we will drop one survey team. Then we will continue north to Barrington[4] island where we will leave the team that will survey the central islands. Only then will we turn back east to survey Chatham."

"And when would that be?"

"We should be back here tomorrow or the day after."

"Very well, then the mystery of the leafless trees will have to wait a couple of days."

Two days later the *Beagle* was back at Chatham. They anchored in Stephen bay. It certainly was an odd place. In the middle of the bay, which was at least thirty fathoms[5] deep, a huge, vertical rock emerged. On the north-western shore there was a low mountain that the Captain climbed painstakingly, since he found that it was covered with very loose volcanic sand, which his legs sank into and his boots filled with.

An American whaler was also anchored in the bay to stock up with the large tortoises, called Galapagos, of which they had caught a great many and had them hemmed in on the shore waiting for the boats, that, trip after trip (they could only take a few at a time),carried them on board.

Darwin disembarked and struck up a conversation with the American sailors. He wanted to know how many tortoises they had caught.

"We must have caught around two hundred," said one of the seamen.

"Where did you catch them?"

"Several of them were close by. We also divided into three groups that went a bit further inland and they brought the ones they found. You can't bring them from very far because they are too heavy. But come, you are a naturalist, there is something that will interest you."

They walked about two hundred feet to where a very large tortoise stood, apart from the rest.

"Look here, on the shell."

Carved with a knife were the words Fantôme 1786.

3. Today known as Española.

4. Today known as Santa Fe.

5. The fathom is unit of measure for depth and is equivalent to 1.83 m, so the bay was at least 55 m deep.

"What is this?" asked Darwin.

"French. A French ship that came to stock up and were not able to take this one."

"Why not?"

"Too big. We also tried to but four men couldn't pick it up, let alone put it on a boat."

"But what does the inscription mean?"

"Fantôme is probably the name of the ship and 1786 the year this happened."

"That's impossible. It's over fifty years ago," said Darwin, surprised.

"It is said that these tortoises can live as much as two hundred years. That's why they are so large, they never stop growing. If they live very long they get very big. Who knows how old this one is."

Darwin took out his notebook and started writing. Then he took out his measuring tape and recorded the length and width of the shell. He then had the crazy notion of standing on it, which the animal resented and stood up. Darwin lost his balance and fell off awkwardly. The American howled with laughter.

On the way back to the beach the American told him that there were two types of tortoises on the island: these that he could see there, that lived in the lowlands, and others that lived in the higher part of the island. Those had a different shell with a very pronounced arch over the neck which allowed them to lift their head higher. "Very interesting," said Darwin as he made another entry in his notebook.

"Why are you taking so many tortoises?"

"It is the ideal food to stock on a ship because there is no need to preserve them in any way. We put them in they hold, where they can live several months without eating. Their meat is very wholesome and allows us to eat adequately during the whole of the crossing of the Pacific. We do the same with the giant tortoises of the Seychelles islands."

"But I imagine that if all the ships that go past here take this amount of tortoises, soon there will be none left."

"There are still a lot. There is some truth in what you say, though. I was told by an old salt that on a trip many years ago they loaded seven hundred tortoises in four days work. It took us three days to gather these two hundred, so I can confirm that there are a good deal less than thirty years ago."

On the beach he found Stokes who had just landed.

"Mr. Darwin, the Captain has given us permission to cross the island on foot so I can make topographic measurements while you collect as many specimens of animals and plants as you can. How about that?"

"I think it is a splendid idea. But what will the *Beagle* do in the meantime?"

"They will survey the north of the island where it is said there is a fresh water spring, the only one in the archipelago."

"How will they find us?"

"We agreed to meet at St. Mary's beach the day after tomorrow at noon."

"You have a deal. Should I carry your theodolite?"

They walked all afternoon. As they slowly climbed the climate changed from very dry to very humid. The vegetation was now luxuriant, a lot more like what could be expected in the tropics.

On the way they found several tortoises that had their shells as described by the American seaman. Darwin made an entry in his notebook: "Perhaps in the highlands the shells have this curvature because these tortoises stretch their heads up to eat the leaves of trees and bushes, while the lowland tortoises only eat cacti sprouts and never lift their heads."

"Mr. Darwin, doesn´t the high curve of their shell leave them exposed to the attack of some predator?"

"There are no predators on this island. The animals do not attack each other. That is why the birds allow us to come near them."

"It was the same at St. Paul's Rocks, wasn't it?"

"Not only there, at Fernando de Norohna and the Falklands (Malvinas) too."

"What do they have in common?"

"That these islands were uninhabited by humans, until recently."

"How interesting. So it would seem that animals change their behaviour patterns when man is present."

"It would seem so."

Due to the absence of roads or paths they did not make much headway. The vegetation and fields of lava forced them to make frequent detours, while the amount of loose stones and rocks had them picking their way carefully to avoid twisting their ankles or tripping. That was why, in spite of having walked for hours, they had not advanced very much.

In the evening they found a place to set up camp.

Night had fallen; they had dined and were having a lively conversation while they enjoyed some brandy that Stokes had brought with him.

"So, what is your verdict on the origin of life in these islands?"

"It is too early to come up with a final theory because there is still a lot of classifying to be done, but in my opinion most of the plants and animals arrived here from the continent, mainly from Ecuador and Peru, several thousands of years ago and then slowly changed to adapt to their new environment."

"I have not seen tortoises of the size of these on the continent."

"No, but there are smaller ones that are very much like them. For some reason here they grew enormously."

"What about the iguanas? On the continent there are land ones but not marine ones."

"As I said before, we still must study their anatomy, but I believe the marine species is very much like the land ones. Perhaps it was on these islands that they turned marine."

"What can you tell me about the birds?"

"The birds here fly and swim, so they could have come from far away. I have not come to any conclusion yet, but remember that at St. Paul's Rocks and here we find the same type of birds. I believe that St. Paul´s will follow the same process as the Galapagos. Probably the birds were the first to populate the islands."

Stokes poured them a little more brandy.

"What do you think, now that we are so near our return to England? Aren't you anxious to arrive and work on your theory?"

"The truth be said, I feel rather depressed regarding my theory."

"Why?"

"Because, according to my promise in Valparaiso, I must have FitzRoy's approval to publish it."

"And what is wrong with that?"

"I am sure he will never allow it to be published, he will probably find some excuse or other based on some technicality."

"Mr. Darwin, he is duty-bound to act in good faith. If he doesn't, then you will be set free from your promise."

"I don't understand what you are getting at."

"What I mean is that the promise works both ways. Not only are you obliged to submit your theory to the Captain for his review, but he is also obliged to analyse it objectively. He cannot reject it without a valid motive. If he were to act selfishly he would not be keeping his side of this gentleman's agreement and you would therefore be free to act as you think best."

"You are so right! I hadn't thought of that."

"Nevertheless I do not think that Captain FitzRoy would do what you fear. I am sure he will be objective."

"I have my doubts."

Stokes drank what was left of his brandy.

"Very well," he said, getting up, "I will take advantage of the fact that the stars can be seen clearly to take some readings before turning in."

"And I will try to collect some nocturnal animals."

Next morning the two young men, burdened by the theodolite and their rucksacks, climbed, with a considerable effort, the island's main mountain. The vegetation was lush and the ground damp. Darwin explained that the higher ground was more humid than the lowlands because the humid air from the sea, as it rose, condensed and turned into a persistent drizzle. "The same happens at the Cape Verd and Canary Islands."

They reached the summit at midday just in time to take the readings.

"Mr. Darwin, look over there," said Stokes, pointing at some level ground below them.

"Fabulous! There must be dozens of them!" exclaimed Darwin, excited.

What he marvelled at was to see over fifty conical craters, irrefutable proof of the island's volcanic origin.

"On our way down I want to go through that field of lava so I can take some geological samples," he said while he sketched the view in his notebook.

"That will mean diverting from our original course, but I suppose we can do it."

"When must we meet the *Beagle*?"

"Tomorrow at noon. They will surely be there before we arrive at the rendezvous."

At midday of the following day the two young men were puzzled, but not yet worried. They were on St. Mary's beach but the *Beagle* was nowhere to be seen. "They must have been delayed surveying the north end of the island," said Stokes.

By mid-afternoon they both kept a watch over the sea but the ship did not appear. When dusk came, they decided to stop waiting and find a place to set up camp. They had no food left.

"I will never be as good an explorer as the Captain is. He always calculates the provisions to last at least two days more than expected. If I were as thoughtful as he is we would now have food."

"I hope the Captain hasn't decided to get rid of me and my theory by abandoning us on this island," said Darwin half in jest.

In the dark they were only able to gather a few sticks and light a small fire where they boiled a little water to brew some tea. Fortunately there was still some brandy left over.

They both went off to sleep convinced that they would wake up to find the *Beagle* at anchor there.

The morning proved them wrong. The *Beagle* was nowhere to be seen. They still had some water left in one water bottle but they were starting to feel hungry.

Darwin decided to do something about it instead of just waiting, so he walked down the beach where he found some blue-footed boobies. Taking advantage of their tameness, he caught two and quickly wrung their necks – he had secured breakfast. Meanwhile Stokes gathered firewood, which was scarce in that part of the beach. They put the two birds to cook over the fire on skewers. They had had a similar experience at Punta Alta, in Argentina, only that time they had eaten seagulls.

"What a strong smell! It reminds me of the medicines my father used to prepare," said Darwin.

"It is the wood."

"What wood is it?"

"From those leafless bushes we saw from the ship."

"Interesting ..." Darwin made an entry in his notebook.

"What was that?" said Stokes.

"What was what?"

"I heard a twig break ... as if stepped on."

Darwin listened intently and thought he could hear voices in the distance. They both checked that their guns were loaded and ready.

"Darwin! Stokes! What are you doing here, calmly having breakfast while eighty people are worrying about you?"

"Captain!" cried Stokes, "we thought you had abandoned us."

View of Chatham Island, by Philip Gidley King

"Maybe I would have if I had known you were so placidly here," chided FitzRoy with humour.

"But we have been waiting for you since yesterday morning."

"Waiting for us here? But we had arranged to meet at St. Mary's beach."

"Isn't this it?"

"No, it is the one on the other side of yonder headland. We've been waiting there since the day before yesterday. Let me see your map, Mr. Stokes."

They compared their maps. They were two different versions of very old maps. Poor, but the only ones available

"You are excused, Mr. Stokes. Your map shows St. Mary's beach at a different place than on mine. Which just goes to show how much the drawing of accurate charts of these islands is needed."

"Do you mean that we were in the correct place according to Mr. Stokes' map, but it differed from yours?" asked Darwin.

"That is correct."

"So how did you find us?"

"This morning one of the seamen saw some white smoke towards the south. We imagined it would be from some camp, so we landed and here we are."

"Thank goodness," said Darwin, "I don't think these boobies would taste very good."

"You will not have to verify that. A good breakfast awaits you aboard the *Beagle*."

Darwin thought it odd that an Englishman were the governor these islands which belonged to Ecuador. FitzRoy explained that Nicholas

Lawson had lived in this South American country for many years and their government had decided that he was the perfect choice as governor since these islands depended mostly on what they charged for services rendered to ships that stopped there, mainly American and British whalers.

"He has a perfect grasp of the peculiarities of the Ecuadorians as he has of both the British and Americans. He speaks Spanish as a native and, naturally, English. A man of two worlds. In my opinion this novel Republic has made an excellent choice," said FitzRoy.

"So we have been invited to dinner at the Governor's residence?"

"That's right. Mr. Lawson is a very well-educated man and knows these islands extremely well. It will be a great opportunity for you to question him at length about them and so perhaps clear up some of the oddities you have found. It promises to be an interesting evening."

"So then, Mr. Lawson, you are not really the Governor of these islands?" asked Darwin, curious about his official status.

"Strictly speaking, I am the Vice-Governor. The authorities in Quito were not bold enough to leave the archipelago officially in the hands of a foreigner. The Governor is Don José Villamil, who resides permanently in Guayaquil. He has no interest in these islands, except for his Governor's salary."

"Didn't the lack of confidence shown by the Ecuadorians bother you?" asked FitzRoy, sipping Peruvian pisco.

"I must admit that at first I thought of not accepting the post on those grounds, as you say, Captain. However, I then found some interesting advantages to this arrangement: every time the people on the island make a request that is impossible to be satisfied, I have an easy way out by saying that I need the Governor's approval. Naturally, Don Villamil's answer will take months and the final decision will always be what I had suggested in the first place ... which means that I always have an elegant way of saying no whenever I need to. But please," he said opening the door that led to the dining room, "please be seated. As they say here: come in, the house is small but the heart is large."

FitzRoy, Darwin, Wickham and Stokes sat on the heavy dark wood chairs. "They're Spanish," explained Lawson, "we do not have that sort of timber on these islands." As they sat at the table, two servants brought in several dishes of Ecuadorian food. Their host warned them of the ones that were especially spicy, since the visitors, after four years at sea, had grown unaccustomed to spicy dishes. "When we return to England, I believe we will never be able to eat curry again without shedding tears," said Wickham; everybody laughed.

"Tell me, Mr. Darwin, as a naturalist, what do you make of these islands?" asked Lawson.

"Well ... if we take into account the craters, the lava fields, the dry plants and the wealth of reptiles ... I would say that the Galapagos Islands are the most cultivated area in Hell." They all laughed heartily at his remark.

"The lowlands on these islands are very dry, perhaps they actually look a bit like Dante´s Hell in the Divine Comedy, wait till you see the islands that have active volcanoes."

"There is a plant, or rather a tree, on Chatham Island that I find mysterious."

"Which one? What is it like?"

"The trunk and branches are very thin, it has no leaves, is about ten feet tall and grows upwards and little sideways ... oh, and when burnt it has a most peculiar smell."

"Like medicine?" asked the Vice-Governor.

"Exactly!"

"It is palosanto."

"Palosanto? Why that name?"

"It has healing properties. Palosanto is the contraction of palo (stick or wood) and santo, (holy) which would translate as 'healing stick' We ship a good amount of this wood to the mainland. I must note that the only property I have personally verified is that it keeps mosquitoes away, which is of little use here since there are no mosquitoes on these islands."

"Do they grow leaves at some other time of the year?"

"I have never seen the ones on Chatham with leaves. I have seen them with leaves on other, more humid, islands. It never rains in Chatham's lowlands, at least since I live here."

"Perhaps these trees only sprout when it rains. It may very well be that they are dormant, then, when it rains, they use this humidity to sprout, flower and reproduce. When the ground dries up they return to the dormant state."

"Perhaps ... though I've never seen it. So what do you think of the animals on these islands? Which one did you find more interesting?"

"The tortoises, without doubt."

"Is that so? You might find it interesting to know that the origin of the name Galapagos is that of a saddle, the 'galápago', which in turn has the same origin as the word 'galopar', to gallop."

"How is that?" asked FitzRoy.

"The Spaniards use a type of saddle they call 'galápago'. The tortoises of the highlands have a dent on the top of their shells in the shape of a saddle, which is why they called them 'Galapagos'. Later on that name was adopted for the islands."

"You should have taken advantage of this saddle, Mr. Darwin, when you climbed on the tortoise the other day, instead of trying to stand on it and falling off so awkwardly," said Sokes.

"Correction, if you don't mind, Mr. Stokes," Darwin answered in the same tone, "that tortoise was not from the highlands, so it had no saddle."

"Nevertheless, that was no reason for you to bite the dust," retorted Stokes.

They all laughed at the anecdote and toasted the tortoises with pisco.

"And talking about tortoises, how many species are there on these islands? Two, three?" asked Darwin.

"Oh no, there are fourteen species."

"Fourteen?!"

"Yes, sir."

"How can you tell them apart?"

"By their shell. One could say that each island has its own species, except for Albermale, or Isabella, as it is known here, where there are four."

"Who could tell me the differences between them?"

"I can, Mr. Darwin," said Lawson proudly, "by just looking at the shell I can tell what island it came from."

"Mr. Lawson knows these islands extremely well," explained FitzRoy, "tell me, Mr. Lawson, in your opinion which is the most interesting animal on these islands?"

"The finches."

"The finches?" asked FitzRoy, puzzled, "what is so interesting about them? They are practically an ordinary sparrow!"

"True, but there are thirteen different types of them. Each island has one peculiar to it, although on some islands there are two or even three distinct types."

"In what do they differ?" asked Darwin, curious.

Galapagos´ finches, taken from "Zoology of the *Beagle*"

"In the beak. As with the tortoises, I can tell what island they are from by the shape of their beak."

"Very well, then, Mr. Darwin, make sure you study these little birds thoroughly," said FitzRoy, and added, "I propose a toast to the finches."

"Hear, hear!" they answered and downed their pisco.

They continued enjoying the delicious dishes of local cuisine which the servants kept bringing, while the Vice-Governor explained in detail what each one was. The islands being a fisherman's paradise, most of the dishes were seafood.

"You seem to be very fortunate as far as culinary delicacies are concerned, but not so with fresh water. We only found one spring, and that on Chatham," said FitzRoy.

"On Chatham there is a large spring, and there is a smaller one here, near our town."

"Was that why the town was established here?"

"Indeed, when Ecuador took control of these islands, three years ago, they decided to establish the capital here because there was fresh water. Also, the mail box had been here for over a hundred years."

"Mail box? What is that?" asked Stokes.

"It is a very old practice by seamen to make sure their mail reaches its destination," said FitzRoy, who was well versed in these matters, "When these islands were uninhabited, there was a box here where ships that stopped to stock up left their mail. They also would see if there was mail for their next destination and if there was, would take it and deliver it. The Portuguese used this method in South Africa as they rounded the Cape of Good Hope on their way to India. The ships on their way out would leave their mail, and the ones that returned picked it up and delivered it. Only there the mail box was a tree, which still stands at Mossel Bay. They would leave their mail in boots which they hung from the branches of the tree that, just as in this case, was near a fresh water spring."

"Well yes, it was a similar case. This was where ships crossing the Pacific, in either direction, would stop to stock up," explained Lawson. "The history of these islands is linked to the lack of fresh water. Most of the islands are uninhabited because they have no fresh water. In fact those who discovered them almost perished from lack of water."

"Is that so? What happened?" asked FitzRoy.

"In 1535 Bishop Fray Tomás de Berlanga was on his way from Panamá to Lima. As there was a lengthy windless spell, the trip was taking longer than expected and they started to run out of water. To make matters worse the ship was adrift and was taken off course by the currents. They had already given up hope when they sighted one of these islands, which were unknown at the time. Full of hope they landed to fill their fresh water tanks, but after searching all over the island they found none. Several crew members died as they sailed to another island, where they finally found a fresh water spring and were able to continue their trip to Lima. There they disclosed their discovery."

"Is that why they are known as The Enchanted Islands?" asked Darwin.

"Not quite. Having heard of this discovery, a few years later Spanish seafarer Alvaro de Mendaño tried to find them without success. He gave them that name, since he believed he had not found them because they were bewitched."

"Let us toast water and the Enchanted Islands," said FitzRoy raising his glass of pisco.

"Captain, let this be the last toast, because if not I will need to mount a Galapago to get back to my bed!" said Stokes, to which they all laughed.

On Albemarle Darwin had a hint of what was most important to his theory, but his state of mind was such that he missed the opportunity, and it would not be until several years later that he came to understand the significance of what would later be the cornerstone of his thinking.

A few days later Darwin landed on Albemarle. He was accompanied by Adrian, the guide that Lawson had recommended.

His aim was to make geological observations, and Albemarle seemed the perfect island since it was one of the few with volcanic activity, and, being larger than most, promised to have more secrets hidden in its interior.

On an ancient map his guide marked the main points of interest: craters, chimneys, rivers of lava, etc. They decided on a route.

As they walked they chatted animatedly. The animals, their lives and habits were the main topics.

One of the most interesting places they visited was a large crater, almost a mile long. Inside, the depression was almost five hundred feet deep. At the bottom of it there was a lake, in the middle of which a smaller crater formed an island. They both walked down the steep slope on the inside of the crater until they reached the lake, and were able to determine that the water was brackish. He noticed that the main crater was made of hardened volcanic ash, but he also found many volcanic rocks, which he assumed were from the depths of the earth and had been thrown there during some violent eruption. He collected some samples, put them in his rucksack, and they then started their long climb to the top. The crater's sides were so steep that they blocked the breeze from the sea, and this, coupled with the midday sun beating relentlessly upon them, made their ascent a true ordeal. As they stopped to rest, yet again, Darwin told his guide that during the crossing of the Andes in Chile he had climbed mountains as steep as these, but on mule back, so it had not been so strenuous. "We could do with a couple of mules here," quipped Adrian.

Nearby there was an expanse with more craters, although these seemed to be extinct as they did not show signs of recent activity. The dryness and the presence of iguanas reminded him of his previous comment on how this island resembled Hell as it was depicted by Dante in the Divine Comedy. Adrian laughed at this comparison, and just to reinforce the demonic image, he pointed at a red iguana that was attempting to eat a cactus with enormous thorns.

Land Iguana from Galapagos, taken from "Zoology of the *Beagle*"

"I wonder what the marine iguanas eat?" asked Darwin, not expecting an answer.

"Sea weed," said Adrian, to Darwin's surprise, "they eat seaweed that grows near the shore."

"How strange," said Darwin doubtfully, "I find it hard to believe that animals so closely related have such different diets. I would like to confirm it."

"Sure, it is only a short detour to the coast, where they live."

They continued walking; only now the fresh breeze from the sea kept their temperature down.

"There is something you might like to know concerning land and marine iguanas."

"What is that, Adrian?"

"Now that I heard you mention that these iguanas are closely related, I remembered something I saw on a plaza island."

"Plaza island? Which are those?"

"Small islands, only large rocks, really, usually just one or two miles from the main islands."

"I see ... and what did you see there?"

"On some of them, both types of iguanas share their territory. Once I landed on one of these islands and saw a marine iguana copulating with a land one. And I am sure of what I saw because I know these animals well."

"I wonder what the result of such a crossing is."

"I cannot prove it, but I suspect it would be a slightly modified land iguana."

"Why do you think that?"

"Because on these islands the land iguanas are smaller and darker than those on the larger islands, that is, more like the marine ones."

Darwin, now very interested, made an entry in his notebook. He must try to convince FitzRoy to allow him to land on one of these plaza islands.

Their long walk finally took them to where there were some black rocks on the sea shore. Several iguanas sunbathed on them and every so often one would slip into the water and swim away, their only propulsion being their tail, which they moved from side to side. Darwin timed them from the moment they entered the sea until they returned to the rock, and wrote down the results meticulously. They then caught one that had just returned. Darwin deftly killed it and then opened its stomach, where he found reddish sea weed.

"Very well, Adrian, you were right, they eat sea weed."

"These sea weeds grow very near the shore, about twenty feet deep."

"Clearly, that is why they only take six to eight minutes to go to feed and return to their rock."

Nearby, a bird caught his eye. It was a booby, but one he had not seen before. This one had a black mask across its eyes.

"It is a Nazca booby, one of the three booby species in Galapagos," explained the guide.

"The other ones are the blue-footed ones and the ones with the light blue beak, correct?"

"Yes, although the one you mention with light blue beak is the one we call red-footed."

"Tell me, Adrian, apart from their looks, do they also differ in their habits?"

Darwin was trying to associate their physical differences with the way they adapted to their habitat.

"They differ in many ways. Each species fish in different areas: The blue-footed ones, close to the shore, the Nazca boobies out at sea, and the red-footed ones somewhere in between. They also nest in different places. The blue-footed boobies nest here, close to the shore, the Nazca boobies nest in the trees, a bit further inland, which is why you don't see many of them."

"What use are the blue feet to them?" Darwin was trying to establish if this distinctive feature had any effect on their success as a species.

"Easy, Mr. Darwin. Come, I'll show you."

Adrian led him to a place, not far from there, where there were several couples of blue-footed boobies. Darwin studied one couple that Adrian had pointed at. The male stood on a rounded rock, and looking in the direction of the female, performed a sort of dance where he alternately picked up one foot and then the other as if showing them to the female. He repeated this movement several times until the female approached him and imitated his prancing. They picked their feet up in unison a few times and then made their beaks clash as if fencing.

"Their feet and beaks are very important in their mating dance," said Adrian softly, trying not to disturb the birds.

"Would that be it?" thought Darwin. Several species, not only in Galapagos, showed striking features that could not always be explained as the result of evolution. Some of these features were the antlers on deer, the yak´s heavily armoured skull and the male peacock's multicoloured tail.

In his notebook, next to his entry, he drew a large question mark, and on the margin he wrote: "in the courting process, some species will give certain physical aspects great importance, which will then be exaggerated over the next generations. These might probably have the sole object of calling the female's attention."

They continued their walk inland. Soon after noon they stopped to rest and eat. Ther meal consisted of rice with raisins. At one moment Darwin left his plate on the floor beside him while he took out his map of the islands so that Adrian could show him where they would find the rivers of lava they were going to see next. But when he turned back to his plate he found there were three finches busily picking at the rice. The guide deftly caught one.

"This did not happen to me on Chatham. The finches there did not care for rice," said the Englishman, curious.

"Those finches are different to these. Look at its beak, it is different to the finches on the next island," he said showing him the bird's beak, "On each island the animals are different. Not just the finches."

"I know. The tortoises and even the palosanto trees are different, and now that we are about to leave I see that I have not taken separate animal specimens from each island."

"Very well, then, here you have a finch from Isabella's (Albemarle) lowlands," with a quick movement he broke the bird's neck, "for your collection," and offered him the bird.

As he was really interested in the island's geology at the time, he did not give this little incident the importance it really had. Several years later, while attending a banquet held by a scientific society, something that was said made him remember the rice-eating finches of the Galapagos, and this would give him the key to escape the stranglehold FitzRoy had placed on him.

With more than fifty tortoises on board, the *Beagle* sailed across the Pacific Ocean towards mythical Polynesia, although, after four years, all we really longed for was to arrive in England as soon as possible. We were still half a world away.

Chapter 16

A Proposal That Could Not Be Refused

The voyage of the *Beagle* was nearing its end. Captain FitzRoy was very enthusiastic about what the future held for him. He had decided to publish a book on his explorations.

The conversations over breakfast between Darwin and FitzRoy had become less and less frequent since they left Galapagos. The naturalist's ideas and the commitment he had made at Valparaiso had created a rift that would not be easy to bridge. It was a subject they did not want to dwell on, so they avoided these conversations which put them in such a predicament.

However, as the *Beagle* sailed northward in the Atlantic, headed for the British Isles, the Captain wished to share breakfast as they had before, and for a while things were as they used to be.

"I would very much like, Filos, to share and discuss what we have observed in the places we have visited on our way across the Pacific and Indian oceans."

"That would be splendid, Captain. In almost a year we have seen so many fascinating places that it is important to stop and take stock so we can determine which things are really outstanding."

Darwin had brought his diary, in which the events of the last year filled two volumes. It seemed very little, however, when compared to what FitzRoy had written in the same period: the ship's log, copies of letters to London, written orders for the officers, maps, drawings, his personal diary, and dozens of loose sheets. The table was stacked with documents, so they hardly had any room for breakfast.

The Captain was leafing through some of his notes.

"I suppose we should start with Tahiti," he said.

"I would say it is a singular place. I have been thinking on how the islands were formed. They are evidently volcanic, but they seem to be in a slow sinking process. Around them a ring of coral keeps growing and keeps them above water. As a result, there are islands with volcanic mountains, like Papeete, and others where only the coral ring emerges, the atolls. This effect could be clearly seen at the Keeling Islands."

"I remember you took samples of corals at different depths in order to verify that the deeper, the older," FitzRoy paused, "but I really do not wish to discuss these places from a scientific point of view, but rather from a more descriptive one, mainly regarding their inhabitants. I would say that I consider myself an amateur anthropologist."

Darwin could see that FitzRoy was making an effort to avoid topics directly related to his theory, which could potentially lead to conflict.

"Well, from that angle, I would say that I was impressed by the cheerfulness, simplicity and common sense of the natives of Tahiti."

"I totally agree. When I visited their Parliament I was agreeably surprised by the organized way in which they debated matters of state."

"I have an entry in my diary on Queen Pomare's visit to the *Beagle*," said Darwin, "quite a political event for such a small nation, and for the ship's crew too, I believe."

"Of course it was ... may I read a little of your diary while we chat?"

"Certainly, Captain, go ahead."

FitzRoy picked up one of the volumes and read parts of it with interest.

"You make an observation here I agree with completely: the racial and cultural similarities between the natives of Tahiti and New Zealand. Not only are they physically alike, but they also share certain customs, like the tattooing of their faces, although it is more widespread in New Zealand. Another similarity I would point out is their languages, which are very much alike and clearly have a common root. We could extend this to the natives of Hawaii, where Captain Cook died."

"Dos this not suggest that these people have a common origin in spite of the enormous distances that separate them?" asked Darwin.

"That it does, Filos. They are all great seafaring nations. The canoes used by the New Zealand Maori are huge; they can carry as many as eighty persons. They often lash two or three of them together with long poles when they venture on the open sea. So nearly three hundred people can travel on a fleet of them; enough to start a colony on any group of islands."

"On this I can add what I heard: there is a legend by which the Maori claim that their ancestors arrived in New Zealand on twelve canoes. They have very strong feelings for their ancestors, whom they worship in many ways. One is by carving statuettes that represent their forefathers."

"I have seen a couple of them; they remind me of drawings I have seen of the famous statues on Easter Island."

"The moais, the giant stone statues that depict their ancestors," exclaimed Darwin, "of course! They are very much alike ... do you think the same people settled on all the islands in the Pacific? Were they able to sail across such distances in their canoes?"

"I am positive that that was what happened. Many must have perished; possibly entire fleets ... men, women and children ... but some of them made it ... see what I found here, in your diary," he read from it, "'the Maori natives greet each other by rubbing their noses.' I saw them do the exact same thing in Tahiti, it cannot be by chance!"

"No, surely not," there was a short silence, "then these people reached out across the whole of the Pacific, except the Galapagos."

"A couple of centuries more and they would surely have gotten there. Anyway," he said leafing through the notes, "they also have many differences."

"You reminded me of one great difference between the Maori and the Tahitians, Captain. The Tahitians are peaceful while the Maori are warriors."

"So they are! I witnessed a war dance they call Haka at one of their villages. It was really impressive and extremely aggressive. It is surely meant to intimidate their enemies."

The Captain poured Darwin some more tea.

"These conversations are fascinating. By comparing our notes and sharing our ideas we have concluded that we have met the people that are the greatest travellers in the world."

"What can you say of the Australian aborigines?" asked Darwin as he put sugar in his tea.

"There is no doubt that they have a completely different origin. They seem to me to be half way between the black Africans and the darker skinned Indians. Their language and traditions have no point of contact with that of the rest of the people in the Pacific, not even with those on nearby islands like Guinea."

"Perhaps they arrived earlier by land from India or Ceilan."

"What do you mean by land?"

"As I mentioned earlier, the islands in the Pacific seem to be sinking. It is possible that all this land was higher and there may have been a strip of land connecting India with Australia."

Maori family, by T. Landseer and A. Earle

"Of course, Filos. That would mean that man originated at one place and from there he populated the whole World, don't you think?"

"Possibly," said Darwin.

The Captain thought for a moment.

"And which would you say was this place of origin?"

"I cannot be sure, but it must have been Europe, Asia or Africa, since they are all connected. From there America, Oceania, and the oceanic islands like the Canaries, New Zealand, Easter Island, Papua and so on."

"Aha," said FitzRoy, thoughtful, "and the different races could be the result of their need to adapt to the environment in each place, according to your theory, is this not so?"

"It would have to be proven," answered Darwin trying to avoid any adverse reaction from the Captain.

"Yes, it would have to be proven ... but it seems very interesting," he said with a smile, "very interesting ..."

FitzRoy continued to leaf through Darwin's diary.

"Filos, I'm sorry that when we stopped at Mauritius we were not able to make a detour to the Seychelles islands to see the giant tortoises that live there."

"Yes, it was a real pity."

"I would really like to know why there are giant tortoises, like the ones in Galapagos, on these islands. I have a notion that they were taken there by pirates."

"Why would they do that?"

"For them to breed and then be used for food."

"I don't quite understand, Captain."

"Let me tell you of something that happened on the Chilean coast. At the time when Chile, Peru, Ecuador and Colombia were rich Spanish colonies, British privateers would attack their ports to snatch the gold and silver that was stocked there waiting to be shipped to Seville. Their problem, however, was where to replenish their supplies of food and water after such a long voyage without being spotted by the Spaniards. Someone had the brilliant idea of leaving a few goats on one of the islands off the Chilean coast. A few years later there were thousands of goats on the islands and all the privateers had to do was land and load as many goats as they needed. The interesting thing is what happened next. The Spaniards soon found out about the goats, so to eliminate them, and thus leave these privateers without food, the Spaniards took wild dogs to the island and let them loose. They certainly killed a great many goats, but there was always a good amount in the mountains where they could keep away from the dogs."

"Very interesting story, Captain, especially because it goes to show how one species controls another. Surely when the number of goats was greatly reduced, many dogs must have died of hunger, which in turn allowed the goats do multiply again until finally they must have got to the point of equilibrium. But what does that have to do with the tortoises?"

"Simply because I imagine that some pirates might have seen the utility of having an island full of tame and wholesome tortoises, would have got the idea of taking some to an isolated island in an area they operated in and so have ample supply of food. After many years there would be hundreds of tortoises and all they had to do was to land and load as many tortoises as they needed."

Darwin found the idea rather clever, but thought it was not probable. The tortoises' reproductive cycle was very slow, so that sort of growth would take centuries. He did not believe that a pirate would do any long-term planning, especially if he would not see the results. Darwin believed

Tahiti, by Conrad Martens

that the tortoises must have lived all over the world at one time, but were probably driven to extinction by predators, and only survived in these isolated islands where there were no predators. But he did not want to argue with FitzRoy.

"If it is as you say, Captain, then the tortoises at Seychelles would belong to the same species as the ones in Galapagos. To do this we would have had to land in Seychelles to compare the tortoises."

"Of course, it was a real pity that we were not able to."

"But I believe something similar must have happened in Galapagos with the mice."

"How is that?"

"The only mammal in the Galapagos is a mouse with rather long and dark ears. It is very similar to one that is found on many islands in the Indian Ocean. I believe they must have got to the Galapagos on some ship, and as there are no predators there, they multiplied."

"Interesting ... but you always make interesting observations, Filos ... more tea?"

FitzRoy continued leafing through Darwin's diary, lifting his eyebrows in interest over certain passages.

Tahiti, by Conrad Martens

"What can you say about Cape Town? What struck you about the place?"

"From a geographic point of view, the people or the animals?"

"Everything, Filos. Let's leave it open. Tell me what your general impression was."

"Very well ... one thing that I noticed was that the settlers, which are mainly of Dutch stock, have a great dislike for England, in spite of how the colony has grown since England took over."

"It may be because the bloody takeover of this colony was only thirty years ago. Most of the Dutch settlers fought against the British troops, so many of them have brothers or fathers or friends who were killed during the hostilities. It is understandable. Let me tell you something curious. The same fleet that took Cape Town in 1806 went on to attack Buenos Aires ... but changing the subject, what do you think of the African animals?" asked FitzRoy.

"There is no doubt that the animals in Africa are truly magnificent. The variety and concentration of great mammals is not found anywhere else in the world."

"I suppose I could add something in that sense. There were many large mammals that lived in South America, of which you collected many fossils, such as the mylodon, toxodon, glyptodon, mastodons, etc.; if they were still alive the concentration would be very much like the one in Africa."

"But the fact remains that they are extinct."

"That is what I'm getting at, Filos. Perhaps those animals were there because humans had not yet arrived, and, as you said yourself, when they did they hunted them into extinction."

"But in Africa humans have always been present, and the large mammals are still around. Something tells me that in Africa there is, or was, something that differed greatly from the rest of the continents."

"Which takes you to the conclusion that Man originated in Africa, is this not so, Filos?"

"I could be, although it would have to be studied in depth." Darwin would rather not pursue this subject because he did not know what the Captain's reaction would be. Even though he knew he was talking to Fitz, he was aware that Roy could appear at any moment and that would be the end.

"And what can you say of the Cape of Good Hope? I remember that when we arrived there by land there was a very thick mist that hid the whole Cape. Apparently this is very common there because that is where two currents meet, a warm one from the Indian Ocean and a very cold one from the Atlantic. The warm current generates very warm and humid air which, when it encounters the cold current, condenses and creates this thick mist."

"I measured a difference of forty degrees Fahrenheit between the Water east of the cape and that west of it. That explains the great diversity of fish in the area."

"And the amount of sharks. Bad place to shipwreck," said FitzRoy with irony.

The Captain poured some more tea.

"The truth be said, I like your style of writing, and I also notice that you write about different subjects than I do. One could say that our diaries complement each other. I concentrate on the actual problems of the organization of the voyage and the difficulties encountered sailing, and I describe the geography as a means to help future seamen while your descriptions are of a more scientific nature for these little-known lands."

He drank some tea and returned Darwin his diary.

"As I have mentioned before, Filos, I plan to publish a book on the two exploratory voyages I have made. But now that I have read some of your work ..."

FitzRoy paused and drank some more tea to increase the suspense for what he was about to say.

"... I got the notion that it would be a great idea for you to publish your diary together with mine, in separate volumes, mind you, but all part of the same edition. What do you think?"

Under different circumstances Darwin would have jumped for joy at such an offer, but now things were not the same. He did not relish the idea of publishing his work under FitzRoy's scrutiny. However, he could not think of any excuse to wiggle out of it.

"I would not know how to thank you for such an opportunity, Captain," he said in an unconvincing tone, "but I am not sure the quality of my writing is adequate for such an important book."

"Nonsense, Filos! Your work is excellent. Our book will be a great success," and lifting his cup he added, "let us toast, with rather cold tea, the beginning of our writing careers!"

The mountains of St. Helena could be seen silhouetted on the horizon. As they had done so many times before, Stokes and Darwin chatted leaning on the handrail and enjoying the view.

"So, Mr. Darwin, you should be delighted to have your diary published together with the work on the *Beagle*'s exploratory voyages. The prestige this will give you will be a great boost for your career. I do not notice you overjoyed, however."

"The idea of publishing it fascinates me. What worries me is that the Captain will be the one to supervise and proofread the whole book."

"What is wrong with that?"

"That he would probably censor anything to do with my theory. I fear FitzRoy will attempt to modify parts of my text. The first published work is of utmost importance since it establishes in what direction you will take your investigation."

"Let me see if I understand you correctly ... there is a saying that says that a person owns his silences and is a prisoner of his words."

"Exactly! I fear the Captain might induce me to write something I will not be able to escape from."

"You say this because of your promise in Valparaiso?"

"Of course, he does not really want my theory to be made public."

"I don't believe the Captain will change a comma of your manuscript."

"I wish I could be as sure as you are ..."

They remained silent for a while, gazing at the mountains they were slowly approaching.

"What do you believe will be the most interesting feature of St. Helena, Mr. Darwin?" asked Stokes-

"The geological origin of these islands lost in the middle of the Atlantic Ocean."

"Come on! How can you say that, we've seen dozens of islands like this one!"

"So you tell me, then. What do you think will be the most interesting feature?"

"The tomb, obviously."

"What tomb?"

"Napoleon's tomb, man!"

"Of course! I had forgotten. Now that we are getting closer to Europe its history is catching up with us."

"He did not die long ago. We might find some soldier in the garrison who knew him and who might tell us what he was really like. Wouldn't that be good?"

But Darwin was still thinking how awkward he felt writing a book with the Captain, or his jailer, as he thought of him now.

Chapter 17

The Emperor's Death

Although in St. Helena Darwin made some interesting geological and zoological observations, the most interesting thing we discovered was what really happened to Napoleon. The true story had been carefully guarded and was too serious for us to make public. Both Darwin and I were amazed at how far court scheming could go. Like an octopus' tentacles they reached out from Europe to these little islands lost in the middle of the Atlantic.

The island was forbidding. It appeared to be a great fortress whose walls rose vertically from the sea. Darwin explained that it was an ancient volcano that rose from the bottom of the sea. The black lava dominated the place, an unrelenting gale blew from the south-east and enormous waves beat at its shores.

On the *Beagle* a small group that included FitzRoy, Darwin and Stokes prepared to board the boat that would take them ashore to Jamestown, the only settlement on the island.

The Captain sat in the boat next to Darwin.

"I did not expect to find a settlement of this size on such an isolated island. I wonder who the first settler was and why he chose it."

"It was a Portuguese soldier called Fernando Lopez," answered FitzRoy, "it is a fascinating story I read about last night."

"Tell me about it, Captain."

"In 1512 there was a battle between the Portuguese forces and an Indian Maharaja; one must remember that the Portuguese were the first to get to India and acquire spices, not always peacefully. Apparently some corrupt Portuguese had been bought over by the Maharaja, but, unfortunately for them, the Maharaja lost the battle and decided to hand the deserters over to the invading forces, after securing the Portuguese general's promise that their lives would be spared. The Portuguese general kept his promise, but he had their right hands, the thumb of their left hands, their ears and noses cut off."

"Did they survive this butchery?"

"Not all. The survivors were taken on board one of the ships that was bound for Portugal where I imagine they would surely have been executed. On the way they stopped here, at St. Helena, to replenish their fresh water, and that was when one of them, Fernando Lopez, escaped while their guard was temporarily distracted. The crew made quite a thorough search of the island but never found him."

"Without one hand and missing the thumb of the other his chances of survival on a desert island were very poor."

"Apparently that is what the crew believed also. The felt pity for him, so they left him some food on the beach and left. The Portuguese Navy decided that the next ship to go past this island should pick up his body and give him a Christian burial. To the surprise of the crew of the next ship that stopped at the island, the food that had been left had disappeared. They searched for him again to no avail, so they left another batch of supplies, including a live cock, and left."

"And he was never heard of again?"

"The story continues ... every Portuguese ship that went by left him supplies, but no one had seen him. Until one day ... "

"They found his body!" interrupted Darwin.

"No sir ... until one day a young Malay prisoner also escaped from one of the ships. Time went by and the ships that stopped at St. Helena left supplies on the beach, and they kept disappearing. Until almost twenty years later, when a ship stopped at St. Helena, the Malay prisoner gave himself up and told them where Fernando Lopez was hiding. They went to fetch him, took him prisoner and carried him back to Lisbon."

"They killed him and that was the end of the story?"

"No, the story continues. Once in Portugal he confessed his treason and begged forgiveness for his acts. He also gave them information on which ships would stop over to replenish or rest at this island on which Spain had laid a claim. The King rewarded him by sparing his life and awarding him a lifetime pension. But the man could not get used to life in civilization and asked to be taken back to St. Helena. He was brought back and lived here until, one day, a ship found that the supplies they had left on the previous trip were still on the beach. They looked for him but he was never found. They assumed he had died, but his body was not found either. It was over thirty years from the day he escaped. And that is the end of the story."

"So, what happened to the cock?" asked Darwin.

"The cock had become Lopez' best friend. When the young Malay escaped and joined Lopez, they formed a strange sort of family. But driven by hunger the young Malay ate the cock while Lopez was away. Lopez was furious and tried to kill him, but he escaped, but would surely have been killed if the Portuguese ship had not shown up."

"What an interesting story. It reminds a bit of the story of Robinson Crusoe and the aborigine he named Friday."

"Daniel Defoe probably based his novel on the story of Fernando Lopez."

The boat had arrived at the jetty in Jamestown's port. A mulatto servant helped them step off the boat that was rocked by the persisting waves.

"Stokes, Darwin! Come with me to the Governor's residence. I have documents I must deliver, but we can also ask him to recommend a place where you can lodge while you do your job during the five days we will be staying here."

The governor had found, for Darwin and me, a pleasant cottage which had the appearance of a typical English one. That made our homesickness even worse. The owner, the kind and talkative Mrs. Watson, welcomed us with tea and scones.

"Tell me, Mrs. Watson," asked Darwin, "I was surprised by the amount of coloured people on the island, do you know that the reason for that is?"

"A great many slaving ships, loaded with Negroes from Africa, en route to America, went by close to the island, so St. Helena sort of turned into the centre of the fight against the slaving trade to the United States of America, which, as you well know, is the country with by far the largest slave population. This is from where the Royal Navy ships leave to try and intercept them. When one is captured, the blacks in the holds are set free at the closest African shore, but many end up here, in St. Helena. That is why the African community has grown so, to the point that they are now the majority."

"I see, now it makes sense."

"What is your interest in this island, Mr. Darwin," asked Mr. Watson, and added in jest, "I will not ask you, Mr. Stokes, since it is clear that your main interest is marmalade."

The Island of Saint Helena, by Louis Choris

"My interest, as opposed to Mr. Stokes', is in rocks and animals."

"You will find a great variety of rocks, but very few animals. Just a few birds, I'm afraid."

"I imagined as much, but I need to separate those that were introduced from Europe from those native to St. Helena."

"Well ... I do not know much on the subject, but from what I have heard the only native bird is the wirebird. They usually nest in a plain near Longwood."

"I would very much like to visit the place."

"I will tell old Joshua to take you. If you are interested in climbing High Knoll or some of the many hills on the island, Joshua can be your guide for that also."

"I am very interested, and I suppose Mr. Stokes is too."

Stokes was in the process of spreading whipped cream on a scone; for a man who had been five years at sea whipped cream was more valuable than gold.

"Of course I will go with you; I must take some readings to establish coordinates and heights."

"I haven't a clue of what you are talking about," said Mrs. Watson.

"The coordinate calculations are used to draw maps," explained Darwin. "Another question, Mrs. Watson, why are there so many fortifications and cannon on the island?"

"Oh, they are the Emperor's legacy."

"What do you mean?" asked Stokes, since this subject interested him even more tan scones and whipped cream.

"When Napoleon was brought here, the British Government was afraid he might escape, as he had done from Elba."

"But how could he escape from here," Darwin asked in astonishment.

"They feared a French man-of-war would appear, attack the island and rescue him. This would be an embarrassment for the crown and a danger to Europe. So they decided to make the island a fortress. But none of that happened. Napoleon died, the garrison was reduced and now we have more guns than soldiers."

"Did you meet Napoleon?" asked Stokes.

"I saw him several times, though we were not allowed to speak to him. I did socialize with many from his circle."

"What do you mean by his circle?"

"Napoleon arrived here in the company of at least thirty members of his entourage. They all stayed at Longwood, as if they were a small court. They would sometimes go for walks and often stopped here for a meal or a drink."

"I am not surprised, I would come all the way from England to eat these scones," quipped Stokes.

Mrs. Watson smiled and continued:

"They were not very pleasant, the French rarely are. Even after six years they could not speak even passable English. I am from the isle Jersey where I learned to dislike them."

"Did anyone on the island know the Emperor?"

"Only Sergeant Rourke. He was his personal guard and had to follow him all over the island."

"Where could we find Rourke?" asked Stokes.

"He is on guard at Napoleon's tomb every day. You shall find him there when you return from your outing tomorrow. It is very close by."

"Standing guard at the tomb? I wonder why."

"It is a sort of lifelong punishment the governor has handed him."

"Why was he punished?" asked Darwin whose interest in the matter was increasing by the minute.

"He can tell you why. Although … don´t believe everything he tells you."

"Are you sure he said to meet him here?"

Yes, Mr. Darwin. On the way back from taking some readings I saw

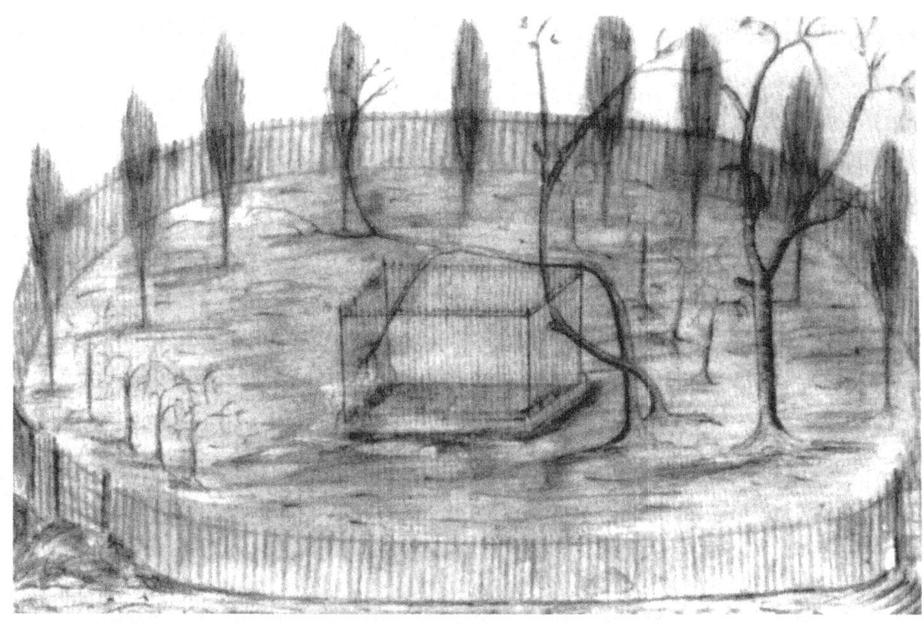
Napoleon's tomb in Saint Helena, sketch by Syms Covington

him on guard at Napoleon's tomb, so I went to speak to him and we arranged to meet at this tavern (pub?)."

"So, Mr. Stokes, did he tell you why he is on guard there?"

"Yes and no. He said that it was to avoid people from damaging it, but he also said it was some sort of punishment also."

"Punishment for what?"

"He said that was part of the story he would tell us today. There he is now."

A soldier had just come in. He was rather old, with white hair and a beaten look and was looking around the tavern, searching. John caught his attention by waving his arm. The soldier spotted them and made his way to their table.

"Lieutenant Stokes, please pardon me for arriving late."

"Sergeant Rourke, please, I have not forgotten British punctuality even after so many years away from England. Anyway, you can't consider three minutes as late. Let me introduce you to Charles Darwin, naturalist aboard the *Beagle*," Darwin stood up and shook his hand, which Rourke pressed very hard, "please sit down. What will you have?"

"Some ale."

They ordered and then chatted about life on the island, the weather and animals until the soldier's ale arrived.

"Very well, Sergeant, you said you could tell us the real story of Napoleon on St. Helena, is that not so?"

"Actually it is the real story of the death of Napoleon on St. Helena."

"Didn't he die from a stomach ailment?" asked Darwin.

"That is British Government's official version."

"The French insist that he was killed by the English," said Stokes, "which of them is the correct one?"

"They are both wrong. I will tell you what really happened."

"The first thing you must keep in mind," continued Rourke, "is that the Emperor was one of a kind. A fantastic personality that ..."

"Excuse me," interrupted Stokes, "you call him Emperor but I understand that by Government decree you could only call him General."

"That is true, but those of us who had direct contact with him always called him Emperor."

"Why were you so close to him?" asked Darwin.

"Because the Governor had assigned me to be his personal guard whenever he left the residence. I had to be less than ten feet from him at all times."

"But I thought that only officers were assigned that duty, and you are a sergeant," said Stokes.

"I was an officer before."

"What happened?"

"I was demoted."

"What? Why?"

"Gentlemen, if you keep interrupting me I will not be able to finish my story. I was demoted, and when I finish you will understand why."

"I am sorry," said Darwin, "we will not interrupt you any more, please continue."

Rourke took a swallow of ale before continuing.

"As I was saying, Napoleon was a very special person. He seemed to understand everyone's problems and always knew what everyone was thinking. He took an interest in large or small problems. He took an interest in my problems and, amazingly, suggested solutions that really worked. Furthermore, his conversation was enthralling, he had a vast knowledge. He could explain what had happened and continued to happen in Europe in clear and simple terms, based on his deep insight of what drove and what weaknesses the main characters had."

"Of course," said Stokes, "he knew them all personally."

"Perhaps; but he also had a great understanding of human nature. He could explain why Julius Caesar did what he did, or Hannibal of Carthage, or Scipio the African, or Alexander the Great himself. ... everything, every decision, every one of their actions he would analyse and explain, and it was then clear why they did what they did. Obviously he had not met them ... what he was able to do, as no one I have ever met, was to get into their minds and feel, think and act as they would. That was how, in politics, he could anticipate what other monarchs would do and, on the battlefield, know what decisions the opposing generals would make. The secret behind his political and military victories was that he knew what his opponent would do so he moved first. Knowing what to do is easy when you already know what will happen, he used to say."

"He was defeated in the end, however. How do you explain that?" asked Darwin.

"The Emperor's great weakness was his ego. It made him always double the stakes. If he defeated Austria, he then had to go for Prussia, and then for Russia and he then would have gone for England ... with this sort of personality each battle he won only guaranteed that he would then go for another more powerful foe, while a defeat would mean the loss of everything he had already gained ... that was how after his defeat in Russia the whole Empire crumbled. He knew exactly what would happen, just as a drunkard knows where his first swallow will take him." Rourke took a long swallow from his glass.

"When you so sympathized with Napoleon, were you aware that he was England's greatest enemy?" asked Stokes.

"Of course! I would never have done anything that would put my King or Country in danger. But apart from his military genius, I could not help admiring his republican ideas. All the absolute monarchies in Europe, including the British Government, were mortally wounded by Napoleon. If any one of you is a Whig[1], you will know what I am talking about."

Darwin felt that this comment was addressed to him. All his family were Whigs and, although he was only a child at the time of Waterloo, he clearly remembered how careful they were to avoid mentioning Napoleon in their conversations over and after dinner, since they sympathized with

1. Whig was the name given to the followers of what is now called the Liberal Democratic Party.

his ideas but feared they would be considered traitors if it was known. He knew exactly what Rourke was talking about.

"But if he was such a republican, how come he had himself proclaimed Emperor?" asked Stokes, who was not much into politics.

"The republican experience had plunged France into a period of terror. Thousands were killed by a government that was driven by hate and bitterness. Not only was Louis XVI executed, but all those who had voted for his death were also taken to the guillotine: Danton, Robespierre and the current King's father, Phillip of Orleans, who had himself referred to as Phillipe Egaltié. Napoleon insisted that an uneducated population, like the French, was easily misled by a corrupt minority. According to him a 'pure' Republic would only turn France into a dictatorship, just as bad, or probably worse, than the monarchy it would replace."

"So what did he propose, then?"

"An enlightened Dictator. Someone who could enforce the Republican ideals with an iron fist. In short, someone like him. That was why the rest of Europe was against him."

Darwin believed they were treading dangerous ground, so he changed the subject.

"How did you communicate with Napoleon? As far as I know he did not speak English and I believe you do not speak French."

"The Emperor actually spoke English very well. He chose to have everyone believe he did not, however, to keep his distance with the Governor. Napoleon was a great actor, and could also be a great liar."

"What was his great lie?" asked Darwin who could feel that this statement held a secret.

"His stomach ailment."

"Then what did he die of?"

"That is what I'm about to tell you."

"When Napoleon was sent to St. Helena, he knew there was no chance he could escape as he had done from Elba. From the moment he arrived he endured, without complaints, all the mistreatment and indignities the Governor, Sir Hudson Lowe, subjected him to. He believed that the European royalty, once they found out about his predicament, and thinking of their own future, would force England to send him back to Europe, perhaps to a forced exile; In the meantime he concentrated on writing his memoirs, aided by his friend and confidant, the Count of Las Cases. At the time the retinue that waited on him resided at the old Logwood mansion, which they called 'le petit Fountainbleau'."

"The little Fountainbleau, after Napoleon's summer palace near Paris," added Darwin.

"Exactly. As time went by, however, he came to the conclusion that no one in Europe would move a finger in his behalf, so he changed his strategy. He was now convinced that he had no chance of retuning to power so his only hope was that the little King of Rome were crowned Emperor of France and thus continue the dynasty."

"Who was the King of Rome?" asked Stokes.

"Napoleon's son. He was born four years before Waterloo and while Rome was in France's dominion, Napoleon had him crowned King of Rome," answered Darwin.

"I see you have ample knowledge of the subject," said Rourke, "Napoleon treasured a lock of his son's hair, which he somehow had smuggled in. After four years in captivity he got the notion that his death as a martyr might help put his son on the throne. It was then that he started to fake a stomach ailment."

"How did he fool the doctor?" asked Darwin, who could not believe his ears.

"The physician in charge was Dr. O'Meara, a republican, as I am. He was part of the sham."

Darwin ordered a new round of drinks.

"I still can't see how a stomach ailment would help his son be crowned Emperor," said Stokes, who didn't quite grasp the plot.

"After Waterloo the British reinstated an absolute Monarchy in France by getting the decapitated King's brother crowned as Louis XVIII, but France, and the rest of Europe for that matter, had changed. Louis was hated, while Napoleon was still immensely popular. Louis' situation was unstable and he kept his throne only thanks to England's and Austria's armies. There was no doubt that Little Bonaparte had a good chance of being crowned. All that was needed was a little push for the weak King to topple."

"I still don't get it."

"This was the plan," said Darwin who believed he understood, "when the French found out that Napoleon was dying as a result of being ill-treated by the English while Louis XVIII did nothing to defend their hero, his kingdom would collapse."

"But how would the French find out what happened to him on this God-forsaken island?" asked Stokes.

"The Count of Las Cases asked to be sent back to France since he was not a prisoner, just company for the Emperor, and the Governor allowed him to. Once back in France, Las Cases spread the rumour that Napoleon was being poisoned by the British. The ensuing popular outcry put Luis XVIII in a spot, but all he did was send a physician to St. Helena to supervise the famous prisoner's health."

"When he arrived he discovered the deception, then."

"No, because he really was not much of a doctor. He was, in fact, a spy who had been sent by the King to report on what happened here. The situation in France was getting progressively worse and the British Government ordered the Governor to make sure there was no unfortunate outcome."

"But what could he do?"

"Sir Hudson did not trust O'Meara, the Whig doctor. He had him watched and they discovered incriminating correspondence in his possession. Lowe had him removed, arrested and sent back to England charged with high treason. He appointed a military surgeon in his place."

"So the deceit was finally discovered."

"Not yet. The Emperor still had an ace up his sleeve. He had convinced O'Meara to get him some pills that would, when taken, make him suffer an extremely painful death; a true martyrdom. To avoid being discovered, he gave them to me for safekeeping until he was ready to use them ... the moment was near."

"Did you not have any qualms about acting against England?" asked Stokes.

"Lieutnant Stokes, this would not affect England in any way. I was acting against Louis XVIII, a monarch despised and hated by his subjects."

"I can understand you," said Darwin in his defence, "then what happened?"

"As he was watched closely, there was always a soldier on guard in his room."

"You also had guard duty as part of the detail," guessed Darwin.

"Precisely. Napoleon then told me to give him the pills, and I went giving him two a day, as O'Meara had recommended."

"What happened next?" asked Stokes.

"They had terrible effect. He started to suffer severe stomach pains, vomiting blood and convulsions ... in spite of such agony, his resolve did not wane and he insisted on continuing. He finally died the night of the 5th May, 1821, after six years in custody."

"You were never discovered, then," said Darwin.

"I was. The Governor was beside himself with rage, so he ordered the doctor to discover the cause of death or face the consequences. The doctor performed an autopsy and found the last two pills he had swallowed in his stomach. The Governor now knew what had happened, so he had Longwood and the belongings of everyone that had been in contact with Napoleon searched."

"And did they find the pills?" asked Stokes.

"Yes."

"How come they did not have you shot?"

"Sir Hudson could not allow the truth to be known in London; if he did, he would be singled out as the fool who put England in the spot as Napoleon's killer. His political career would be finished, so he chose to cover up and let the official story be that Napoleon died of a severe stomach ailment. He could not have me shot, so he made up a reason to have me demoted and make me serve on guard duty at Napoleon's grave for life."

They all remained silent for a few moments.

"In the end it was all to no avail, since his son was never crowned Emperor," said Stokes.

"The issue is not closed yet," Darwin knew this part of the story well, as his family had discussed it at length over dinners, "the French are convinced that Napoleon was poisoned by the English with Louis XVIII's approval. The Bourbon dynasty, weakened by discredit, was overthrown by a popular revolt in 1830, shortly before we left England. Most of the French were in favour of the King of Rome, but the rest of Europe, England included, favoured a King from the established dynasty. They finally came up with an intermediate solution: they crowned Louis Phillipe d'Orleans, son of Louis d'Orleans, revolutionary follower of Robespierre, who called himself Louis Egalité. His Bourbon lineage and his revolutionary past was an alternative which, although it did not satisfy everyone, both sides were ready to accept. As far as I know his government is very weak, so there may still be a chance for the young King of Rome"

"The King of Rome will never be Emperor of France," declared Rourke.

"Why not?" asked Stokes and Darwin, almost in unison.

"Because he died, childless, almost four years ago. There is no heir."

"So then it was all to no avail." uttered Stokes.

"And how is Louis Philippe getting on?" asked Darwin, interested in how republicanism was faring in Europe.

"Louis Philippe is very shrewd. When the King of Rome died he felt that his only competitor disappeared, as he knows he is detested he went about trying to win over the people's favour by honouring Napoleon's memory. He built all sorts of monuments, and even a mausoleum where he plans to lay Napoleon's remains. On this issue he has already started talks with England."

"London will never return the body." assured Stokes.

"On the contrary. The British Government needs to keep Louis Philippe on the French throne to keep the Republicans at bay. I am sure that after going through the motions of a discussion, they will surrender the Emperor's body. The idea seems to be to convince the French that it was Louis Philippe who snatched the body of their beloved Napoleon from the hands of the vile English. I am sure it will not work, however. Even Napoleon's bones will show him up as the usurper he is ... the end is near," said Rourke bitterly.

"Anyway, to no avail because there is no other Bonaparte that could be crowned," added Stokes.

"Don't be so sure of that."

"What do you mean?"

"His nephew, Louis Napoleon Bonaparte. That young man is an eagle. There is no doubt that the Emperor's blood runs through his veins. Perhaps he will have the opportunity to implement the republican reforms that France, and Europe, need so badly."

This stop at St. Helena, one of the last, reminded us that after five years on a voyage during which we only had time to explore and research we were approaching Europe where hate and intrigue were dominant. Were we ready for it?

Chapter 18

The Rubicon

We were all happy to return to England, but the closer we got, the more we wondered what the future had in store for us. After being away for five years, would our families receive us with open arms or would we be strangers in our own homes? How would our careers continue? Would we travel again? All these questions increased our anxiety and dampened the happiness of our return.

Seeing their home country again was something most had dreamed of for a long time. In spite of the foul weather and the heaving ship, the whole crew was on deck, divided into groups discussing their future.

Darwin and Stokes were talking animatedly. Their expectations were totally different. The young lieutenant wished to go on a new exploratory voyage. He believed that after two trips on the *Beagle* he could hope for a position of higher responsibility on a third one. Wickham had promised to recommend him as his second in command if FitzRoy managed to get him to be appointed Captain on the *Beagle*'s next mission.

"How about you, Mr. Darwin, what do you have in mind?"

"I wish I had such a clear-cut plan as you have, Mr. Stokes. In the first place, I must deal with my father, and try and get him to understand that I will not be a preacher. No mean task."

"But you must have something in mind."

"Actually I am totally at loss. My wish is to make a future of studying nature. Perhaps classify all the specimens I collected on this trip. I might consider a teaching position at Cambridge, about which I must speak to Professor Henslow, my tutor."

Smart in his full-dress uniform, Captain FitzRoy approached them.

"Waiting to behold the English coast, Gentlemen?"

"Aye, sir," answered Stokes, "and while we wait we were talking about our plans and expectations for the future, now that we are back,"

"What are they, then?"

"Mine is quite simple, Captain, to go on a new voyage to explore new places, but with a higher rank than today. On the other hand Mr. Darwin tells me he would like to teach at Cambridge, but fears he may not be accepted."

"Don't you drown in a glass of water, my friend," FitzRoy told the naturalist, giving him a friendly pat on his back, "once our book is published you will be so well-known you will be able to pick the offer you like best from all the ones you will receive, you'll see."

"What about you, Captain?" asked Darwin, "I take it you will not request a new command."

"No, I have already served on two long voyages, almost nine years. I must now see about a career in London."

"Do you have in mind a position in the Admiralty?"

"Not quite. I thought of a political career ... after publishing our book, of course"

They were interrupted by a loud cheer. The English coast had been seen and everyone on deck was shouting with glee. FitzRoy lifted his telescope and scanned the horizon.

"What can you see, Captain?" asked Darwin, eagerly.

The Captain quietly put down the telescope, turned to look at Darwin and said, smiling, "Our Rubicon."

After his return Darwin spent the first few days visiting his rather large family. First he went to see his father and sisters at their estate, The Mount, on the Severn. Meeting his father had him worried. He expected him to insist on his future in the clergy, but, surprisingly, the issue was not brought up. He had also been prepared to retell, ad nauseam, all his experiences, but found that his family already knew most of them. They had received not only all his letters, but also his diary. "We would read them after dinner," his younger sister told him, proud to be able to know every detail of his adventures in faraway places.

"A mountain with our name!" his father exclaimed, beaming, "you should send Captain FitzRoy a complete set of Wedgewood cutlery." Wedgewood was the largest china manufacturer in England, owned by his deceased mother's family.

After spending a few days at The Mount, the young man went to visit the Wedgewoods at their estate, Maer Hall, a few miles from the Darwins. The first thing he wanted to do there was to thank his uncle Joshua for having convinced his father to allow him to go on the *Beagle*'s voyage. His cousins welcomed him as they would the proverbial prodigal son, which delighted him, and he noticed that Emma seemed to be especially happy at his return.

Another mandatory stop in this family tour was to see his elder brother, Erasmus, who had moved to a very comfortable flat in London a few years earlier. Charles and Erasmus had lived together in Edinburgh while they both studied medicine, during which time they developed a very close, mature relationship, in which Charles valued his elder brother's opinion and advice.

Erasmus had been their father's great disappointment, since he had had great hopes for his future in the medical profession. He was very intelligent, affable, full of fun and handsome, but when he received his share of the income the Wedgewood industry generated, he decided that the good life was more interesting than a physician's practice. Race horses, social events, cigars and women were his main pursuits, although he still entertained a healthy interest in intellectual matters.

When they met they gave each other a long, affectionate embrace. Five years absence had not diminished the fondness they felt for each other.

"Let me look at you, Charles! You are wider, stronger, I would say, your face has filled out and ... your hair has thinned."

"Thanks, Ras," he had always called Erasmus that, "I, don't know if what you say is good or not, so I will not mention the extra pounds that can be noticed nor the receding hairline ... " they both laughed heartily, "it must be part of the Darwin heritage."

"Come, Charles, take a seat," he poured a glass of whisky, "how did it go with father?"

"I expected you to ask me about my voyage."

"I know all about your voyage, I have read your diary and all your letters. I know nothing of your visit to The Mount, however."

"Well ... I must admit I was surprised that father did not ask me what my plans were for the future. He was there when I mentioned I would publish my travel diary with FitzRoy and concentrate on classifying the specimens I collected during the trip. He never mentioned joining the clergy and, frankly, I did not either. I suppose I did not really want to."

"I believe you don't have to worry about what the Old Man expects of you anymore. A couple of years ago your old Geology professor at Cambridge, Mr. Sedgewick, came by The Mount and spent a whole afternoon speaking of you. In short he said that your reports from the *Beagle* had made you one of the foremost Geologists in the United Kingdom. That made quite an impression on father." he sipped his whisky, "Charles, I believe you are not yet aware that during your absence you have become an eminent scientist." "Ras, you are my brother, so you are biased. I am just an amateur naturalist who made some observations on places he visited around the world."

"Let me show you something."

Erasmus got up, took a key from his pocket and opened one of the drawers in his desk. He took out a file full of letters.

"You may not know it, but your tutor, Professor Henslow, read some of your letters and other writings at several scholarly meetings. They were very well received by the audience. Several societies have contacted me requesting I hand you their invitation to join them. Here are some of their letters." He opened the file and showed Charles the letters in it, "The Royal Geographic Society, The Royal Society and The Geological Society, for example. I also have here a letter from Cambridge inviting you to lecture on the botanical, zoological, geological and anthropological aspects of your voyage... little brother, you have certainly turned into a very important person. I must let you know," he added, "that I have confirmed your presence at over six dinner parties with several members of London's society who wish to meet you."

Charles read, in awe, the letters from such reputed societies. He was flattered, but also feared he might let them down.

"Ras, this is all very nice, but I must think of how I will earn a living from now on. None of these societies will pay my expenses."

Erasmus smiled. He found his younger brother's tendency to find problems where there were none amusing. Before answering he refilled their gasses.

"Kiddo, I believe you should return to The Mount and have another chat with father."

"I don't understand."

"Charles, you have come of age. Since our mother, who was a Wedgewood, died, father has been investing and saving the dividends you were due. I can tell you that although you are not rich, you do not need to work to survive. If you are careful and don't squander, you can pursue any activity you desire. I believe you should be getting about seven hundred pounds per annum, but father will give you the details."

Charles whistled, "Seven hundred?! Wow!!"

"That's right, kiddo. So let's forget about how to survive in London and tell your brother what your plans are, now that earning money is no longer a problem."

Charles' situation was now so different from what he had expected that his mind was in turmoil. He decided to start with what he considered simple.

"Well ... first, I will edit and publish my diary of the voyage, and in the long term I will put together the supporting evidence and rationale for my theory on species transformation. Although I fear I am up against some trouble there."

Charles gave him a short summary of his theory, which he would call the Theory of Evolution, of FitzRoy's stance and the details of the promise he made in Valpariso.

"Let me tell you what I think," said Erasmus, "I find your theory very interesting. I agree with FitzRoy, however, in the fact that it will cause a great commotion and you will probably suffer attacks from many quarters for which your best defence will be to have a well-developed scientific support. I am not worried at all by the promise you made in Valparaiso because, firstly, FitzRoy's career is also tied to whatever effect your theory might have, and second, because I am positive that he will be absolutely fair when evaluating your grounds."

"But Ras, he said he will pursue a political career. He will never allow my theory to get in his way; he will never let me publish it."

"I don't believe he would do that. FitzRoy is a true gentleman; it would be a breach of ethics to block your theory without reason. But if it were to happen, your promise would no longer be binding, as Stokes said, due to the Captain´s hypothetical bad faith."

"Very well, Ras, now returning to my immediate plan, that is, to publish my diary, I need to be free to publish what I believe I should and avoid any censoring on his part."

"How could he censor your work?"

"Simple, he told me to send him my part as soon as I finish it so he can proof-read both his and mine."

"Do you know who the editor is?"

"Yes, Henry Colburn."

"Perfect, I know him. Then you will do the following ..."

Erasmus gave him an idea of how to avoid FitzRoy's censorship. Charles, relieved of his worry, thanked him.

Darwin also went to visit his tutor, Professor John Stevens Henslow, at Cambridge. He took Charles to see where he had stored all the specimens he had sent to England during his trip. The amount of space needed to store such a large quantity of material was remarkable.

The other remarkable thing was what Henslow told him of the effect his letters had had on the scientific community. A dinner would be held in his honour at the University shortly.

"Lyell wishes to meet you, Mr. Darwin," said Henslow.

"Lyell? The one who wrote Principles of Geology?"

"The same."

"His book was my main reference book. I can't believe a scientist of his standing would want to meet an amateur like me."

"Actually, you are not an amateur any more, Mr. Darwin. Everyone, myself included, believe that not only are your observations brilliant. You have the knack of converting a complex matter into a simple model from which you arrive at conclusions that are very clear."

"I am glad you think that, although I hope I will not let you down."

During the following months Darwin worked full time transcribing his diary, including data from his notes. He wanted it to be more than just a diary, so he tried to include or outline some of his ideas on a changing world. It would be a good way to measure the effect his 'heresies' would have.

FitzRoy was also very busy. Shortly after their return he became engaged to Mary O'Brien, a young high society girl whom he had met in Plymouth before leaving on his voyage, and with whom he had been in permanent contact with through their correspondence during the five years he was away. He gave many conferences which received very favourable reports from the press. FitzRoy was the wonder boy of the British gentry, so everybody that was somebody attended his wedding. He then moved into a very comfortable flat in London, close to where Darwin lived, but they hardly saw each other, however. They both worked hard on their respective parts of the book, that FitzRoy had announced to anyone who would listen to him would be printed soon, which created great expectation. The Captain had decided to include a volume on the first voyage of the *Beagle*, so he was obliged to include the diaries of the former Captains, Philip Parker King and Pringle Stokes, which added months of hard work and several headaches.

Due to the length of the manuscript, the editor had suggested it be published in volumes which would be able to be purchased either as one block or individually. The Captain thought it was a good idea and had decided that the first volume would be about the first voyage of the *Beagle*, authors Parker King, Pringle Stokes and himself; the second volume his own diary of the second voyage of the *Beagle*, the third volume Darwin's diary; and finally, a fourth volume including all the calculations, statistics, tables, etc. and other attachments.

Overwhelmed by the need to be precise while making the narrative entertaining, plus the need to include notes from two persons he could not confer with[1], FitzRoy was taking longer than expected to finish his part of the work. Finally, after over nine months of intense labour, the greater part of it was finished. What remained to be done now was to review and combine the different volumes, especially the second and third ones. If he did not, there might be incongruities, since, in this case, there were two authors referring to the same voyage.

As he knew that Darwin had finished his part, he sent him a letter requesting that he send it to him. The following day he received a perplexing answer:

My dear Captain FitzRoy,

I surely must have misunderstood. I had the impression that as soon as I finished my volume I should deliver it to the editor directly so he could review and start the diagramming, and so save time while you finished your own two volumes.

In any case, I do not think it will be a problem since you can request a copy of it from the editor.

Sincerely, Charles Darwin

FitzRoy could not believe that it was a misunderstanding. He was sure he had told Darwin clearly that the copy should be sent to him first. It was no use making a scene over this at this time, so he quickly dressed and went to the editor's offices. There he was told that he indeed had a copy. "I have read it, and it is extremely well written," said the editor, Henry Colburn, "it is both entertaining and erudite, full of very interesting data. It targets well-educated people."

FitzRoy returned home with his copy, sat in his favourite easy chair and started reading it as quickly as possible.

1. Parker King had moved to Australia several years earlier and Pringle Stokes had committed suicide in Tierra del Fuego.

After two hours he was almost blind with rage. This was not what Darwin had shown him aboard the *Beagle*. This was not a day-by-day diary, but a summary of ideas and rationales arranged in accordance with the way the voyage evolved. It was not that it was not interesting, on the contrary, in this way it was really superb. The problem was that the piece was full of hints and clues that led to Darwin's novel ideas of a world in perpetual change. Here and there one could read bout islands that emerged from the sea after millennia of volcanic activity, fossils of animals that had become extinct, animals that had moved to new territories and may have grown larger or smaller to adapt to their new environment. All along one could find hints that suggested that the story told in the Bible was not altogether true.

Perhaps a reader who had not much training in such matters would not be aware of the direction these ideas and comments were going, but to FitzRoy the conclusions were self-evident. And to make matters worse, published in the official account of the *Beagle*'s voyage! There could not be anything more embarrassing.

The Captain continued reading, but he had already made up his mind that he would confront Darwin the very next day.

"But Captain, these are not even clues! You think they direct you to the theory of evolution because you already know it, but it is not so. There is no theory suggested here. Obviously I cannot but say that the megatherium is extinct. Could I say otherwise?" Darwin said in his defence.

"So what is this you say about the Falkland (Malvinas) fox? That it is the same as the Patagonian fox but with longer legs to adapt to the environment of the islands. Or what you say about oysters found high in the Andes, or why mountains rise? What will the Church think?" said the Captain glaring at Darwin.

"Again, what could I say? I could leave out the oysters, but that would be lying by defect." Darwin paused a moment to allow the Captain to calm down, "Believe me Captain, no one arrives at the conclusions you already know of. Many different people have read it and no one believes it could harm the Church."

"There is no acknowledgement to the Admiralty for giving you the opportunity to travel and gain such knowledge either!"

"Captain, you know how grateful I am for the opportunity you offered me. It did not occur to me to thank you in the book what I have thanked you for in person so many times. But I accept my mistake and will amend it by including, in a prologue, my gratitude to you and all the officers on the

Beagle for the opportunity of joining the voyage and the support I received from all of you during it. As to the Admiralty, I do not believe I have much to thank them, since the position was not created by them nor did I receive a penny or a word of encouragement from them, Captain. However, I will include them in my acknowledgements as a favour to you, not them, because I can see now that if I did not it might hinder your career." He drank some coffee and continued, "In fact, Captain, if you think of it, it was not only I that received no support from the Admiralty, you did not either, since they did not accept to refund any of the expenses you incurred in to comply with your mission. That is why I am delighted that you have chosen to pursue a career in politics, away from the Admiralty. A person of your qualifications has no future in an organization full of petty jealousies."

In spite of these kind words, FitzRoy went directly to the Editor's offices. He would not allow them to publish Darwin's volume.

"That's impossible, Captain," Colburn answered after hearing FitzRoy's request, "In the first place we have made a commitment to Mr. Darwin to publish his volume which we cannot go back on. In the second, I have read his work and I found it exceedingly good, the public will love it. And finally, the famous geologist, Charles Lyell, said in his column in the Times that he was eagerly waiting for Charles Darwin's account of his voyage to be published." Colburn looked out the window, let a few seconds go by and asked, "But tell me, Captain, what was it that made you change your mind and exclude Darwin's volume from your book on the *Beagle*'s voyages?"

Things were not going as FitzRoy had expected. First Colburn's refusal to accept his request surprised him, and now this question put him in a spot.

"I read the whole volume, and although it is, as you say, very well written, he makes certain assumptions I do not care to go along with."

"What sort of assumptions?" asked Colburn, leaning forward, very interested.

"Well ... assumptions about fossil remains of extinct animals, according to him, and oysters in the Andes, which would suggest, according to him, of course, that the mountains rose from the bottom of the sea ... in short just assumptions with no scientific support. I do not want my name or that of the Admiralty to be seen to approve of them."

"I see ... Look here, Captain, the Admiralty is not participating in this venture in any way, they have not invested any money or given any sort of support, so we do not have to worry about their position on these issues. I do understand, however, your fear of being involved in scientific matters that may affect your reputation by implicitly adhering to assumptions which may later be rejected by the scientific world. In that case I would suggest that in your volume you set down your position on these matters clearly so no one can say that you agree with these assumptions."

"But how would I include this in my work?"

"Very simple. Add a chapter in which you can write at length on these matters and establish your position clearly. I can tell you that from an editor's point of view having two opposite stances is very good for business. The people will pick the volume that they prefer. Sales promise to be very good."

FitzRoy took his leave and went home chewing his impotence. He now was obliged to write in defence of a position he did not believe in. If he wrote in defence of the biblical version he would be the laughing stock of the scientific world. He would do it if that was what was needed to defend his King, the Church and his own way of life. If it was his duty, he would do it, as he had done so many times before.

So, it was now decided. The last chapter of the second volume would be titled 'Remarks with reference to the Deluge'.

Erasmus' strategy had worked. Charles sent his work directly to the editor with a letter of introduction from his brother, who knew him from having frequented the same poker games. In his letter Erasmus asked Colburn to read Charles' work to comment and correct his style, since he was an inexperienced writer. That was why, when FitzRoy went to see him, the editor had already read Darwin's part and had a positive opinion of it. In addition, through Henslow, Darwin and Lyell had met and they had immediately struck up a friendship. Lyell, who had a scientific column in the Times, did not hesitate to promote Charles' writing.

Several months went by before the work was finally published. The Captain had to finish his part; then there was the editing, page layout and printing. In a last effort to undermine the interest that Darwin's volume had generated, FitzRoy decided that all the illustrations would be included in the first two volumes. The third, Darwin's, would have none in spite of the fact that it described plants and animals.

A few months later an event moved Darwin deeply producing bittersweet feelings: on 9th, June, 1837, the *Beagle* cast off on its third voyage, to survey the Australian coast. Wickham had been appointed Captain,

Young Emma Darwin, by George Richmond

but the great, and pleasant, surprise was that his friend, Lieutenant John Lort Stokes had been appointed second in command. The *Beagle*'s sending off ceremony at Woolwich pier on the Thames was quite an event and Darwin was among the guests of honour. To come aboard the *Beagle*, inspect its cabins and decks, shake hands with his former mates who were preparing to set off on a new adventure, was both glorious and rather strange. He found it odd to be aware that the *Beagle* would set sail without him. At Woolwich he met FitzRoy who was a little aloof. He nevertheless greeted him with a strong handshake, and addressed him as Filos once again. He was moved too.

"Mr. Darwin," said Stokes, his eyes watery with emotion, "it will be several years until we see each other again, but we shall always be ship brothers."

"What is a 'ship brother'?"

"It is a special relationship between two people who have lived aboard and shared unforgettable experiences. A ship brother is more than a friend, it is for life."

"Then, Mr. Stokes, we definitely are 'ship brothers'!"

They gave each other an embrace, as brothers who part would. Darwin begged him to take care and write ... as any older brother would do.

The *Beagle* weighed anchor and sailed, while people on the pier slowly dispersed. Only two remained for a while. Darwin and FitzRoy strolled back to where the carriage they would share to return to London waited for them. 'Their' ship had sailed and they were deeply moved. Whatever had come between them seemed to have disappeared.

Shortly after Darwin married his cousin, Emma Wedgewood. When she became pregnant the couple decided she would be better taken care of at her family home, Maer Hall, with her sisters. A small makeshift laboratory was put together for Darwin's use next to the large family library, and it was there that he started to put together the work that would take so many years to see the light.

He was in the middle of this when the three volumes, plus the appendix, of the Narratives of the Voyages of the *Adventure* and *Beagle* were finally put on sale at bookstores. A few weeks later, anxious to know how it was doing, he took a sheet of paper, drew a large question mark, put it in an envelope and sent it to Colburn in London.

Two days later he received Colburn's answer. Everyone crowded around Charles as he opened the envelope. No one but Charles, who jumped for joy, understood what the message meant, since all they could see was a large exclamation mark.

A couple of days later he received a letter from his brother, in which he summarized the reactions, all positive, the book had had. He had also included a few newspaper clippings. A final item made Charles feel a bit sorry for FitzRoy. According to Erasmus the third volume, Charles', was a great success. Volumes one and two had hardly been sold.

Chapter 19

The Defeat

Although I was absent for some time, I knew that Darwin and FitzRoy's relationship was becoming exceedingly stressed by a sort of chess game they were involved in regarding the possibility of publishing the Theory of Evolution.

"So, what do you think?" Darwin asked, anxiously, when the Captain finished reading.

"It seems to be a good beginning," answered FitzRoy.

Since the Narratives had been published, Darwin had spent months putting together a document, of no more than ten pages, in which he explained the basic concept of the Theory of Evolution. He hoped that the clear and simple, but thorough, way in which he did so would convince FitzRoy of the soundness of his arguments and he would then be allowed to publish it. That was why he had brought a copy for him to read.

"What do you mean 'a good beginning'? I have developed the idea in a simple and direct way, with a linear reasoning that, as I see it, will help the reader arrive at the same conclusion I laid out in the introduction."

"It is true that it is simple and the logic and reasoning are flawless; however, it is still no more than speculation ... that is, a theory, not a proven fact."

"What do you mean?"

"That you are not following a scientific method."

"What do you understand a scientific method is?"

"You should know that better than I, man. The scientific method starts with a hypothesis, followed by observation or experimentation, then the analysis of the results and finally a conclusion that confirms the original statement," he handed the document back to Darwin who stared at him, "what you set out here is a very good hypothesis, but you do not submit the results of any experiment or observation as supporting evidence."

"How can one make an experiment on a process that takes millennia to occur?"

"You are the scientist, Mr. Darwin," said FitzRoy as he poured two glasses of whisky, "as I said before, your document is a very good beginning; a very well-developed hypothesis." He handed Darwin the glass and sat in the armchair facing him. He did not call him Filos any longer, noted Charles.

"The only experiment I can think of is to modify animals through selection, as the pigeon breeders do by only allowing the best specimens to breed," said Darwin.

"That seems to be a good idea," said the Captain, "but then you will be proving that Man can alter a species, but it will not be proven that it would happen in the wild without human interference. You need to find what drives animals to change in the wild ... you would have to find that driving force."

"Then I´m at a dead end."

"Of course not, Mr. Darwin. If it is not through experimentation, you may be able to prove it through observation. Everything you documented during our voyage, properly analysed, could be of use."

Disappointment was written all over Charles' face.

"You have a formidable job to do, Mr. Darwin. You have the opportunity of publishing several books on geology, botany and zoology from the observations documented during our voyage. This work will surely turn you into one of the most prominent scientists in England. Only then will you have the scientific knowledge and widespread recognition which will give you the reputation you will need to make the Theory of Evolution public."

"It will take years," said Darwin discouraged.

"Years of fascinating work," retorted FitzRoy.

"I shall have to consult and interchange information with other scientists."

"Do so, but you must always make it clear that the theory must not be disclosed outside the closest circle."

During the years that followed this conversation Darwin's life changed significantly. He purchased a grand old house in Down, outside London. He used to call it 'my china house' because he had purchased it with the proceeds both he and Emma, his wife, received from the very successful Wedgewood china works they both had stock in through their family ties. Every year a new child was born and a new book was published.

Darwin was not proud of what he had published, however. He considered them merely data collections; he felt that he had not really contributed anything to them. His only merit, he used to say, was that of collecting and arranging the information. Scientific circles did not agree with him, however. His peers considered Charles Darwin the foremost naturalist in the United Kingdom.

Due to this recognition he was often surrounded by admirers and sycophants, but it also helped him meet and befriend some charming people; Huxley, Hooker, Henslow and Lyell were more than consulting scientists, they were true friends.

On one occasion Lyell invited Darwin to dinner, as he had done countless times before, with a number of personalities from the scientific community. This time it was different, however; one of the guests was an elderly gentleman with a mane of white hair who spoke with a thick German accent. It was no less than Alexander von Humboldt.

"So you met Iñiguez and he spoke to you about me?" asked the German.

"Yes, I met Iñiguez in Talcahuano, a few days after the earthquake."

"A remarkable character."

"He is that. My conversation with him made me perceive religion in a different way."

"I met him near Quito, shortly after he had joined the Jesuits. There were two events that had affected him deeply ... his conscience gave him no peace for his responsibility in the death of his father and his brother"

"Responsible for the death of his father? He drowned like so many fishermen do. What was he responsible for?"

Humboldt looked at Darwin gravely and asked "Didn't Iñiguez tell you the truth about his father's death?"

"I don't know what truth you are talking about, Doctor von Humboldt. He just told me he had drowned."

"Of course ... that was the official version, but not what really happened."

Humboldt drank some wine, marking time, generating suspense.

"In his youth Iñiguez was very spirited, and he was often dominated by rage. He would argue and quarrel over anything anytime. On a really bad day, when he was out at sea fishing with his father, they started arguing over something and blinded by rage, the young man threw his father overboard. He drowned."

"When he returned, overwhelmed by guilt he ran to his mother, in tears, to tell her what had happened. She decided that, as her husband

Alexander von Humboldt

was lost, she would not lose her son too, so she made up the official story that he fell overboard and drowned. This kept him out of prison. But the young man was so consumed by guilt that he couldn't look his brothers in the eye. As soon as they were able to keep the family, he decided to go to America. His younger brother's death was a blow he couldn't handle. He tried to commit suicide several times until he was rescued by the Jesuits."

Darwin was lost in thought. He had always felt there was more to Father Iñiguez' life than he had been told; but that he was his father's murderer never crossed his mind. Now he understood what he meant when he said he had come to terms with God.

Humboldt's account was followed by silence, which ended when two waiters entered carrying trays laden with food, and the conversation switched to light banter about hunger and appetite.

"Mr. Humboldt, you have travelled extensively," asked Lyell, "what can you tell us of the eating habits and customs of different cultures?"

"Certainly," Humboldt loved to be in the limelight. With his anecdotes he always ended up being the centre of attention. "Most of the primitive natives eat with their hands, as was the case in Europe until the Middle Ages. Other more advanced cultures have been using utensils for centuries."

"Who are those," asked Lyell whose field was geology, not anthropology.

"The Orientals, for example."

"What do they eat with?"

"With wooden sticks. They handle both with one hand, like so," and he clumsily demonstrated how it was done with the knife and fork.

"It must be very difficult to eat rice with them," quipped Lyell.

"It is. If I had used sticks to eat rice when I was a child I would surely have starved, because my brothers would have gobbled everything up before I even started." replied Humboldt in jest.

"Could you repeat that?" asked Darwin.

"I beg your pardon?" Humboldt did not like to be interrupted.

"If you could repeat that, please?" insisted Darwin.

"I said that if I had used sticks to eat rice when I was a child my brothers would have eaten it all before I even started and I would have starved." said Humboldt, serious now

"Eureka!" exclaimed Darwin, "do you have paper, pen and ink, Mr. Lyell?"

"Certainly," answered the host, bewildered, "in my study."

"Then ... gentlemen, if you will excuse me."

To everyone's surprise Darwin rose and walked towards the door Lyell had indicated.

Darwin was writing furiously in Lyell's study when the door burst open and young Huxley came in.

"Mr. Darwin! You almost made us choke. Humboldt is livid and Lyell is trying to calm him down."

"My apologies, Mr. Huxley, but something that was said made several things come together in my mind that explains the driving force of change and I need to write them down before I lose them."

"What? I do not understand!" said Huxley, both angry and intrigued.

"Do you remember what I explained of my theory of evolution?"

"Yes, and you know I consider it brilliant."

"What needed to be explained, and was missing in my theory, is the driving force that compels animals to change, to adapt."

"So, what is this driving force?" asked Huxley, now more interested than annoyed.

"Food."

"You've lost me."

"Humboldt's example is good. If he tried to eat rice with sticks while his brothers had forks, he would have starved. But what would have happened if the situation were reversed and he had a fork and his brothers sticks?"

"He would have filled his belly ... and, judging by the way he eats, his brothers would have starved."

"Exactly. That was what made me remember that on one of the islands in the Galapagos a finch hopped on my plate to eat the rice, while on other islands the local finches did not. You see ... the finches on different islands have differently shaped beaks. Surely this one had a beak with which it could eat rice while the others could not."

"I still do not see the connection with the sticks."

"Imagine that one island is populated with finches that eat a specific type of seed with a tough husk. Now imagine that for whatever reason a finch is born with a deformed beak, but luck would have it that this deformed beak is better adapted to cracking the husk of this particular seed. What would happen to that finch?"

"Well ... I suppose it would be able to eat more than the rest" Huxley was starting to grasp where Darwin's reasoning was taking him.

"Correct. This finch will be stronger and probably live longer and have more offspring."

"Now I get it!" Huxley exclaimed, "its offspring would have the same beak, would therefore eat more and have more descendants than the common finches. The population of 'new' finches will grow and the common finches will have less to eat."

"The common finches would eventually disappear and there would only be the new ones on the island. That is how food is the driving force in change. It is this driving force that FitzRoy said was missing in my theory."

"Brilliant, Mr. Darwin! And now what?"

"Now I must review and analyse my observations to determine if they support this theory. If they do, then there should be a type of finch peculiar to each island with beaks adapted to the available food. The task ahead will be fascinating."

The door opened and the host, Lyell, came in. He was visibly annoyed with Darwin and Huxley for having left the table the way they did.

"Gentlemen," he said, "could you please return to the parlour to bid Dr. Humboldt farewell? He is leaving."

Darwin was back at FitzRoy's house. When he arrived he was greeted by Mary, FitzRoy's wife. Being a good hostess, she asked after his family and sent her love to Emma.

"I hope we can meet again before we leave," said Mary.

"Leave? Where to?" asked Darwin.

"New Zealand." she said smiling.

Charles stared at FitzRoy. After publishing the Narratives FitzRoy got involved in politics and had quite a successful career so far. He ran for, and won, a seat in Parliament representing his county, and his reputation gave his opinions weight.

"I received the appointment this morning. The Governorship was left vacant and the House of Lords decided that one of its Peers should be appointed. I suppose I have been chosen because I am one of the few who know the place."

"Congratulations, Captain. I am sure that your talent and commitment were also valued for such an important post. How long will you be there?"

"It is hard to tell, but I would imagine about four or five years."

"So you have work for several years."

"Of course ... several fascinating years."

They sat on easy chairs and Darwin steered the conversation to the subject he was interested in. He gave FitzRoy a short explanation of his assumption that food was the driving force that drove animals to evolution. FitzRoy just looked at him.

"What will you do next, Mr. Darwin?"

"As you said, ... analyse my observations to determine if they support my assumptions."

"And what brings you here?" by FitzRoy's tone and expression Darwin could tell that he was not inclined to help him, but he pushed forward anyway.

"You see, Captain, I started studying the finches, but I have now discovered that my collection is far from complete. Going over my notes I see that there were over ten species of finches in the Galapagos, but I only have four."

FitzRoy had his gaze fixed on him and did not move a muscle.

"I got in touch with several of our crew and some of them had some finches in their collections. They all agreed to lend them to me for my research but I am still short of at least four. That was when I remembered that you had the best collection of finches ..."

"Let me guess," interrupted FitzRoy, "you would like me to lend you my collection so you can advance your theory, is that not so?"

"Yes."

Darwin, who could now see that the Captain's attitude was worse than he had expected, was not prepared for what happened next. FitzRoy went red in the face and rage took hold of him. "Roy is taking control" Wickham would have said.

"Let me see if I understand you correctly," said the Captain raising his voice, "you expect the Governor of New Zealand, appointed by His Majesty, the King of England, to lend you his collection of animals for you to advance a theory that threatens the Church and the King? Did you think for a moment that I would make such a fool of myself?"

Darwin could not believe he could lose control in that way.

"Captain, I must warn you that your denial to help me put together the evidence you suggested yourself, will only set me free from the promise I made in Valparaiso."

"Get out of my house! And don't you dare return!"

Darwin got up and walked to the door.

"Traitor!!" shouted FitzRoy, beside himself.

Next morning, at his home in Down, Darwin was still shaken by what had happened at FitzRoy's house. Emma tried to understand what had happened, but as she did not know the nature of her husband's work, and Charles did not explain what the consequences were, she could not understand the cause of the problem.

They were both enjoying a cup of tea when one of their servants came in and announced that Captain FitzRoy had turned up and wished to see Mr. Darwin.

"Tell him I do not wish to see him," said Charles.

"He gave me this note for you, sir," answered the servant and handed it to him.

Darwin opened it. It said "I am terribly sorry."

"Show him in."

Two minutes later the Captain entered followed by the servant who carried a box which he laid on the floor.

"Mr. Darwin, I beg pardon for my behaviour yesterday, I am terribly sorry I acted in such a manner. I wish you could pardon me, not forget. I was not thinking, it just came out. I beg your pardon once again."

"Do not fret, Captain, it is forgotten."

"Then we are still ship brothers?"

"Of course we are," they shook hands.

"Emma!" said FitzRoy when he saw her, "how nice to find you here. I have not seen you for quite some time."

"True, Captain, but let me congratulate you on your appointment."

"Thank you, I only hope I will do what is expected of me."

"I am sure you will. How are Mary and the children?"

"They are all very well, thank you for asking. She sends you her love."

Darwin was looking at the box that FitzRoy had brought, and when the latter noticed his quizzical look, he said:

"These are the finches you asked me to lend you, Filos. I am sure they will be of great use to you."

"I trust you will be staying for lunch, Captain," said Emma.

"I am afraid I must be back in London before that, but I would not mind a cup of tea." Darwin's wife went off to arrange it.

The men sat down.

"Excuse my bluntness, Captain, but I am a bit bewildered. Yesterday you fervently opposed my pursuing the theory, and today you bring your collection to help me with it."

"I apologise again for my behaviour yesterday. You are free to continue your research and I will not hinder you in any way."

"I will keep the promise I made in Valparaiso."

"I thank you. I will keep my part of the promise, which is to analyse your results with an open mind."

"But ..."

"I beg your pardon?"

"There is always a but, Captain, please continue."

"Well ... I simply wanted to understand your position, Mr. Darwin. You see ... science must have some useful purpose, if not it does not make sense," Darwin listened attentively, "as a seaman I am especially interested in the science of Meteorology. What use is it? You might ask. Well, if one could predict storms with at least a day to spare, how many lives could be saved? I would say many. Warnings could be sent to all ports on the British and French coasts, ships would wait until the storm blew over before leaving and many shipwrecks could thus be avoided."

"You are absolutely right, Captain."

"So my question is, Filos: what is the use of the Theory of Evolution?"

The question caught Darwin unawares, he had no answer.

"Hmm ... the Greeks used to say 'knowledge for knowledge's sake'. They did not need a reason, just the need to learn."

"But that can be applied, Filos, to knowing the habits of the storks or the breeding cycle of the dragon flies, or any other subject of not much consequence. But your theory, that destroys the very foundations of the Church, will divide society. Many will suffer ... you will suffer attacks yourself ..."

"That is of no consequence."

"But do you not care what your wife and children may suffer as a result of your theory?"

That hit home.

"I believe, Filos," continued FitzRoy, "that even with sufficient proof you must answer that question, what is the point of the theory ... if it is worth the trouble."

Darwin remained silent.

"Emma!" beamed FitzRoy, "I was starting to think that I would have my tea on the train!" he said in jest.

Darwin's wife poured the tea and they changed the subject.

"When I came in with the tea I overheard something rather disturbing," said Emma.

The Captain had just left and Darwin and Emma were alone in the parlour.

"Is it true that your work attacks the Church?" Emma was a very religious woman who brought up her children accordingly. She and Charles rarely spoke about his research. She was not really interested in the subject and Charles preferred to keep her ignorant of his conclusions.

"Well ... not really."

"That means 'yes', correct?" she asked.

"In truth my work does not attack the church. The fact is that the conclusions at which I am arriving would prove that the Bible's account is not altogether true and that could put the actual existence of God in doubt."

Emma's face had a troubled expression.

"Are you sure of that?" she asked.

"Almost," he lied.

"Now I understand why the Captain appealed to your sense of responsibility before you publish it," she paused, "remember, Charles, you are not alone. Your decisions have consequences." She picked up the Wedgewood set and left.

It was late night and it was dark in Down. Darwin couldn't sleep. He quietly slipped out of bed, put on his dressing gown and went down to the library. He poured himself a whisky and sat in his favourite armchair.

"Why publish my theory?" that question kept pounding in his head, and the answer had to be within him. He took a pencil and paper and wrote down the possible answers, he then started to analyse them one by one.

"Prestige?" No, he already had that. He had published countless books and papers and was considered one of the foremost scientists in Britain. It was not for prestige alone.

"The world needs to know the truth?" People are just interested in living well. They can live with lies or truths, they really don't care that much. So this was not a reason either.

"Money?" Certainly not. Emma and Charles were not rich, but they had no wants.

The reasons for not publishing his theory were clear; he did not need to write them down. The way society would be split, the attacks he would receive, and, most important, how those attacks would affect his family.

He had made a decision. He drank down the last of his whisky and went back to bed.

"Congratulations on your book, Mr. Stokes. I read it, enjoyed it immensely and couldn't help remembering all the adventures we were on together. And congratulations on your Commission as Captain of the HMS *Beagle*. After eighteen years sailing on it, who would deserve it more than you?"

John Lort Stokes had returned from the third voyage of the *Beagle* a few months earlier. Wickham, who was Captain when she sailed, had to disembark in Australia for health reasons and Stokes was appointed Captain in his place, a responsibility he took on and executed with great professional success. Once back in England, and following FitzRoy's example, he published a book on his voyage as Captain of the *Beagle*.

Since his departure, that afternoon on the pier at Woolwich, Darwin and Stokes had not met again. That was why that week-end Charles had insisted he visit them at Down.

"Thank you, Mr. Darwin," answered Stokes, "I often recalled our conversations during this trip, and on countless occasions I would ask myself 'what would Charles have said about this place? What would have he discovered?'"

"Let me be solemn for a moment, Mr. Stokes, I was moved to learn that you had named a bay after me. I am most grateful for that honour."

"You certainly deserve it. Someday there will be a city there named after you."

"Ha, ha, perhaps," Darwin laughed, "you also named a river after FitzRoy, is it not so?"

"Yes. You remember that we often mentioned in our conversations how unfair it was that an explorer of FitzRoy's calibre did not have some important landmark named after him. But I failed."

"How did you fail?"

"I was hasty. We were searching for a river connecting some inland lake with the sea. This would be very important because it would surely be the place where a colony would be established. I found this river which I was positive was connected to a lake, so I immediately named it FitzRoy. The subsequent exploration found that it did not connect to any lake, so FitzRoy's name remained for an ordinary river, not an important one as was my intention."

"I see ..." Darwin was pensive, "what news of the Captain after his ill-fated spell as Governor of New Zealand?"

Stokes settled into his armchair. "Do you mind if I smoke?" he asked as he took out a large cigar. This conversation promised to be a long one.

After two years in office, the British colonists had almost evicted FitzRoy, and London had no choice but to replace him and hurry him back to England, where his political career was over as a consequence of his failure.

It had all started with one of the recurrent violent clashes between British settlers and Maori natives. In the North Island the Maoris killed some white settlers in retaliation for an attack they had suffered from a group of dishonest settlers who wanted to drive them from their lands so they could then take them. The tension increased as the British apprehended the Maori chief and several of his lieutenants. They were about to be hanged when Governor FitzRoy turned up in order to get first-hand information on the conflict and dispense justice. He heard out both sides and came to the conclusion that they were both equally at fault. In consequence he set the Maoris free and issued a set of rules for a peaceful coexistence of settlers and Maoris. The settlers could not believe he had set the 'murdering Maoris', as they called them, free and a settlers' uprising ensued that demanded the immediate removal of FitzRoy.

"The Captain does not grasp the political subtleties. He believed his duty was to be fair, when a Governor is expected to govern for the British subjects," said Stokes. "if London had wanted to uphold the Maoris' rights, they would have appointed a Maori Governor. But you know FitzRoy, when he returned he insisted that he was right and should never have been dismissed. He quickly became the laughing stock in Parliament, no one could back him up, so he lost his seat and ended up with nothing.

"To make matters worse his personal finances had suffered and were now in very bad shape. He applied for a position in the Admiralty, but after so many years away, most of those who were once his subordinates, like myself, had been promoted to ranks above the one he had when he left the Navy, which must be quite hard on his self-esteem."

"I see ... " said Darwin, "so what will the Admiralty do with him? I would like to think they would want to take advantage of his talent."

"No one doubts he is talented, but no one really knows how to take advantage these talents. Who would want to put someone so unstable in a position of command? Someone who will fly into a rage for no apparent reason and then slump into a deep depression. Believe me; I want to give him a hand. It was he who got me my first assignment; I owe him what I am today in the Navy. But I cannot figure out how to help him."

"I believe I know how you can help."

"Really? How?"

Darwin poured them some more whisky.

"By creating a Department of Meteorology and putting him in charge."

"What use would a Department of Meteorology have for the Admiralty?"

"To save men's lives."

"How would it do that?".

"If storms could be predicted, ships could avoid leaving port until the danger was over, for example"

"Well put, Mr. Darwin. Do you think FitzRoy would be interested?"

"Believe me, he'll love it. It will also be good for his self-esteem."

Stokes relit his cigar.

"Changing the subject, how is your theory doing? When will it be published? You would think it was Penelope's knitting, never-ending."

"I will not publish it."

"No?! Why not? Has it to do with your promise in Valparaiso?"

"No, that promise still stands, but there is a different motive. If I were to publish it I will be attacked from all quarters. That would be of no consequence if it were just me, but my family would suffer. I cannot be so vain."

Stokes raised his eyebrows. He could understand the reason and could tell what an enormous sacrifice Charles was making to protect his family. Very commendable.

"Is this decision final?"

"I wouldn't know ... as things are today, yes. But in the future, my children will grow and eventually Emma and I will not be around ..."

"What do you mean?"

"I thought I would write it all and send it to my editor with instructions to publish it after our deaths."

"I understand ... One can imagine how hard that decision must have been. The work of a lifetime ..."

"No, it is not that at all. I am working on other things. My current work has to do with the analysis of certain animals; their lives, their breeding cycle, their feeding habits, etc. It is far less controversial than the subject of evolution and the scientific community seems to appreciate my work in this field."

Darwin had found his place in the scientific world and he wanted to be happy with it. But deep in his heart he felt that he was deceiving science by not pursuing the line of research related to evolution. And this would continue for many years. His ailing health bore evidence of the conflict inside him. Darwin's body always reacted to tension through sickness. He used to tell anyone who would listen that since he returned from the voyage of the *Beagle* he had not once felt well for a full day.

Many years later, in 1858, the house was in turmoil due to the illness of two of the Darwin children. Henrietta had suffered a high fever but seemed to be pulling out of it. The youngest son, however, who was only a year old, did not seem to be reacting. The doctors' prognoses were not encouraging.

Darwin found solace in his work; Emma in religion.

On one of those mornings, Emma brought him his tea, and, as usual the mail. Charles received a lot of mail as a matter of course and had taken the habit of starting by reading the return addresses to decide which one he would open first. This time there was one that caught his eye. The stamp was from Malaysia. He did not know Alfred Wallace, who had sent it, but he often received letters from people he did not know since his reputation made him an authority in his field.

He opened the letter and started reading it. Suddenly he frowned and clenched his fists.

"Oh, no!" he exclaimed.

"What is it?" asked Emma.

He dropped the letter and buried his face in his hands.

"And now this!"

Chapter 20

The Betrayal

When his defeat seemed inevitable, Darwin's friends intervened and caused his glory but also his misery.

"My friends, I have asked you all to come to Down today because I need you to do something that has been requested of me which, due to the delicate health of my youngest child, I will not be able to comply with."

His friends and eminent scientists Lyell, Huxley and Hooker sat in his study. On the way over, on the train, they had wondered what Darwin's summons was about. They were almost positive that Charles had finally decided to go ahead with his theory, but his opening words baffled them.

"A few days ago I received a letter from a young English scientist who lives in Malaysia, one Alfred Wallace. He has done some very interesting research on butterflies and has sent me his paper. He asks me to read it and, if I consider it of merit, to submit it to the Royal Society."

"What does he say about butterflies?" asked Hooker.

"How good is his work?" asked Huxley, not waiting for Hooker's question to be answered.

"Patience, gentlemen, patience. I have prepared a copy for each of you; please read it and then we shall discuss its merits. After all, you will be the ones to submit it."

While they quickly read the ten-page manuscript, Darwin poured them each a drink. He was aware of the importance this day had for science: evolution would see the light in a manner he had not expected, but he was devastated by the prospect of losing a son.

After a few minutes the three men finished. They were dumbfounded.

"This is incredible," exclaimed Huxley, "it cannot be published."

"Do you think it is not good?" Darwin asked him.

"Why, no, it is excellent, but the conclusions Wallace arrives at are the same you arrived at twenty years ago. The Theory of Evolution is your idea and work. Wallace is late," complained Huxley.

"Wallace is not late, my dear Huxley, because I never published my work," said Darwin.

"Then submit yours together with Wallace's paper," interposed Hooker.

"Never! In the first place it would be unethical, and second, there are reasons of a personal nature that made me decide not to publish it and the situation has not changed. Gentlemen ... please let us not discuss my work but the merits of Wallace's work, so we can determine if it deserves to be submitted to the Royal Society or not."

The silence in the study was heavy.

"Mr. Darwin," Lyell was the one who knew him best and longest and was closest, "you are aware, then, that if this work is submitted, Wallace will be the one to receive the recognition? All your work, over twenty years of hard labour will be buried ... all for naught ... the work of a lifetime, Mr. Darwin."

"I know," answered Darwin, "several years ago I decided that my work on evolution would never see the light."

What he said was not altogether true. A few years earlier he had given his editor a sealed envelope to be opened after his death. He had also given him instructions to the effect that it should be published only after both Emma's and FitzRoy's death and after all their children came of age.

"Gentlemen," he resumed, "again I beg you not to mention my work anymore, but let us evaluate Wallace's work."

"This paper is good," said Hooker, "we are all aware of this and that it deserves to be published, in spite of it being limited to butterflies and that the mechanism that drives the change is not determined, while it is in yours, Mr. Darwin."

"So you will submit it?"

"I will do it," said Hooker.

Darwin felt he was being executed for a crime he had reported himself. It was a sentence that would bring about the scientific death of the work of a lifetime.

"Gentlemen, I thank you from the bottom of my heart for having come. I must now retire, however; my son's plight has disturbed me deeply," his eyes watered, a tear was nigh, "the death of a son is the worst thing that can happen to a man ... nothing can prepare you for such a tragedy."

Thomas Huxley

A child's funeral must be one of the saddest scenes one can imagine. The Darwin and Wedgewood families assembled at the small cemetery in Down for this one. Although no obituary had been published, several friends had heard of the tragedy and had turned up.

Emma overcame grief a lot better than he had expected. Darwin remembered Father Iñiguez' premonitory words that morning in Talcahuano: religious faith makes these situations more bearable. Charles was grateful for that, since Emma was his support in that terrible moment.

After the funeral, carriages took them all to the Darwin residence, where they paid their respects to the mourning couple.

Huxley, Hooker and Lyell gave their condolences first to Emma then Darwin.

"Mr. Darwin," Huxley said to him, "I know this is not the right moment, but I wanted you to know that the day before yesterday Hooker read the paper at the Royal Society."

"And what was the reaction?"

"On Wallace's work, not much; on yours, however, a standing ovation"

"What do you mean 'my work'?"

"Yes, Mr. Darwin," said Hooker, "I decided that, apart from Wallace's paper, I would read some of the letters you sent me twenty years ago where the theory is explained in more detail."

Darwin couldn't believe his ears.

"You read my work on evolution? Without my consent?"

"It was a very old letter, so I did not think there would be a problem. In fact, it went down very well, and it is fair that it did."

"Gentlemen, you have no idea the harm you have caused me. You have made me default on my word," said Darwin, visibly annoyed, who turned and left.

"Sir, Mr. Charles Darwin is here to see you."

"Please show him in" answered FitzRoy.

The budget the Admiralty had assigned for the study of meteorology was small. Nevertheless, with scanty means and a small staff FitzRoy had managed to produce some impressive results. In recognition for his efforts and achievements, the Admiralty had promoted him to Vice-Admiral.

"Come in, Filos," he took Charles' hand in his and said, "my deepest sympathy, please sit down. How is Emma?"

"She is fine, thank you, Captain," many still called FitzRoy 'Captain', it was a term of affection, as friend and leader, not rank, "I do not know where Emma gets the strength to keep the household going."

"You are aware, Mr. Darwin, that I know exactly how you feel."

A few years earlier FitzRoy had lost his wife and eldest daughter. This tragedy had come upon him at the worst possible moment: his finances were in trouble and he was suffering from a severe depression. After pressure by friends, the Admiralty had finally agreed to re-incorporate him; he was given several assignments, but in each one he was soon in conflict due to his tendency to take offense over anything. When they were at their wits end as to what to do with him, the Admiralty decided to create a department for the study of meteorology, at the head of which they named FitzRoy. As from that moment his life seemed to take a turn for the better. He remarried shortly after this, was promoted and then the new couple was blessed with a daughter, which, due to his age – he was then fifty-two -, he used to refer to as his 'almost grandchild'. Having come to terms with the world, his humour had changed and he was more like what he had been during the first year as Captain of the *Beagle*.

"Of course we know. We thank you for your telegram."

"I regret I did not go to the funeral; I did not find out about it until the following day."

"Emma would rather not have anything published. Only the family was there and a few friends who had found out by chance"

"A cup of tea?"

"That would be nice, thank you," Darwin looked at the maps hanging on the walls, all of them with large arrows drawn on them in a north-south direction, "how is your work getting on?"

"Very well, indeed; look at this, Filos," he pointed at a map where the British Isles, the west coast of Europe and the North Sea Islands could be seen. We receive weather reports from Edinburgh, the Shetland Islands, Copenhagen and Iceland. Guess what we discovered?"

"I haven't the faintest idea."

"Every time we have a storm in London, I find that a day before there was one in Edinburgh, and two or three days earlier in the Shetland Islands and Copenhagen."

"Is it the same storm moving south?"

"Exactly, so if we could know that today there is a severe storm in Edinburgh, we could close down our ports and thus save the lives of many seamen."

"And why don't you?"

"Because the information takes three days to come from Edinburgh, let alone the Shetland Islands and Copenhagen. My proposal is to treat this information as urgent and therefore have it sent by telegraph ... but I cannot manage to get it assigned that priority. I am simply called the Mad Barometer," FitzRoy smiled, his humour at its best, "but I suppose this is not what brought you here."

"That is correct. I shall try to be concise. A few weeks ago I received a letter from a young man named Wallace. He sent me a paper and asked me to read it and, if I considered it had merit, to submit it to the Royal Society. As my son was dying, I gave it to my friend Hooker, who read it at the Society's meeting. Only my friend decided to also read an old letter of mine on the same subject. "

"What was the subject of Wallace's paper?" asked FitzRoy.

Darwin braced himself for FitzRoy's fury when he told him, "on the evolution of species."

"Do you have a copy of this paper?" asked FitzRoy calmly.

"Here you are, Captain."

FitzRoy read it quickly.

Hooker, Lyell and Darwin together in Down

"Well ..." he said when he finished reading, "I suppose someone would eventually arrive at the same conclusions. Your friend Hooker is a true friend. Your work, my friend, is a lot better than Wallace's. It would not be fair for him to get all the credit."

"I did not want you to think that I had betrayed you by making my work public without your consent."

"Forget that. Once the subject has been made public, the best we can do is to make sure it is channelled in the right direction."

Darwin was surprised at FitzRoy´s reaction. He had expected him to fly into a rage and accuse him of coming up with this trick to sidestep what he had promised in Valparaiso.

"What do you mean by channelling it, Captain?"

"I believe you should take the lead and publish your work being careful not to affect the values we want to preserve."

"You are actually asking me to publish my work on evolution?"

"Of course! If Wallace publishes his it will be out of our control, while if you do, it is manageable."

"What do you mean by my being careful, Captain?"

"Quite simple, Mr. Darwin; that what you publish does not imply that God does not exist or that Man evolved from animals. That is, limit your discussion to the evolution of plants and animals. By leaving Man out of it those who want to can believe we were created by God."

"I remember now ... leave room for the Great Clockmaker, like Newton."

"You have a good memory, Filos."

In November 1859 the first edition of On the Origin of Species by Natural Selection was published. At first it was sold mainly in scientific circles. Only a year later, when the second edition was published, did it start to be discussed in universities, and therefore the idea started to spread to the general public.

In June 1860 a series of conferences on scientific topics were held at Oxford. FitzRoy was one of those invited to speak, in his case on the progress made in the field of meteorological forecasting. The Vice-Admiral had become quite well known in this field, especially since the Times of London started publishing his weather forecasts.

FitzRoy's presentation was sober, clear and detailed. The audience, although scarce, showed their appreciation. Once his presentation was over, he also hurried to attend the day's big attraction, which had already started: the debate between Darwin's friend and follower, Thomas Huxley, and the Bishop of Oxford, Samuel Wilberforce. The subject: Evolution.

The hall was packed. The debate focused on the logical conclusion of the theory: the origin of Man. The audience, mostly university students and teachers, were massively in favour of Huxley, who had on his dais a copy of Darwin's On the Origin of Species. The Bishop, on the other hand, with his Bible, was booed after each intervention.

At the end of the debate, Bishop Wilberforce tried to get some effect by asking Huxley if his descent from a lowly monkey was on his mother's or his father's side.

After the ensuing bedlam had subsided, Huxley answered: "I would much rather have a lowly monkey, as you call it, as an ancestor than be related to a foolish man like you." The audience burst into laughter, which only made his ridicule more evident.

FitzRoy, almost blind with rage, took his leave. "This will not remain unpunished," he thought.

"Good morning, Captain. What a pleasant surprise to see you here in Down," exclaimed Darwin.

"It may be a good morning for you, a man who cannot keep his word."

The contorted expression on his face showed that rage had made him lose control.

"I do not understand. Why do you treat me this way?"

"It is I who doesn't understand. Why did you have to send Huxley to ridicule the Bishop of Oxford? We had agreed that you would not attack the Church and would not mention the origin of Man. You have done the exact opposite."

"Calm down, Captain. I did not send anyone. I heard that Huxley was going to a debate, but he did not represent me nor did he follow any instructions of mine. I do not give Huxley orders. Whatever he does or says is his own business, not mine."

"Lies! Huxley is one of your supporters. Surely Wallace is another of your followers, whom you instructed to write about evolution so you could, through this ruse, trick me into allowing you to publish your work."

"That is not so, Captain, I don't even know Wallace."

"You lie! You are a liar, a man with no word. You have betrayed me!"

FitzRoy was beside himself. Darwin did not know if he should try to make him see reason or answer back in kind.

"I have not betrayed anyone! And you should remember you called me a traitor once and returned the next day to apologise."

"This time I will not apologise. I would cut my throat first!"

He turned on his heel and marched off. That was the last he saw of FitzRoy.

One spring morning in 1865, as Darwin returned from a walk, he saw Emma waiting for him at the door, a paper in her hand.

"Emma! Is something amiss?"

"We have received terrible news of FitzRoy, Charles."

Emma knew that her husband and the Vice-Admiral had had a dreadful discussion five years earlier. They had not spoken or written to each other since. She knew it would be a terrible blow to Charles.

"What happened?" Darwin could almost guess what he was about to hear. He had imagined the scene many a time.

"He died ... he committed suicide yesterday morning."

Darwin sat down. It was a severe blow, after all they had gone through so much together ... but he sensed there was more to it.

"How did he kill himself?"

"I don't know how he could have ... he slit his throat with his razor."

Alfred Russell Wallace

"Oh, no! He slit his throat!? It was my fault, all my fault ..." Darwin buried his face in his hands, "I knew he might do this. He cut his throat ... it was a message for me. He was telling me I betrayed him ... he had said he would ... but I didn't betray him!"

Emma could not understand her husband's ravings.

"How can it be your fault, Charles? You had an argument five years ago; it could not have been that. FitzRoy was a person with a tendency to suffer depressions."

"No, Emma, if he slit his throat it was on my account ... a six-year-old girl has lost her father because of me, Emma. This is terrible!"

Darwin went to lie down, he had tachycardia. The next morning he refused to get up, nor the next day nor the next, and so on for weeks. Emma wrote to Stokes, if anyone could pull him out of it, it would be his old friend.

"Mr. Darwin! Wake up, Please! Can you hear me?"

Darwin slowly opened his eyes. It took him a moment to get used to the brightness in the room; the curtains had been opened wide. A gentleman with long grey whiskers and wavy hair was looking at him.

"Vice-Admiral Stokes, what a pleasure," said Darwin trying to sound jolly, "what brings you here?"

"Emma called me. She and your children are very worried about you. You must make an effort to get over this depression, even if it is only for their sake."

"But it is not a depression that has me bedridden, I have a heart condition."

"Come on, Mr. Darwin, you can't fool me. I know you better than my own children. Every time you get depressed you feel sick. I remember the same thing happened to you after the incident in Valparaiso."

"It very well may be, but I do not do it on purpose, I really feel my heart is weak."

"This is about FitzRoy, isn't it?"

"It was my fault that he killed himself. I cannot forgive myself."

"That is not so. It is not that at all."

"The publishing of the Theory of Evolution and the aftermath had a deep effect on him."

"But that was over five years ago! This was for another reason. I know."

"What reason?" asked Darwin, distressed.

Stokes took the London Times from his briefcase and handed it to Darwin.

"Look for the weather forecast," he told him.

Darwin looked through the whole newspaper.

"I can't find it," for the last four years the Times had published the Admiralty's weather forecast, "did they stop publishing it after his death?"

"That is the point; they stopped publishing it a week before his death. To make matters worse, that Friday they published a very cruel editorial in which they made fun of his lack of accuracy," explained Stokes, "very unfair, I must say, because he would always say that if the information did not reach him by cable on time he could not make a forecast. But you know the press."

"Are you saying that the editorial in the Times drove the Captain to his death? I think you are just trying to make me feel better."

"What I'm saying is the truth, my friend. I spoke to his wife who, I might add, is in a very delicate financial situation. I am trying, through contacts I have, to get her appointed lady in waiting to the Queen."

"I shall volunteer money, too. I do not want the little girl to want anything."

"Very well, Mr. Darwin. I see you are in better spirits now. Get up so we can discuss your plans for the future; I will be in your study. I will ask Emma to brew some tea for us."

Darwin got up, dressed and combed his hair. On entering his study he said to Stokes:

"I have no plans for the future. I don't know what you want to talk about."

"What do you mean no plans? You now have to write about the origin of Man."

"But that is precisely what the Captain did not want me to do."

"Come on, man! You are an adult now, and as such you do not have to take orders from anyone … let alone a dead man, who did not have a good reason to do so when he was alive in the first place."

"It may be as you say … I had not given it any serious thought … I find the subject fascinating. But …" he sipped his tea, "I was thinking of FitzRoy … how could we pay tribute to him?"

"True," said Stokes, "he has not been treated fairly. We must think of something that will honour his name … but what?"

Darwin published his book about the origin of Man a few years after that, but neither of us could figure out a way to pay homage to the late Captain FitzRoy.

Chapter 21

The Other Promise

Dear Mr. Moreno,

You have now finished my story, and should understand how Mr. Darwin and I feel about the late Vice-Admiral FitzRoy's remembrance. I feel that I have failed him because I could never name a place with an importance equivalent to my gratitude towards the man who taught me everything I know and who gave me his unwavering support in everything I tried and achieved. In like manner, Mr. Darwin feels indebted to him, in part because deep in his heart he considers he contributed to the state of mind that drove the Captain to the most terrible and final decision.

Your letter and your planned trip, however, have given us, as our own end is nigh, the chance to honour his memory and settle our debts.

As I mentioned before starting this story, you must promise to comply with a request in exchange for my help. This request is that, on your trip up the Santa Cruz River and its headwaters, you name the most important geographic feature you find after FitzRoy.

As Vice-Admiral of the Royal Navy I will make sure you and your country are rewarded for such a noble gesture.

Sincerely,

Vice-Admiral John Lort Stokes

Dear Vice-Admiral Stokes,

At this moment I am in the Chilean city of Punta Arenas from where I hope to return soon to my country, and from where a British ship will take this letter to you. You may well receive this envelope, and the rock that goes with it, before I arrive in Buenos Aires. I have just completed the trip you started over forty years ago. I have accomplished what I had set out to do, reach the headwaters of the Santa Cruz River.

I do not wish to burden you with details, which I hope you will be able to read in a book I plan to write shortly. I simply would like to dwell on some of the points that have a bearing on the debt I have with you.

The data you sent me was tremendously useful. Not only did I recognise every landmark, but I also found two messages your expedition left. One of them in a cave which, I daresay, must be the one where you thought you saw a child's hand. The other one I found at your last bivouac: Western Station. From that small hill I compared the silhouette of the mountains that can be seen from there with the sketch you sent me. I was able to identify each peak, including Mount Stokes that stands out as it is the highest in that range.

It might come as a disappointment to learn how close you were of finding the lake you were searching for. After three gruelling weeks, just a two hour brisk walk would have taken you to its shore. I can confirm that its blue-grey waters are of glacial origin, even though I could not see any glacier from where I was. I did see icebergs adrift, however, that proved the presence of glaciers on some of the branches of this lake which I called 'Argentino'.

My trip did not end there. Captain FitzRoy had noticed, from Western Station, that the valley of the Santa Cruz seemed to run north. I verified that and I found a river that flowed from the north and into lake Argentino at a point quite close to where the Santa Cruz is born. I studied the place and the currents and I have come to the conclusions that this river, I have called 'La Leona', and the Santa Cruz are in fact the same river. Only the lake's expansion flooded part of its course.

We went up this river, whose water is the same colour as the Santa Cruz. The landscape was the same, that is, an arid valley, delimited by steep cliffs, in the middle of which flowed the winding river. With much effort we travelled close to sixty miles and found the headwaters. This was another great lake hemmed in between the desert and the Andes. Its waters are also of that greyish-blue you saw the Santa Cruz River had. I named this lake 'Viedma' in honour of the first white man to lay eyes on it.

On the western shore of the lake, at the foot of the Andes, a gigantic glacier thrusts its immense mass of ice right into the lake's waters. This glacier, the Viedma, is without doubt the main tributary and origin of the Leona and therefore the Santa Cruz Rivers.

But my description of the area does not end here. To the right of the glacier an enormous rock formation can be seen. One could call it a mountain, but unlike those around it, this one is not conical nor is it formed by an accumulation of rocks. This mount is formed by a single rock, shaped like a tower, with vertical walls. It is higher than any of the surrounding mountains, (including Mount Stokes). At its summit, the perpetual snow, battered by furious winds, creates a permanent wispy cloud that caused the local Indians to call it 'Chalten', which means volcano in their language.

I named this one Mount FitzRoy. It marks the beginning of the Santa Cruz River and hopefully will one day mark the limit between two countries that should be closer, Chile and my Argentina.

The rock I am enclosing I knocked off Mount FitzRoy with my geological hammer, my idea being that it be placed on Vice-Admiral FitzRoy's grave as a symbol of the Mountain in far off Patagonia that pays him tribute.

I remain, sincerely yours,

Francisco Pascasio Moreno

"Francisco Pascasio Moreno! Naturalist and explorer of faraway lakes. Come in."

The Minister of Foreign Affairs, Dr. Rufino de Elizalde, was asking him into his office as he had done a year and a half before. After a warm greeting they sat comfortably in armchairs.

"So, Francisco, you actually went up the Santa Cruz, found its headwaters, discovered lakes, glaciers, mountains ... you even brought a mummy, am I right?"

"That is correct. I found it in a cave near lake Argentino."

"Just what we needed," the Minister sounded satisfied, "an anthropological discovery that proves you were there and did extensive and detailed surveying. Congratulations."

"Thanks."

"We are still missing something, aren´t we?"

"What?" asked Moreno, puzzled.

"A sort of endorsement from England for your expedition, since they will probably be in charge of the mediation we have been trying to secure. I take it we have none of that," he said, sadly.

"Don't be so sure."

Moreno rolled out a chart he had brought with him.

"Look at this," he told the Minister.

"This is the same chart as the one FitzRoy had, only it has lakes Argentino and Viedma added. Did you draw it?"

"No. This is and Admiralty chart. I received it from Stokes yesterday."

"Aha ... very interesting," lied de Elizalde, "and what use is this to us?"

"Look at it closely here and here. Don't you see anything special?"

The Minister examined it closely and could now see that where Moreno pointed it said "Mt. FitzRoy (Arg.)" and "Mt. Stokes (Arg.)".

"Fantastic! An Admiralty chart indicating those mountains that separate Chile and Argentina. It is perfect for our plan! This deserves a toast."

He poured two glasses of brandy and they toasted success.

"Before I leave I would like you to have this," Moreno handed the Minister an old, frayed and decoloured Argentine flag.

"Feilberg's flag!" exclaimed the Minister, "You found it!"

"As you said once, 'if you can't find it, you find it anyway'," said Moreno imitating de Elizalde.

"Very funny. But is it really his flag?"

"I'm afraid you will never know for sure," answered Moreno, mocking

"Come on, man, tell me the truth."

"Doctor, please, do not doubt my word."

"How can I doubt if you have not answered me."

"Do not doubt when I say you will never know, because you will not."

A carriage bearing the Arms of the Admiralty pulled up to All Saints Church in Upper Norwood parish, London. Two elderly men stepped out; one had thick whiskers and the other a long white beard. The latter carried a parcel that seemed to be quite heavy. The rector met them at the entrance.

"Mr. Stokes, Mr. Darwin, it is a pleasure to have you here."

"Thank you, Reverend Pearson, as I mentioned in my letter we bring something we would like to put on FitzRoy's grave."

"No problem at all, Mr. Stokes, you have his widow's consent," said the rector, "but, if I may ask, what is it you will be putting there?"

"The contents of this box," said Stokes.

Darwin opened it and showed him the contents: a rock.

Since his wife's death, John Coghlan felt very lonely; he had decided to return to London, where he would live near his brother and nephews. The small scientific community in Buenos Aires had gathered at Moreno's house to honour him and bid him farewell as you do an old friend.

Mount FitzRoy, by Francisco P. Moreno

In the crowd, Coghlan finally spotted Moreno.

"Let us go to your study, Francisco, I want to ask you something."

"Certainly, this way."

They climbed the stairs and went into the room. The study was far more cluttered than when they had sat down to write that first letter to Stokes. During the last few years, pictures, bones, stuffed animals and weapons had been added to Moreno's collection, but what was in a prominent place was a document by which the Argentine Government had named him 'perito' (expert) for Argentina in the mediation with Chile that would define sovereign rights over a large portion of Patagonia. He had become the Perito Moreno.

Coghlan motioned him to a map that hung on one of the walls. There the main areas of conflict over borders were detailed. One area where Argentina had been particularly successful in the mediation was that which include Lakes Argentino and Viedma.

"Francisco, the mediating commission decided that the border would be the line joining Mounts FitzRoy and Stokes. There is no doubt about Mount FitzRoy. But on your map Mount Stokes is here," he said pointing at a place on the map.

Charles Darwin, taken from *The London Sketch Book*

"Correct," answered Moreno.

"If this is so, then FitzRoy could never have seen it from Western Station," he indicated its position on the map, "since Mount Cristal is in the way."

Moreno regarded him with a puzzled look.

"We both studied all the drawings Stokes sent us very carefully and the real Mount Stokes was this one you now call Mount Cervantes. I do not think it is a mistake." Declared Coghlan.

Moreno poured two glasses of whisky and handed one to the Irishman.

"The truth is that the Chileans had already accepted that the border was determined by Mounts Stokes and FitzRoy, but they did not really know the exact position of Mount Stokes. They did not have the charts and the Admiral had already died."

He sipped his whisky and went on.

"If Mount stokes were the one you mention, Argentina would have lost close to forty square miles of fertile land. I know the area well; Mount Stokes had to be further south."

"Then you, with a bit of viveza criolla[1], mislead the Chileans and the arbitration committee by moving Mount Stokes fifteen miles south, am I right?"

"I did nothing," said Moreno in his defence, "If anyone moved Mount Stokes, it must have been the hand of God."

Coghlan burst into laughter, and Moreno followed suit.

"So the hand of God, eh?!" said the Irishman, laughing, "you are a cheeky devil, man, but one that has done his country a great service."

They toasted with whisky, and Moreno declared, "As my grandfather used to say: ask me no questions and you shall be told no lies."

1. Quickness of wit, slightly dishonest, which Argentines are proud of.

A note from the author

The idea of writing a historical novel about Darwin, FitzRoy and Moreno in Patagonia came to me after I had made the same trip they had up the Santa Cruz River. There were times that, with my fellow travellers, what we saw, felt and experienced coincided so closely to what these explorers described, that we could not help feeling a kindred with them.

Internet allowed me to access their diaries, memoires and correspondence. I slowly started to know them, understand what drove them, their fears and desires; their personalities came alive in my mind. I felt I knew Darwin, FitzRoy, Stokes and Moreno and I felt I was starting to understand what had happened.

Just as one can imagine the final picture when one puts together a jigsaw puzzle, I started to understand the plot. But there were pieces missing in this puzzle, there were historical gaps that did not allow me to complete the story. That was when I decided to write a historical novel, in which fictional "pieces" would allow me to complete the puzzle.

I made a point of keeping the fiction to the barest minimum, for which I not only visited several of the places where they had been (the Galapagos, for example) but also read and consulted on palaeontology, anthropology, geology, bird watching and camping life. The idea was that as I wrote the fiction to fill the gaps, they would be as close to reality as possible. I created a few fictional characters, but always taking care that they would be consistent with the story.

I would like to invite those readers who are interested in how this puzzle was put together to join me to discuss these topics in my website:

www.GerardoBartolome.com

or contact me through my Facebook page or my email:

Info@GerardoBartolome.com

Gerardo Bartolomé
Buenos Aires, November, 2005

Este libro se terminó de imprimir
en el mes de diciembre de 2024
en DP Argentina S.A.

Panamericana km 37,5
Centro Industrial Garín
Calle Haendel, Lote 3 (B1619 IEA)
Buenos Aires, Argentina